Alex Porter's life goes up i
bookstore catches fire. Pow
nothing but stand by and watch as ᴜₕₑ ᴏₙₗᵧ
loved is taken from him.

Fire sergeant Matt Fields is ordered to Cliffside, Maine by
the privileged Porter family, which doesn't mix well with
his quick temper, to investigate exactly what happened.
When he meets Alex, he can almost taste the sexual
tension hanging between them and fights to focus on his
job to find out what started the blaze.

Once Matt discovers arson, a simple case of accidental fire
becomes much more dangerous, and Alex's life is
suddenly at risk. Someone is out to get him...and Matt
wants to know who. As he digs deeper to find the person
who torched the shop, he and Alex finally give in to the
wild heat between them. From hot as hell phone sex to
even hotter face-to-face encounters, they grow closer
together as the case spins out of control.

In the end, their newfound love will be put to the test
when secrets come to light and arson turns to murder.

OUT OF THE ASHES

M.J. James

A NineStar Press Publication

Published by NineStar Press
P.O. Box 91792,
Albuquerque, New Mexico, 87199 USA.
www.ninestarpress.com

Out of the Ashes

Printed in the USA
First Edition
September, 2019

Print ISBN: 978-1-951057-48-0

Also available in eBook, ISBN: 978-1-951057-45-9

Warning: This book contains sexually explicit content, which may only be suitable for mature readers, murder, kidnapping, depictions of infidelity by secondary characters, mentions of emotional abuse by a sibling, and fire..

For Richard

Chapter One

BLACK, BILLOWING SMOKE splattered the night sky like paint on a canvas long before Alex reached the tiny bookstore he owned and loved more than anything. The glow of streetlamps skittered over the car's windshield as he sped through the quiet streets of Cliffside, Maine, the idyllic town he called home. Their measured illumination tossed shadows across the interior of his sedan. He zipped past darkened storefronts and empty parking lots, praying he wouldn't get pulled over because he didn't have time to try to haggle his way out of a ticket. His life teetered on the edge, and he was desperate to stop the fall.

He had worked tirelessly to turn the shop into something he could be proud of, and now all his efforts were going up in flames. Even as a little boy he had dreamed of having his own business, and his intense love of the written word was the perfect motivation. For almost three years, it was his lifeline. Now, after a midnight phone call from the local police, said lifeline would be forever severed... He couldn't even comprehend what was happening.

"No, no, no..." His protests faded away when he turned onto Shemwood Drive. The historic brownstone was blazing red-hot, thick black smoke pluming into the night-time sky. "NO!" He slammed the silver sedan into Park and leapt from the car, leaving the engine running and the headlights on. Smoke swirled in the light of their beams like venomous snakes on the prowl as he raced across the street toward the fire, heat blasting him in the face with every inch closer he got. He winced but charged forward.

"Stay back!" A firefighter approached as he headed for the roaring blaze. He stared at her, wide-eyed, the large shield attached to her helmet teetering above her head, the orange glow of flames reflecting off the shiny surface.

"This is my store!" he yelled at the petite blonde woman now standing between him and the fire. She gripped his arm like a vise when he tried to sidestep her, and he snatched free. "Let me go."

"I don't care. You're not going in there." She yelled to be heard over the roar of the inferno churning behind them. Alex's determination faltered between the rumble and heat of the fire and the woman blocking him. "What the hell are you gonna do, anyway?"

"I..." What *was* he going to do, put out the fire with his bare hands?

"Step back!" She pushed against his chest and he skittered backward. She then turned her attention to the other firefighters manhandling a hose clearly losing the battle as it spewed water on the Book Nook.

"My God." Alex ran his hands through his hair, his emotions like a caged animal, trying to claw their way out. Frustration and anger swirled among the panic settling into his chest and he gritted his teeth to keep from losing control. This couldn't be happening. It just couldn't. He tugged at the tie around his neck to try to ease the suffocating feeling in his throat and undid the top button of his shirt. He sucked in a deep breath and held his breath until his chest began to ache and throb before forcing all the air out, letting some of the dread twisting his stomach go with it. He had spent the majority of the night at his shop, hosting a pretty successful author signing and then cleaning up afterward, and all he had wanted to do was go home and relax. One phone call and his plan was literally up in smoke.

He wanted to scream, hit something, shatter into a million pieces right there in the street because everything was gone.

All those books, the artwork created by kids in the neighborhood during Saturday story times... Everything was burning.

His life was gone.

The pain of the realization swept over Alex like dense, choking fog, consuming him, turning him inside out. He sat on the curb across the street from his store, a thick huddle of sightseers from the bar on the corner now crowded together behind him, ogling the scene like vultures over roadkill. He could hear their "ohs" and "my Gods" and the words were making him sick. Sick because there was nothing he could do to stop them. Stop their taunting and awe and shock. He couldn't stop any of it. The fire, the onlookers, the pity pulsing all around him; he could do nothing.

Nothing but stand there and watch as the life he had worked so hard to build turned to ashes right before his eyes.

AFTER A LONG night of standing powerless on the sidelines while his life burned, Alex finally gave up and headed home—even though he wanted to do the exact opposite. He *wanted* to stay. Fix things. Turn his life upright again. How could he just walk away when the only thing important to him was gone? But he did. He left. Went home. He was a zombie as he peeled off his smoke-drenched clothes and sat naked in his living room, burying his erratic emotions in more than a few glasses of vodka and cranberry. Once his mind was good and chemically altered, he stumbled to his bedroom at the back of the house and collapsed into bed, falling asleep just as daylight began to peek through the curtains. He woke an hour later to incessant pounding on his front door and dragged himself out of bed, his head pounding like a thousand drums. He snagged a pair of boxers from the floor and slipped them on as he rubbed sleep from his eyes and wound his way through the house, using walls and furniture to stay upright.

"Yeah?" Alex swung the door open wide, the low sun blasting his face like pepper spray, almost blinding him. He lifted a hand to shield his eyes and fought to focus. "Oh, Sorry. Good morning, officers."

Two stern-faced uniforms stared back at him, both with their legs shoulder-width apart and backs awkwardly straight in an overly masculine TV cop fashion. Alex wanted to laugh at how ridiculous they looked but held back. Their presence didn't feel like a joke. Police at your door first thing in the morning didn't typically scream social call.

"Mr. Porter?" The woman spoke first, her tone more a statement than a question.

"That's me. Are you here about the fire?"

"We are, sir. Could you come down to the station, please? Answer a few questions for us?"

"Questions?" Alex's gut lurched. "What questions?"

"Standard in this type of thing, sir. We need to find out what happened last night."

"Yes, you do. But I don't see why you need to question *me*. I wasn't even there."

"Then you'll have nothing to worry about." The woman shifted on her feet, and Alex noticed her grip tighten on the Glock at her side.

"Wait a minute...do I need a lawyer?" His stomach turned, like at any second his already obliterated life was about to get much, much worse.

"Do you have a *reason* to need a lawyer, Mr. Porter?" The male officer spoke this time, pulling Alex's attention from the agitated woman. The man was good-looking, what some might even call hot, but all Alex could see was the accusation hidden beneath his words.

"Sure sounds like I might." Every nerve in Alex's body was screaming at him, putting him on edge. He had seen enough true crime television and episodes of *Law and Order: SVU* to know how things like this typically played out.

"Well that's certainly up to you," the male officer said. "Either way, we need you to come with us."

He didn't want to—he wanted to slam the door in their faces and crawl back into bed and forget the last twelve hours even happened—but Alex knew he had no choice. If he didn't go with them willingly, they would just make him. His neighbors would see him dragged off in cuffs and the entire town would know what happened before he even arrived at the station. He ran a hand through his hair and huffed.

"Fine," he said, stepping out of the doorway and onto the porch. A cold northern wind swept around them, but Alex was too upset to care.

"Um, sir?" The female officer gestured toward him, and Alex stopped.

He lowered his hand from above his eyes as he moved to the side and, to block the sun, stepped into the shadow cast by one of the large columns flanking the porch steps. "Yes?"

She glanced over at her partner who nodded to Alex's lower half. "You might wanna get dressed."

Though he had slipped them on only a minute ago, Alex had forgotten he had answered the door in nothing but a pair of black boxer briefs.

He darted back inside and stood behind the door. "I think I'll need a minute." Both officers nodded as he stepped away from the door and headed back to his bedroom. He was wide awake now, embarrassment and fear jolting his mind. He got dressed in record time, throwing on some jeans, a T-shirt, and a pair of old sneakers while trying not to dwell on what would no doubt happen once he got to the police station. How in the world was any of this happening?

First, he lost his store, and now...what, he was about to be grilled by the police? Maybe even arrested? No, the officers standing at his door didn't come right out and admit anything, but Alex knew they suspected him. Even the simplest mind would only take a second to realize it made sense to think he burned down his own place, but that didn't help quell his uneasiness. By the time he locked the house and crammed into the back of the police cruiser, his hangover had moved from his head to his stomach, and he had to fight to keep from throwing up.

"OKAY, MR. PORTER, let's go over this again." A detective sat across from Alex in one of those dull gray rooms seen in every police interrogation scene in every movie and cop show on TV, nothing but a nondescript metal table and two matching chairs occupying the space. And, of course, the wall-sized mirror no one with any measure of common sense would ever believe wasn't see-through. "You say you left your shop about eleven thirty, right?"

Alex fought hard to remain presentable. He sat tall and kept his shoulders back even though his body ached from the neck down; he had been sitting there close to an hour. "Yes. Like I said earlier, the book signing was over around nine, maybe nine thirty, and I left a couple of hours later after I cleaned up the place. I didn't check my watch, but eleven thirty seems accurate." He was frustrated—*beyond* frustrated—because on top of losing everything he had worked so hard to own, now he had to deal with the beady, disbelieving glare from this half-rate detective.

"And you received a call from dispatch around midnight?" the officer continued. Alex nodded. "Please speak your responses, Mr. Porter." The man tapped the short microphone sitting on the table between them, a dull thrum bouncing around the room.

Alex rolled his eyes but leaned forward a bit and cleared his throat. "Yes," he said. "I received a call from someone here, notifying me of the fire. I had stopped to get gas once I reached Main Street, so I wasn't too far away. I turned around and went straight back. I stayed there until the fire was out, then went home. To be crudely blunt... I got shitty drunk as soon as I got home and passed out. Then your officers woke me up extremely early this morning and dragged me down here. There...all caught up?"

The detective seemed unfazed by Alex's display, his face stoic. His lack of reaction set Alex's nerves ablaze.

"Am I missing something?" Alex asked with a shrug of his shoulders. "Why are you staring at me?"

The detective took his time answering. "Because I'm confused, Mr. Porter."

"Confused? What is there to be confused about?"

"Well..." Another long pause. Alex could almost taste the man's loftiness. "I'm confused, because we have no record of a phone call made to you from here. In fact—" the detective rummaged through the thin stack of papers "—your number has *never* been called from this precinct."

Now Alex was the one confused. Shock seized his muscles, his nerves, his ability to focus.

No phone call? How?

He shook his head. "No. No... That's impossible. Someone called me. A female officer. She told me my shop was on fire, and I needed to get there as fast as I could."

"She?" The detective scribbled in the notebook in front of him. "The officer was female?"

"Yes. And she clearly stated she was with the Cliffside Police Department. So, unless there's a secret one in town no one knows about, this has to be the one, this office."

The detective made more notes before looking up. "So, even though I can't find a single person, male or female, in this entire building who remembers calling you only a few hours ago, you're still sticking with your story?"

"This isn't a *story*, Detective. I'm telling you the truth. So, yes, I am 'sticking with it,' as you say. Feel free to search my phone if you believe I'm lying." Alex pulled his cell phone from his pocket and unlocked the screen before sliding it across the table. The detective scooped up the phone and skimmed through the contents, writing on his notepad again.

"I see you did, in fact, receive a call at five till midnight, but it wasn't from here." He placed the phone on the table in front of Alex. "Care to tell me who the call was from, Mr. Porter?"

Alex bit his tongue until he tasted blood. *Don't blow this, don't you dare.*

"I've already told you," he said through gritted teeth. "The person claimed to be a police officer. *From this police station.*" The detective crossed his arms and smirked, and Alex's frustration quadrupled. He fought the urge to cause a scene, he was so exasperated. "You know what, Detective—"

The door to the now claustrophobic room swung open and a slender, graying man in an expensive suit strode in. "Not another word, Alex." The man stopped when he reached the table and dropped a briefcase onto the cold metal surface. "I know you're not interrogating my client without me, Detective Singer. Right?"

Detective Singer half smiled. "No interrogating here, counselor. Simply having a conversation. Right, Mr. Porter?" Alex didn't respond.

"Well, suffice it to say this 'conversation' is over." The man didn't budge, staring down Singer for several tense seconds before the detective stood up from the table and left the room in silence. Alex couldn't help but smile. Score one for him; a nice change of pace, given recent events. Once they were alone, the man took a seat across from Alex and promptly switched off the microphone.

"Thank you," Alex stated. "Please don't take this the wrong way, but...Who are you? I know you're not my attorney. I don't have one."

The man smiled as he opened his briefcase and fished out some papers. "You do now."

"With all due respect, Mr.?"

"My name is William Stone, Alex. I'm with the firm Stone and Saber. In Bangor. I work for your mother."

Of course.

Alex was shaking his head again. "Thank you, but no thank you, Mr. Stone. I believe I would rather take my chances on my own."

"I'm afraid this isn't really your call. As I said, I work for your mother. And even though I'm representing you, and you will be afforded all the rights and privileges that come with attorney-client relationships, you don't have the authority to hire or fire me. Those privileges belong to Mrs. Porter."

"I don't have the right to release my own attorney? That can't be legal."

William smiled as he pored over the papers but said nothing.

Alex laughed at the situation and sat back in his chair. "My mother. She is... Well, she is certainly something else, isn't she?"

His mother. Evelyn Porter. Since birth, she had been controlling Alex's life in every way she could. Alex had used everything he had in him to break free from her control, to get out from under her rich but extremely heavy thumb and make something for himself. And now, in a matter of hours, she had managed to root her way back into his life again. This infuriated him to no end.

"I won't pretend to know or understand the relationship you have with your mother, Alex," William said. "That isn't my place. What *is* my place, however, is to see to the welfare of my clients. And since you're now my newest client, I will make certain all of this goes away quietly."

"Ah, there it is. Of course." Alex stared at William for a few seconds before continuing. "You're here for damage control. To make sure the famous Porter name doesn't get tarnished by a fire-starting criminal like me. Am I right, Mr. Stone?"

William clasped his hands together on the table and stared back at Alex almost to the point of awkward before saying, "My job, Mr. Porter, is to ensure you are treated fairly and justly. And if somehow this process ends with criminal charges being brought against you, my job will then be to do everything in my power to defend you. I promise nothing more or less."

"Please, allow me to clarify for myself." Alex cleared his throat. "Even though I didn't ask for an attorney—especially one from my mother—it seems as though I am...stuck with you. Correct?" His lawyer nodded. "Well. This is perfect."

William looked up from his paperwork just as the door swung open again and Alex's day from hell went from bad to a thousand times worse.

"Jesus." He dropped his hands into his lap and gave in to the unstoppable. "Like I said. Perfect."

"You'll remember to watch your tone, young man." A much older woman stepped into the room and stood next to William on the opposite side of the table.

Even though he wanted with every fiber of his being to curl into a ball in the corner of the room and disappear,

- 12 - | M.J. James

Alex instead bit back his rage and regained his composure. The muscles in his back seized up in protest, but he wouldn't allow the pain to show through. No chance he was going to let his mother see just how much she got to him. He swallowed his pride and forced the same fake smile he gave every time she was around. He knew there was no point in fighting her; she always got her way.

"Hello, Mother."

Chapter Two

MATT FIELDS WAS elbow-deep in a backlog of case files when his phone rang. As sergeant of the Southern Division of Maine, his job was to investigate any and all fires for the lower third of the state. And with an already skeleton crew of only four investigators, himself included, the workload was massive. Given the fact his senior investigator Brenda just retired, that load was now quadrupled. Hence the countless files threatening to split his desk in half. He shoved the current case he was working on—a local deli that burned down a week ago he was pretty sure was accidental—to the side and scooped up the phone on the third ring.

"Sergeant Fields."

"Sergeant Fields, this is Captain Nathanial Gregson with the Cliffside Police Department. Hope I didn't catch you at a bad time? I spoke with Marshal Teagues, and he said I should contact you directly."

"Never a good time to call, Captain Gregson, but what can I do for you?" Matt tried to quiet his frustration over his boss freely doling out his number without so much as a warning and made a mental note to discuss this at the next department meeting.

"We had a local bookstore fire last night. Total loss. Family has requested an investigator."

"Doesn't your department have investigators?"

"We do. And I tried to explain that to the family, but this is Evelyn Porter. Not sure if you know her or not—"

"—I know the name." Who within a hundred miles didn't? The Porter name was synonymous with Maine elite.

"Yeah, well, she's a character to say the least. And a major contributor to the mayor's campaign, which is why she pretty much gets her way in this town. So I apologize in advance for asking, but we need someone from your office to come over ASAP."

Matt glanced at the stacks of manila folders towering on his desk, all of which required the same amount of "ASAP" attention Evelyn Porter was demanding. He couldn't even find the time to tear away from his work long enough to take a piss. Leaving town? No chance.

"Arson?" Matt asked.

"Unknown as of yet, but from what I'm hearing from our local fire chief, sure looking like it."

Damn. Just what he needed, another arson case. Half the ones on his desk were the same, and those cases always took more time and a hell of a lot more energy to solve—the two things he was lacking at the moment.

"I'm sorry for your troubles, Captain, but I'm currently staring at about thirty cases on my desk, all of which need my attention before yours. I can't drop what I'm doing for you no more than I could for any of them."

There was a pause on the line before Gregson said, "Teagues told me you might say something like that and said I should remind you of your probationary period? I'm sorry to have to bring this up, Sergeant, I am, but I'm desperate. I got the mayor breathing down my damn neck on this one. Not to mention the Porter family."

Son of a bitch. He couldn't believe Teagues pulled the probation card. Matt had been sergeant for just over a month, and yes, technically he was still in his trial run, but for his boss to give out his information to some random police captain...it beyond pissed him off.

"So, basically, he told you I had no choice, am I right?" Matt was scribbling everything down as fast as he could with the plan to confront Teagues the first chance he got. Which, given the circumstances, wouldn't be for a while.

"Again, Sergeant, really sorry about all this. But Mrs. Porter feels an outside party would be more...*capable* of handling a case of this magnitude."

Translation: the family thought Gregson's department was about as competent as a three-legged dog. Matt kept his thought to himself.

Matt ran a hand through his hair, took another look at the files smothering him, then said, "Okay, Captain. Let me see what I can work out."

"I appreciate you, Sergeant. I'll be sure to let the family know."

"I'll get back to you." Matt hung up before Gregson could respond and plopped his elbows on the tiny square of desktop not covered in paperwork, resting his head in his palms. Jesus, how the hell had a seemingly promising promotion turned to shit so damn fast?

AFTER PUTTING IN calls to his investigative team— basically yielding three "no can dos, boss"—and leaving a message on Marshal Teagues' voicemail requesting a meeting, Matt headed home to pack a bag. As much as he didn't want to, added to the fact he had zero time, he knew he had no choice but to go to Cliffside. Defying orders from his boss was a sure-fire way to lose his job, and getting fired was the last thing he wanted. Sure, being in charge came with a whole new set of headaches, but Matt thrived on the challenge. He loved the excitement of the work he did and the reward of solving a case. But being ordered to do something, being given no say in the matter...nothing raked his nerves more.

He tossed his suitcase in the back of his SUV and navigated out of town, heading east. During the hour drive, he had plenty of time to prepare for what he imagined he would be walking into once he got to Cliffside. Some hoity-toity family and their sense of entitlement wasn't something he was used to dealing with, so he knew he had to be on his game.

He went through a mental list of current state laws and guidelines regarding cases of suspected arson, formulated a general plan of attack, and even brushed up on his sparse bank of vocabulary. Being a simple man from a simple background didn't give way to many "upper class" interactions, but in the couple of instances he had experienced, Matt held his own.

By the time he pulled into the parking lot of The Cliffside Inn, his confidence he could wrap this up and be home by the weekend was on a steady rise. He slipped into the motel office and got a room, choosing to pay the higher nightly rate versus a weekly one to help keep him focused on getting back to Bangor. After unloading his suitcase and making sure his bed had clean sheets—his one and only OCD tic—he hopped back in his SUV and whipped out into traffic.

He had already programmed the police station address into the nav system in his dash and pulled up the directions. He was only a few miles away, so he tried to mentally prepare himself for meeting Evelyn Porter face to face, just in case she happened to be at the station waiting on him. He didn't plan on being a dick or anything, but he also wouldn't let some socialite dictate what he would or wouldn't do. He planned to treat this just like any other incident: look for evidence, compile a case if the cause turned out to be arson, and turn the case over to Gregson and his team. The sooner he could do finish the inspection, the sooner he could get back to the shit-ton of files waiting for him.

Matt noticed a short, round man with a gun on his hip standing outside the side entrance of the building as he pulled into the police station parking lot and slipped his SUV into a slot marked VISITOR. The man looked to be in the middle of a heated phone conversation, his face red and his free hand gesturing wildly. Matt waited until the guy had calmed down, and then grabbed his digital voice recorder from the console before getting out. He learned a long time ago to record his notes. Made his life a hell of a lot easier than trying to decipher his written ones; he had the handwriting of a serial killer and was the first to admit it.

"Sergeant Fields?" The round man greeted him with an outstretched hand as Matt approached, slipping his phone into his pocket. Matt took his hand and gave a firm shake.

"Captain Gregson?" The man nodded. "Nice to put a face with the voice."

"Not a pretty one, but the only one I got." Gregson tugged at his belt. "Let's get inside. This damn heat is killing me." The temperature couldn't have been warmer than fifty-five degrees out and windy as hell. Matt wondered how high Gregson's blood pressure must be.

The inside of the Cliffside Police Department was about as impressive as the outside. The building was old, no doubt there, the walls an ugly green tile every government building from the fifties was decorated with. The small, open floor plan was overstuffed with equally dated desks, which surprisingly held updated computers and phones. A few officers milled about the giant room, but otherwise it looked like the daily grind was a slow one. Matt followed Gregson through the narrow walkway slicing through the middle of the room to a small office made almost entirely of glass in the back.

"Sorry for the mess," Gregson said as he rounded the large desk and attempted to clear some of the haphazard paperwork scattered across the top.

"Don't be. Looks better than mine." Matt smiled and took a seat in one of two straight-back armchairs that looked a lot more comfortable than it was.

"Yeah, well...hazard of being the boss, right?" Gregson gave a deep laugh which turned into a raspy cough as he plopped down into the desk chair. "Appreciate you coming out, Sergeant," he added after his coughing fit subsided.

"Didn't really have a choice, Captain."

Gregson tried to hide his discomfort. "Again, sorry about that. I don't normally like to—"

Matt waved him off. "Forget about it. I'm here." He shifted in his seat, his ass already numb from the hard wood, and fished the recorder from his pocket. He set it on the arm of his chair and pressed RECORD. "Okay, tell me about the case." He took a second to glance around the station. "Is Mrs. Porter here?"

"I believe you just missed her." Gregson stood up. "Wait, there she is." He pointed and took his seat again, and Matt caught sight of Evelyn Porter coming down a short hallway to his right. She looked just as he imagined, hair pulled back into one of those tight-ass buns that had to hurt like hell, a dark gray power suit which somehow didn't look dated on her. Matt could see how she was able to strong-arm the likes of Gregson, but he wasn't the least bit intimidated. To be fair, though, he *was* a bit distracted by the man walking with her.

The guy was slender, the T-shirt and jeans he was wearing fitting him nicely, accentuating what Matt could see was a well-defined body. His hair was thick and dark, maybe black, with the perfect amount of curl to be sexy. A light five o'clock shadow gave him a scruffy, unkempt look Matt had always liked. He was hot. *Very* hot, Matt noted, which he regretted thinking as fast as the thought entered his mind. He needed to stay focused on the job he was there to do, not on the fact he had been...damn, *three months* since getting off with somebody other than himself. Thoughts like those would get him into trouble he didn't need. Yet his eyes were glued to Evelyn Porter and the mystery guy as they rounded the corner, headed straight for him.

Thankfully, they bypassed Gregson's office, but not before the sexy guy and Matt made eye contact. Jesus, there were fireworks going off in his head. There was an instant, undeniable, strong-as-hell connection between them. He could feel the pulse, like when your heart beats in your finger after a bad papercut. His entire body thrummed. He was drawn to the guy, like...he would jump up and storm out after him just on the off-chance he could get a name or maybe even a smile. And the guy stared back hard at him, intensely, almost like...like he felt the exact same way.

Holy. Shit.

"Uh, who...who was the man with her?" Matt asked after turning back to Gregson once the guy and Mrs. Porter had disappeared around the corner. He hoped like hell he didn't look as fucking flustered as he felt. Every inch of him—a few of them more than others—was buzzing with electricity.

"Her son, Alex Porter. He owns the burned-up bookstore."

"Oh. I thought...So, Mrs. Porter isn't the owner?"

Gregson fished around on his desk for a few seconds before pulling a file out of the maelstrom and thumbing through the contents. "Nope. Looks like Alex Porter is the sole owner. Huh. That's a surprise."

"A surprise?"

Gregson looked up a few seconds later as though Matt hadn't been there all along. "What? Oh, no reason, really. It's just the Porters tend to have a hand in everything. And I thought Evelyn would have been part of her son's business. Goes to show you shouldn't judge, huh?" He started to laugh again but was cut short when another round of coughing rumbled in his chest.

"So, who wanted me here?"

"Oh, Evelyn for sure. Called me personally. At 6:00 a.m., mind you. Like I said, she's something else."

"Does Mr. Porter know?"

"Does he know his mother demanded you drop everything and come to town? Highly unlikely, but hell, anything's possible, right?" Matt lifted an eyebrow and Gregson smiled. "From what I know of Evelyn Porter, she's not the type to share what she's up to. No doubt the reason her firm is so successful, yeah?"

"Yeah, probably so." Matt had pretty much tuned out of the conversation, his thoughts on this guy Alex, who he'd bet had no idea his mother had ordered Matt in to investigate. This should go over well.

Dammit. Sometimes he hated his boss.

Chapter Three

"I DON'T NEED to hear the words, son, but I would be grateful if you could show a little appreciation. I did have to cancel my entire morning for this." Evelyn Porter always had a way of making everything about her. Her ability to spin things back to herself was one of the main reasons she and Alex never had a real relationship. Any time something happened to him—awards at school, a broken arm—somehow she became the center of attention and reaped the praise and sympathy. Even now, with his life in ruins and facing possible criminal charges, she was the one suffering.

"Thank you, Mother," he said with as much sarcasm as he could muster. "But I didn't ask for your help." Alex had zero intention of giving in this time. He learned long ago to not feed the beast; doing so only made things worse between them. Over the past few years, they had managed to build a socially acceptable relationship of awkward silence which made life much simpler for him, and he wasn't about to let said simplicity go.

"Fortunately for you, I have clout in this town," Evelyn went on as if he hadn't said a word. He lagged behind her as they left the police department and stood on the sidewalk until a black town car rounded the corner headed in their direction. "Otherwise, you would be arrested by now."

"So, you're the law now, Mother?"

Evelyn cut her eyes at him. "Tone."

He wanted more than anything to tell her to go to hell and just walk away, figure out how to fix this mess on his own. But somewhere deep in the back of his mind he knew—as much as the realization made his stomach turn even more than the hangover he was forging through already had—he did, in fact, need her help.

"I'm sorry," he said, caving. "I'm just...stressed out over everything. I can't believe this is happening." The town car pulled up to the curb, and a tall, slender man in a black suit hopped out and circled the back to open the door. Evelyn slid in and Alex followed.

"Take us to the site, Carl." The driver nodded and pulled out into traffic. "I knew this would turn out badly for you, Alexander," she continued as they headed across town. "From the moment you told me your plans to open your own business, I've been waiting for this."

"Really, Mother? You've been waiting for a phone call telling you my shop burned to the ground and the police think I'm responsible?"

"Don't be acerbic," Evelyn snapped. "It's beneath you."

Alex huffed. "Mother, please. Can't you just be...*normal* for once?" The shock on Evelyn's face only fueled his nerves. "This is serious."

"I know all too well how serious this is, Alexander. That's why I'm here."

"Oh, please. Let's not do this again, okay? We both know the real reason you're here." He was opening the door to the car before the driver had fully stopped, desperate to get away from her. The familiar pressure in his chest when she was around had come back, and he was struggling to take a breath. He stepped onto the sidewalk with his eyes closed and sucked in the crisp northern air, trying to calm his nerves. He hadn't seen her in months, and yet after a five-minute conversation he was already feeling defeated. Opening his eyes and seeing what was left of his dream in the harsh daylight only crushed him even more.

The store was a complete loss. With the exception of a few feet of front and rear walls and the fixtures from the bathroom, everything was either severely burned or altogether gone. He fought the urge to cry as he stumbled his way through the debris of his life. The hardback copies of Dickens, Poe, and Bronte he had purchased at an estate sale in Bangor were nothing but ash now, littering the muddy floor of his once-thriving shop, mixed with slivers of burned bookcases and shards of soot-stained glass. The reading area he had been so proud of—a cozy nook tucked in the back of the building with a window overlooking the park, and the inspiration for the shop's moniker—was nothing more than a pile of debris, the expensive Italian leather Nella Vetrina lounge chairs his mother's assistant had given him as a grand-opening gift now nothing more than a heap of rawhide and metal springs.

Alex closed his eyes and tried to ignore the nausea, his stomach doing somersaults and his head spinning. He risked everything opening this place, the one and only time he used his family's status in this town to get special treatment. He needed the bank loan to secure the location, furnish the place, and stock the shelves with books. The fact he threw his name out to get the money had always haunted him.

Since he had been old enough to realize the weight the Porter name carried in Cliffside, Alex had fought against the privilege his moniker brought. He never wanted anything given to him because of who his parents were. Everything he ever had—his first car, the house he was struggling to pay for—he got on his own. The fact his independence upset his mother was merely an unexpected but welcome bonus. She couldn't understand why he wouldn't just take the trust fund she and his father set up for him when he was just a boy, and he had given up years ago trying to make her see he wasn't the type of person who rode on someone else's coattails. Right now, staring at his life, what was going to be his future, he thought about his trust fund, how easily he could just take the money and rebuild, bigger and better as they say. He squashed the idea as quickly as it rose and refocused. No way would he use their money. *Her* money. Like everything else in his life, he would find a way to make things right again. He just had no idea how.

"What is that supposed to mean, Alexander?" Evelyn joined him on the sidewalk outside his burned-out store.

"Seriously, Mother?" he asked. "Do you not see, or are you just choosing to ignore everything?" Evelyn stared at him like a deer in headlights, oblivious to her own self-servedness. "We both know you're not here for me. You're here for *you*."

Evelyn tried to hide her shock, but Alex could see it plain as day all over her face. "How is this for me?" she asked.

Alex laughed. "Let's not play this game anymore. We both know the only reason you're here is to keep our name—*your* name—out of the mud. Our name is really all you care about, right? What everybody else thinks about the all-mighty Porters? To be honest, I would bet my inheritance you're even *happy* my shop burned down."

Evelyn stood quiet for several seconds before pulling her cell phone from her purse. Alex was surprised as she punched in a number and brought the phone to her ear. He couldn't help but notice her demeanor had shifted a bit. She was always stern and off-putting, had been as far back as Alex could remember, but now she held an air of confidence and determination. Though it hurt him to admit, she was impressive.

"This is Evelyn Porter. I need to speak to Captain Gregson." Evelyn stared out at the charred remnants of Alex's shop as she waited on the line, her free arm crossed over her chest. Alex wondered what she was thinking as she stood there silent. Was she worried about him, about what he would do with his livelihood gone? Was she scared for him? Upset at all? He shook his head. No, he already knew the answer to those questions. She was in damage-control mode, nothing else. By the time her conversation picked back up, Alex was angry at her all over again.

"Nathanial," Evelyn said into the phone, "thank you for taking my call. I'm doing well, thank you. I'm calling about the fire at—yes, it is." She looked to Alex for a few seconds, then, "that's actually why I am calling. I wanted to follow up on my request for someone from the Bangor fire marshal's office to come run the investigation."

Evelyn sidestepped Alex—who wasn't the least bit surprised his mother had made such a request to the Cliffside police captain; she was nothing if not full of self-serving privilege—and began pacing the sidewalk. "Oh, you already have? Wonderful to hear, Nathanial, thank you. I appreciate your determination. This needs to be resolved promptly. And I believe our local departments just aren't equipped to conduct an accurate, thorough investigation of this magnitude. This is my son we are talking about here. Surely you understand?" A few more seconds of silence went by before Evelyn was smiling. "Excellent. I appreciate your help with this. And your discretion. And please give Brenda my regards." Evelyn ended the call and returned her phone to her purse. She took a moment to compose herself before turning to Alex.

"I'm assuming you caught every word?" she asked. Alex nodded. "Good. Now, maybe you will see I am not here just for damage control. I'm here for you, Alexander. I will do whatever I can to help get us past this."

Even though he had no doubt of his mother's true intentions, Alex decided to keep his thoughts to himself for once. He was too emotionally drained to fight anymore.

"Thank you, Mother."

Evelyn smiled and put a hand on his shoulder—her idea of affection. "Now, how about some breakfast? I'm sure you're starved." Without waiting for an answer, she signaled to Carl and the man leapt into action. The car was in front of them before Alex had a second to think.

"No, I'm not very hungry," he said as Carl opened the back door for them.

"Nonsense," Evelyn interjected. She eyed Alex. "You look like you haven't eaten in days."

Alex rolled his eyes. "I eat, Mother. I'm just...not hungry right now."

Evelyn stood her ground. "Well, coffee, then? I'm sure you could use some, yes?" Alex glanced at the Book Nook behind them and she added, "And a change of scenery?" He smiled, though only half genuine.

He wanted to just be by himself, to be honest. He wanted to sit and stare at what was left of his store and wallow in the self-pity taking up residence in his heart and not care about anything else in the world other than feeling sorry for himself. But he knew his mother wouldn't back down, so he had no choice but to give in.

"Coffee sounds good."

"Excellent." Evelyn closed the car door and stepped next to him. "You know what? This morning is so lovely. Let's walk instead." She didn't wait for Alex to protest as she took off down the sidewalk, leaving him no choice but to follow.

"So," he said after several seconds of awkward silence. "How was the drive over?"

"Oh, dreadful. I'm always amazed how such a small city can have so much traffic."

"Bangor isn't small, Mother. It's three times the size of Cliffside."

"Yes, and half the size of Portland. Oh, I wish your father had listened to me when I told him to start his company there. Portland made so much more business sense."

"Portland is two hours away. He didn't want to spend all his time driving. And you wanted to live here."

Just the mere mention of his father had Alex missing the man. Unlike his mother, Alex had a real connection to his dad. The man was much more loving than Evelyn, though still somewhat standoffish and reserved.

Charles Porter had been a master at doling out equal parts affection and criticism. He could tell you he loved you while explaining how you screwed up all at once. He was tough but fair. Loving but distant, when the need arose. He had his flaws for sure, loads of them, but Alex had never doubted his father cared for him.

He missed his dad.

"Yes, well, business would be much better had he done what I suggested."

Alex laughed. "Mother, you just told the chief of police to jump and he asked how high. I think business is going well."

"Still, life would be far nicer to not have to worry about some things."

Evelyn always had a flair for the dramatic, making things out to be much worse than they ever were. Alex didn't keep close tabs on the family business, but he knew his mother was in no way hurting for money. Her monthly stipend from the business, along with the insurance money left to her by Alex's late father, kept her much more than well off. But to hear her tell the tale, they were one bad business deal away from poverty. Her blatant disregard for just how privileged she had become was just one more thing frustrating about her.

"Subject change," he said as they came to a stop in front of Maggie's, a small but extremely busy café. "I didn't thank you for your help. Back at the police station. And the phone call. I...I appreciate all you've done, Mother." And he did. Though he hated admitting so to his mother, her effort at kindness made Alex feel special to know even though they had a rocky relationship at best, she would, in fact, come to his rescue if need be, ulterior motives or not.

They took a small table by the front of the café and gave the server their orders. Evelyn waited until they were alone again before speaking.

"Alexander," she said, her voice so low he strained to hear her. "You don't have to thank me. I'm your mother. My job is to take care of you." And he knew she meant every word. More than even she realized. Evelyn had always regarded parenting as a job, nothing more, nothing less. There had never been an emotional attachment for her, not really. No bond most mothers have with their children. Of course, Alex knew she loved him, but her love was more out of responsibility rather than purity. Like being maternal and caring and nurturing was her duty versus a choice she was more than happy to make or simply the course of nature. At least that was the way it came off. Now, far too much time had passed to change anything, which left them in the awkward, almost transactional relationship they'd been navigating for the past few years since his father's death.

"Either way," Alex said, "thank you."

Evelyn gave him a tight smile. "Let's discuss what comes next." The server arrived with their coffees and again she waited until he walked away, always mindful of outside appearance, before continuing. "I spoke at length with William before he arrived this morning. He believes nothing will come of this, but I'm not one to rely on others or their beliefs."

"Of course not." Alex took a sip of his coffee, ignoring the peculiar look he was getting from his mother.

"Which is why I called Nathanial," she went on. "I have it on good authority the marshal's office in Bangor is one of the best. I'm confident they will prove you had nothing to do with the fire and all of this will simply go away."

"I didn't."

Evelyn took a sip of her drink. "Well of course, I know."

"Do you?" Alex asked. "Because sometimes I don't feel like you do." If there was one thing he liked about his mother, it was her ability to finagle her way through anything. A master at the art of bluffing, he gave up long ago trying to determine if she was being honest or merely spinning a web. But he had learned to recognize her tells over the years, and she just showed one.

"Don't be silly. Of course, I know you didn't do this. I didn't raise you in such a way."

"You didn't—" He wanted to tell her she hadn't raised him at all. His father did, though only barely, along with an endless stream of nannies. But he kept quiet before he said something guaranteed to cause an argument—or more importantly, as far as his mother was concerned, a scene.

Evelyn glared at him. "Now is hardly the time to discuss your feelings on your childhood, Alexander. We have far more important things to worry about."

He laughed. "Yes, Mother, let's ignore the real problem, shall we? I mean, there's no point in changing things up now, right?" He signaled the waiter who made a beeline for their table. "May we have the check, please?" The young man nodded and left. Evelyn took another lingering sip of coffee as if nothing had changed even though the tension between them was so thick Alex couldn't breathe.

"Let's try to remain focused, shall we?" Evelyn stated. "I'm sure the day will come when we will get into whatever issues you may or may not have with me, but right now we need to work on getting you out of this mess."

The waiter returned with the check just as Alex opened his mouth to speak. He took a cue from his mother and waited until the man left before fishing a twenty from his wallet and tossing the bill onto the table.

"You've helped enough," he said, standing up. "Thanks again for the lawyer. And the phone call. But I think it's best if we don't spend too much time together. I would certainly hate to know I inadvertently caused you to feel something real and honest about your son."

Evelyn grabbed his wrist as he tried to walk away. "Sit down, Alexander. You're creating a scene."

He pulled away. "Why, Mother? So we can both just sit here and pretend nothing is wrong between us? Keep acting as though this is just part of the norm, the two of us having a cup of coffee together like a couple of gossiping girlfriends?"

Evelyn stood and faced her son. "Don't be uncouth. It's beneath you." Her eyes scanned the room, refocusing on Alex only after confirming no prying eyes were zeroed in on them. "Because whether or not you agree," she went on, "I am the only person who is capable of helping you. And you are mistaken if you think you won't need help getting out of the mess you're in. So. do as I say and sit down." She took her seat again like she knew he would obey.

And dammit, she was right.

Alex stood there a moment longer, hoping to show his mother his resilience against her, before sitting back down. His anger was at near uncontrollable levels.

"Now," Evelyn said, her voice calm, unwavering. "As I was saying, let's discuss what happens next." She sipped her coffee with poise and grace and unbridled stoicism Alex expected. Though he had seen this countless time throughout his life, his mother's knack for taking complete control of a situation was always something to witness firsthand. "I think you should move back home. I can cover any expenses you may have until you finish school, and once you've graduated, you can come to work at the office. I believe it's far past the time for you to begin taking your future seriously."

"You can't be... Are you for real?"

"Don't use colloquialisms, Alexander. You're far better."

He smirked. "I have no intentions of moving back home, Mother. I have a house, you know. And there is absolutely no chance I will be working at the family office. Or any office, for that matter."

Evelyn clasped her hands together on the table and stared at him. "Well then, please tell me, how do you plan to live, if I might ask? How will you pay for things like food, electricity? The house you mentioned? Those things and many others aren't free, Alexander. And don't even think about getting government assistance. You are a Porter. We do not take handouts."

"Oh my God," Alex snapped back, his anger winning the fight and showing itself. "You do know I'm not a child, right? I'm a grown man, Mother. Independent from you. I have been for much longer than you care to admit. I am more than capable of taking care of myself."

Evelyn took another sip of coffee. "I see. So, you would have been fine had I not sent William over this morning?"

"Yes," Alex lied. "I would have. And speaking of... How did you even know I was at the station anyway?"

"I told you, son, I have some clout in this town. I keep up with things of importance to me."

"Of course you do." Alex downed the remainder of his coffee, the still-hot liquid scorching his throat all the way down. "If that's true, which I don't doubt, then you know I'm doing just fine living on my own without any help from you. I've been doing so virtually my entire life."

He caught the twinge of...*something* cross his mother's face. Was it guilt? Highly unlikely, but something registered there.

"Be that as it may," Evelyn said, "Nothing changes the fact you could potentially be facing severe criminal charges. Do you even realize this, Alexander? Because from my vantage point, I would have to say you don't. Your income source is now gone. And you continue to refuse to take charge of the trust your father and I worked hard to build for you. So, you can deny all you want, let your pride be your downfall if you feel you must, but like it or not, you *are* going to need some help moving forward."

"Well, be *that* as it may," Alex said, no longer in control of his emotions, "any financial help I may or may not need will not be coming from you." Enraged and on the brink of crossing a line he wouldn't be able to come back from, he stood up from the table. "And please, Mother...don't bother coming back to the store. I think we've both had enough of each other for one day. I'll send Carl back around to pick you up." He slid the money he'd tossed onto the table earlier over to her, said, "Coffee's on me," and left the café.

Chapter Four

MATT WAS ON the fucking edge by the time he left the station. He had pretty much prepared himself for Evelyn Porter and the demanding, privileged personality he knew she would no doubt have, but he wasn't ready to possibly butt heads with her son who was insanely hot and would be a definite distraction. Put him in a situation with a beautiful woman, and Matt could charm the pants off her. But a guy he was attracted to? He usually fumbled over his words and looked like a total idiot. Which was the last thing he wanted to happen on the job. He needed to be composed and professional, not blushing and stammering like a love-struck teenager.

No, he wouldn't let that happen. He would be an adult, focus on the job he was there to do, even if that job killed him. He wouldn't let his actions be controlled by his starving libido, no matter how hard it might be.

Literally.

He followed the directions from his GPS and was turning onto Shemwood a few minutes later. As he made his way down the street, he noticed how peaceful the small town was. Shop after shop lined the sidewalks, each visually tying into the next like the entire city got together and decided on a matching theme. Cafés had small tables out front; a flower shop was vomiting colorful balloon bouquets and poinsettias all over the sidewalk, signaling the upcoming holiday season; even the local drugstore had its doors opened wide, racks of sale items pouring out. In the past, shit like that would've made his skin crawl. But now...everyone celebrating the time of year kind of warmed him a little. Sure, he loved the fast-paced, hectic life he had back in Bangor, but he couldn't deny how slowing things down carried its own appeal.

Matt noticed the burned-out building before he reached the end of the street. A thin plume of smoke still rose in the air above the site, and the stench of burned wood and debris filled his nose even with the windows up. He wheeled his SUV up to the curb across the street and got out, grabbing his digital voice recorder. A deep voice caught him off guard just as he stepped onto the sidewalk and ducked beneath the yellow POLICE LINE: DO NOT CROSS tape.

"Are you a cop?"

Matt spun around, the recorder twirling through his fingers like a baton before he was able to catch it. Alex Porter. Still in the same T-shirt and jeans, still just as hot and inviting.

Damn.

"Um, not exactly." He slipped back under the tape and walked up to Alex. "I'm Sergeant Matt Fields with the Bangor Fire Marshal's Office." He extended a hand, and Alex glanced down before merging it with his own and giving Matt a firm shake. Alex's hand was warm, soft, *not* the hand of a man used to manual labor, and Matt's body tingled from their touch. Alex smiled, and Matt could feel his cheeks burn red. "Sorry for your loss, Mr. Porter."

"Please, call me Alex. My father was Mr. Porter. So, I guess you're here to prove I, in fact, burned down my own store." Though he spoke with a distinguished air, his tone confirmed what Matt had suspected back at the police station; he wasn't happy about Matt being there. Sunlight bounced off Alex's face, making the green of his eyes almost glow. Talk about a distraction.

"Well, no, not exactly, Mr. Porter. I—"

"—*Alex*, please." Alex gave a forced smile, and Matt tried not to stare.

"I'm here to investigate, nothing else. I don't have a personal investment in this case one way or the other. I know your family *demanded* I drop everything and come look into this, but I won't be altering anything I may or may not find to prove or disprove anyone's innocence or guilt." His cheeks burned again but for a whole different reason this time. He didn't stand for bullshit—not when said bullshit came from someone who thought they were better than others.

"Well," Alex said. "Please, Sergeant Fields, tell me how you feel. Don't hold back." He slid his hands into the back pockets of his jeans, which pulled his T-shirt tight over his chest. So tight Matt could make out well-defined pecs and pert nipples.

God, he needed to focus.

"Sorry if I came across as rude or...socially unacceptable, *Mr. Porter*. But I want to remain nothing but professional during my time here. I'm sure you understand."

Alex nodded. "I wouldn't expect anything less."

"Good." Matt pushed pent-up air from his lungs. "Now, if you'll excuse me, I need to get started." Alex didn't say a word, only stepped to the side and held out a hand toward the debris where his shop once stood. Matt hated being a jerk, but he didn't have time to play nice. And being too friendly with this guy was dangerous, he could already tell. Alex was far too pretty for Matt to be anything but a hundred percent by the book.

"I'll let you know when I'm done." He stepped past Alex, catching a whiff of a sweet, masculine cologne that made his head spin in a good way as he lifted the police tape and re-entered the cordoned-off area. "I, uh... Could you stay here until I finish? I might have questions."

"I don't plan on going anywhere, Sergeant." Matt picked up on Alex's tone. He knew he had pissed him off, which might turn out to be a good thing in the end. He couldn't have someone who didn't want him. Not that he *wanted* Alex. Or maybe he did. Hell, he didn't know what he wanted, or why the hell he was even having those thoughts. He was there to do a damn job, not get laid. But...three months. *Three months.*

"Thank you." He attempted a half-assed smile and left Alex alone on the sidewalk. He shook the inappropriate thoughts from his mind and refocused on why he had just put his life on hold and drove over an hour. He could worry about solving his other problem later.

THE INSPECTION OF the property took all of fifteen minutes for Matt to finish up. Less than half the time to determine arson was the cause. Which meant one thing:

He wasn't getting out of Cliffside anytime soon.

He caught sight of Alex leaning against a metal trashcan beneath an over-pruned maple tree out by the street. He had his hands tucked into his front pockets. The brisk northern wind swept through, lifting and swirling his shaggy black hair. His T-shirt flew up a time or two, revealing a flat, muscled stomach and tanned skin. He was insanely fucking sexy, no doubt about it, and he was getting to Matt in all the right ways. But Matt would be a damned fool to even consider making a move given Alex might very well be behind the fire. But he sure as hell didn't stop from getting all tingly and excited at the notion.

Alex stood straight when Matt approached. "Am I under arrest, Sergeant?" he asked.

Matt could see his fear, hiding just beneath a layer of attitude and feigned confidence. He had to admire his determination, but at the same time, he needed to remember this guy, no matter how incredibly sexy, could very well be an arsonist. He just couldn't let Alex know yet. If Alex skipped town, a shit storm of trouble would fall right into Matt's lap.

"I have to submit my report to Captain Gregson, and to Chief Stevens at the fire department," Matt answered, trying not to stare into Alex's hypnotic eyes. "What happens next is up to them." He wasn't telling the entire truth—he could be as involved with making an arrest as he wanted to be. Hell, he could've put Alex in cuffs and hauled him in right then if he'd wanted to. But that wasn't how he operated. He stuck strictly to investigating the fire to determine cause, leaving the back end to the cops. Sure, a few times he had to see the case through to the end, but he had no intention of going the distance on this one, despite Evelyn Porter's ridiculous demands. If a deeper investigation proved Alex was the person behind the fire, Cliffside PD would make sure he was dealt with.

"You can't even tell me if the fire was accidental or intentional?" Alex crossed his arms over his chest and glared at Matt.

"I know you might be used to things going a certain way for you, but that's not how I work. I don't comment on ongoing investigations."

"What is that supposed to mean?"

"Nothing at all, Mr. Porter. I just know how small towns operate. Which is why I was called in."

"Please don't get confused, Sergeant. You're here only because my mother has overwhelming control issues, not because the people in this town aren't smart enough to solve crimes or too ignorant to keep their mouths shut when warranted. And for you to insinuate—"

"—I'm sorry if I offended you," Matt interjected. "I never intended to. I just meant I can't talk about this case with you. It's not my place. I'm only here to investigate. What I find is for the local police. What they do with the results of my investigation, who they tell...that's up to them."

Alex smirked and stepped back. "Well, excuse me for asking if *my* business was intentionally burned to the ground or if the fire was accidental. I suppose I will just have to wait for the police to show up at my door again to arrest me." He ran a hand through his hair, and damn if the move didn't send a jolt right to Matt's groin.

Not now, you horny bastard. Stay focused.

"Calm down, Mr. Porter. There's no reason to get worked up."

"Worked up? Is that what I'm doing? Sorry for getting 'worked up' over being arrested for something I didn't do."

"No one is being arrested right now. And if you had nothing to do with the fire, then you have nothing to worry about."

"Oh, of course. Why didn't I think of that? Well, thank you. That is so very helpful." Alex turned and walked toward a silver four-door parked a few spaces away. Regardless of his shitty attitude, Matt couldn't help but stare at an impressive jeans-clad ass as Alex sauntered off.

"Don't leave town, Mr. Porter!" he yelled after the man.

Alex stopped and spun around to face him. "Don't worry, Sergeant, I have no intentions of going anywhere." Though Matt could almost feel Alex's hatred for him, he couldn't help but get turned on by the powerful confidence and attitude. He had always been attracted to men like Alex Porter, the overly confident, cocky assured types who demanded respect and always got what they wanted. He had no clue if what he'd seen was Alex's true personality or just a side effect of his overloaded emotions, but the way Alex carried himself was definitely working in his favor. Matt stood silent as he drove off, and even after such an uncomfortable, heated first impression, he knew he wanted to get to know Alex better.

Maybe sticking around in Cliffside for a while wouldn't suck so much after all.

Chapter Five

ALEX WAS BEYOND mad by the time he made it home from the Book Nook for two reasons. One, Sergeant Matthew Fields was a complete imbecile who had basically called him a spoiled, privileged brat right to his face, and two, the man was beyond sexy which was driving Alex insane.

From the second Matt had stepped out of his SUV, Alex was taken by him. He noticed the sculpted body buried beneath slim-fit khakis and a white button-down, muscles tightening the fabric in all the right places as he walked up. But nothing compared to his face. A five o'clock shadow trimmed to perfection dusted a strong, well-defined jaw sheathed in amber-colored skin. Full lips anchored his features nestled beneath a spot-on proportioned nose and deep-brown eyes which sucked him right in. He was the complete definition of Tall, Dark and Handsome, insanely mesmerizing, and Alex had had to swallow a few times before he spoke.

Even after their argument, he still couldn't get the man out of his mind. On one hand, he wanted to steer clear of Matt Fields, but on the other...well, he didn't know *what* he wanted. He was only twenty-four, but he'd had his fair share of scandalous sexual encounters, so being nervous and on edge around men—good-looking, confident men like Matt Fields—wasn't his normal behavior. But Matt had somehow already gotten under his skin and he couldn't shake him. Never had he been infuriated and turned on by a man so much.

But...what if Matt found something during his investigation? What said something might be, Alex couldn't fathom, but if Matt did, it would mean someone had burned down the store on purpose. Someone like...

No. He wouldn't let himself even go there. Brayden would never do something so horrible. Yes, Alex had broken up with him only a couple of months ago, and yes, Bray had been extremely angry and agitated, but he wasn't psychotic. Or a sociopath. There was no chance he would burn down the Book Nook as payback.

Would he?

Thoughts of Brayden and their life together—and how things had gone from magical to unbearable so fast— occupied his thoughts, along with how different his life had become in only twenty-four hours. His bookstore, the most important thing in his life, was gone. Besides the loss of an income—which he didn't need, if he were being honest; the store was never about the money—he also lost the spark that kept him going. And the cherry on the cake? He was positive he would soon be suspected of arson. The realization of what the fire meant had only just begun settling in, and he was fighting against the overwhelming feeling of despair threatening to upend him even more.

No. He wouldn't let dejection have control. He wouldn't let the feeling win, take over his life, end him. He would fight to keep his sanity. He would overcome this. He would survive. He would rebuild. He had to. He would figure out how to clean up the mess he was in and start over. And maybe, just maybe, his life would be better than before.

Before.

Oh, he hated when those memories came back. They didn't show up often—he had gotten good at keeping them locked away deep, deep in his mind—but when they did Alex struggled to move past them all over again. Only a few months had passed since he turned his life on its head by walking away from the man he had once thought was "the one." A silly, almost childish ideology, believing there was only one person in the world who was the perfect fit for another, but Alex couldn't help but hold onto the dream. The dream was what he had wanted most out of life. To find his person. To share the world with someone who held the same feelings he did. He had never witnessed first-hand a relationship built on love—his parents' marriage always seemed more like an arranged one, forged from necessity—but Alex didn't let their lack of love stop him from hoping. Even now, after his almost three-year relationship had crashed and burned, he still believed in soul mates, those two halves of one being who were destined to be complete again. He just had to get out there and find his.

But in the meantime, there was nothing wrong with having a little fun. And maybe "a little fun" would come in the form of a hotter-than-hell fire sergeant. Sure, Matt aggravated Alex to no end—made clear in the first five seconds they met—and the man seemed to have a major chip on his shoulder, but Alex was talking about sex, not marriage. And it was obvious Matt needed sex just as much, if not more, than Alex, so he would relax a little. Plus, the idea of sleeping with the enemy, so to speak, was hot in itself.

ALEX TOOK HIS time in the shower. Thoughts of Matt and what might be under those khakis had him so turned on he had to take care of things before finishing up. Which took him by surprise, because he wasn't the type of man who generally got worked up over a stranger. Sure, it had been a few months since he and Bray had broken up, and even longer since they had been together intimately, but reaching the point of needing release over a guy? Sergeant Fields really did a number on him.

He threw on some clothes once he was done and headed out. After the morning he'd had with his mother, followed by his run-in with Matt, he had gone all day without eating and his stomach was all too happy to remind him. He tried to ignore the grumbling demands as he headed through town. He wanted to stay as far from Shemwood Avenue and his demolished store as possible, so he decided on Dean's Diner across town for dinner. The place wasn't the best by any means, but the food was decent and Wednesday nights were typically slow.

This night, however, seemed to be the exception. Alex had to circle the lot twice before he parked, settling on a narrow spot out by the street. He hadn't seen Dean's this packed in a while and thought about maybe grabbing something to go and heading back home. But...he didn't want to sit alone and eat. Sure, he would be eating by himself at the restaurant, but at least there would be people around and the ambient noise would help keep his mind off his troubles. A lot of people, he realized once he stepped inside.

The interior of the diner was teeming with customers, every table taken and a line of patrons stretching the length of the front wall, waiting beneath a large white "To Go" sign dangling from the ceiling. A few servers were zipping in and out of the tables with expert precision, carrying plates of food and refilling drinks with a frenzy. Alex stood just inside the doorway and glanced around the dining area, searching for even the smallest empty table. He didn't find one, but he did, however, find the source of his earlier masturbation session. Sitting alone in the back of the restaurant, his nose buried in a newspaper and a patty melt plate, was Matt.

There was no denying Matt was gorgeous. He was no longer wearing the department-issued white button-down and black tie, this time dressed in a very tight maroon V-neck tee which made Alex's entire body twitch with marked anticipation. Though he wanted to do the polite, sociable thing and go over and strike up a conversation, he knew doing so was a bad idea. Matt had just finished scrounging through charred debris for evidence Alex had burned down his own business; becoming friends with him wasn't the wisest choice.

Just as he made the decision to forego the diner for some fast food and head back home, Matt looked up. And right into Alex's eyes.

Perfect.

With no other choice now, Alex had to do the honorable thing. He wound his way through the crowded diner and right over to Matt's table.

"Good evening, Sergeant," he said, trying his best to be polite and sociable.

Matt brushed his hands together before extending one to Alex. After a couple seconds, Alex gave it a firm shake, feeling the heat from Matt's skin. His heart rate spiked from a two-second handshake. Jesus. "Good to see you again, Mr. Porter."

"Alex."

Matt nodded with a half smile. "Have a seat, *Alex*," he said, gesturing to the other side of the booth.

"No, thank you. I...wouldn't want to intrude on your dinner." Truth was, he didn't want to sit with the arrogant investigator, regardless how incredibly enticing he currently looked.

"Not at all." Matt smiled and gestured to the empty seat across the way, and Alex feigned graciousness as he slid into the booth opposite him. "Not like there was anywhere else to sit anyway."

"How thoughtful."

A waitress showed up at their table and slid a menu in front of him. "What can I get you to drink, hon?" Alex looked up at her and noticed she couldn't have been but a couple of years older than he was. It really irked him when someone used terms of endearment like "hon" or "sweetie" or "dear" when talking to complete strangers; he cared even less when said someone was his own age. But he didn't want Matt to think he was socially inept, so he kept his annoyance to himself and ordered an iced tea.

"Come here often?" Matt asked once she was gone and lowered his gaze, giving a small laugh. "Sorry, that sounded like a really bad pickup line. I swear it wasn't."

"I didn't think it was," Alex answered.

Matt looked up at him and nodded. "Good."

They spent the next few minutes in very uncomfortable silence, only speaking when the waitress came back to take his order. He didn't want to seem like a copycat, but he decided to go with the same thing Matt had ordered because, despite the rest of their less-than-average menu, Dean's had the best patty melt in the state. After the waitress left, Alex decided to bite the bullet.

"So, tell me, Sergeant...why are you suddenly being so nice to me?" Matt raised an eyebrow as he gulped his drink. "Please don't act like you haven't been brusque toward me since the second we first met."

"I didn't say two words to you when we first met."

Alex rolled his eyes. "I'm not talking about at the police station. I mean at my store. You were...well, you were being a complete jerk."

Matt leaned back in the booth and stared at Alex for the longest time before finally saying, "I'm sorry about that. Really. I just...I was pissed at the whole situation."

"Wow. You have an odd way of apologizing. But I suppose the polite thing would be to accept." Matt gave a smile mirroring Alex's in authenticity. "And to what situation are you referring, if I might ask?"

"Having to come here." Matt sat upright. "Having to drop what I was doing because some rich b—uh, because the Cliffside police department can't handle anything on their own."

Alex smirked. "That's not what you were going to say."

"Yes it was."

Alex raised an inquisitive brow but let Matt's almost-faux pas go. "Please, continue."

"Look..." Matt stared hard at him, his eyes almost hypnotic, drawing Alex in—which fueled Alex's anger at himself even more for even allowing his mind to entertain such thoughts. "I'm not used to all this bureaucratic bullshit, having to play politics every damn day. I just wanna do my job and go home. I don't wanna have to rub elbows and kiss ass all the time."

"So, you think since my mother, the, um, 'rich bitch' you were going to talk about, ordered you here then I must be just like her, right? A rich...bastard, I suppose?" Alex was white-knuckling his knees, he was so infuriated. But he couldn't pinpoint why. Possibly because Matt thought he was a stuck-up, entitled snob, or maybe because his mother yet again meddled and made his life harder than necessary?

"What? No, not at all. I just..." Matt exhaled, and Alex noticed his features change, soften a bit. "I'm sorry. For being a dick. For assuming you were some stuck-up trust-fund brat with too much money and not enough respect for others."

"Wow. Please, Sergeant, don't skimp on the details."

Matt laughed. "Hey, you called me out. Least I can do is be honest."

Alex shrugged. "True."

"But I *am* sorry. It wasn't fair of me to put my issues on you. I'm new at this job. I guess there's a bit of an adjustment getting used to how I have to operate now."

"Wait, you're new? Have you ever even investigated a fire before?" This was news Alex hadn't been expecting. Had his mother inadvertently placed his future, his freedom, in the hands of a man ill-equipped for the job?

"What? Yeah, of course. I'm not new in the *field*, just my position. I just got promoted to sergeant two months ago. Pretty much why I couldn't say no." Alex was the one raising a brow this time. "Ninety-day probation."

"Ah, I see."

"So I was pissed off having to ignore the piles of work on my desk *and* at my boss for telling your police captain I'm basically his bitch for the next month."

Alex laughed. "Being someone's bitch isn't always a bad thing, Sergeant." Matt's eyes widened and Alex wanted to crawl under the table. "I mean, uh...um...hey, you, uh, ever been to Cliffside before?"

Matt laughed. "You sound a hell of a lot more like the rest of us commoners when you're embarrassed."

"I'm not embarrassed, Sergeant. And I'm as common as the next guy. I just..." He was utterly embarrassed and would have given anything for the power to go out or lightning to strike. Since neither those nor any other natural disaster or unexplained phenomenon was going to save him, he would have to himself. "You never answered my question," he prodded. "Have you been to Cliffside before? I don't recall seeing you around town."

"You make a habit to know every face in town?"

Alex smiled and his heart skipped a little. This man before him was much more than a simple pushover. "Touché."

Matt smiled back. "To answer your question, no. I've never been here. Big surprise."

"Why a big surprise?"

"Well, given my profession, you'd think I had been. But no, never. Guess you guys are good at keeping suspicious fires to a minimum."

"Until now."

Matt leaned back in the booth again and dropped his hands to his lap. "True. By the way, sorry about your shop."

Alex faked another smile. "Thank you, Sergeant."

"Enough with the sergeant business, please. Way too formal for me. Call me Matt. And since I'm on the apology train, sorry again about earlier today."

"I'm kind of starting to like all the 'sergeant business,'" Alex said with a slight grin. He should have been just as embarrassed as before being so blatant. But instead, he was almost brazen, like his manners, all the etiquette training his parents had dispensed throughout his childhood no longer mattered. Only what he was feeling, and getting Matt to see it.

Matt's eyes bore into his, the spark between them growing to a tiny ember ready to ignite. "Well, then feel free to call me whatever the hell you'd like. And forgive me if I came off earlier like—"

"—A total asshole?" Alex interrupted.

Matt tilted his head and laughed. "Nicely done. You know how to catch a guy off guard." They shared in laughter which helped lighten the tension. "And yeah, I guess asshole's a good enough word as any. Sorry."

Alex shook his head. "Don't be. I'm the one who should be apologizing. My crazy, obsessive mother is the reason you're here, remember?"

"God, if we have to say we're sorry for things our parents do, I have a lot of apologies to make."

Alex laughed this time. "Same here, believe me."

"Sounds like you have about as good a relationship with your mom as I had with mine."

"Had?"

Matt's face grew somber for a second before he smiled; Alex noticed the emotion didn't reach his eyes, however. "She died about ten years ago."

"Oh. I'm so sorry."

Matt shook his head. "We weren't close."

"Still, she was your mother." Alex thought of his own mother then, and how they rarely got along. He couldn't help but wonder...would he feel as sad as Matt seemed if their roles were reversed? "Did you two make up before she passed?"

"Uh, kind of, I guess. I mean, we weren't best friends or anything, but we were...civil with each other." Matt took a sip of his water then signaled the waitress over.

Alex knew all too well how civility shaped a relationship. "Well, that's good, I suppose." He didn't know what else to say. He knew he had stepped into what was a touchy subject and just wanted to backpedal his way out.

Matt nodded just as the waitress reappeared. "Could I get a beer, please? Whatever you have is fine." He looked to Alex. "Want one?"

"Sure." The waitress nodded and was gone again.

"Cancer, in case you were wondering," Matt added. "My mom. That's how she died. Cancer."

"Oh..."

"Sorry, didn't mean to bring down the mood." He stared at Alex for a second before laughing.

"I guess we didn't hit it off too well, did we?" Alex said.

"Nah, not really. But hey, we can make up for it."

God, there was so much running through Alex's head he wanted to say. "You don't think... It's okay, the two of us talking, right?"

Matt raised an eyebrow. "Why wouldn't it be?"

"The fire. I mean, you're here to investigate me, so—"

"—I'm here to investigate *the fire*, not you," Matt said. "And besides, I'm done for the most part. So, there's zero conflict of interest. And we're just talking. No harm in talking."

No harm in talking was a little hard for Alex to believe, but he found himself not caring one way or the other regardless. Because he wanted to get to know Matt. He couldn't explain why, but there was something there, drawing him in. He had no doubt the "something" was ninety-nine percent physical, he knew, but the one remaining percent...that was the part making him uneasy.

"Okay, then," he said, a bit of the tension he'd held when he first caught Matt sitting alone in the booth fading away. "So, *sergeant*, how long are you in town?"

Matt smiled and shook his head. "Not sure, really. I submitted my report to Captain Gregson today, and tomorrow morning I have a meeting with Chief Stevens at the fire department. After that, who knows. Depends on what they plan to do."

"About me, you mean." Dread quickly replaced the missing tension and Alex's shoulders tightened.

"Hey." Matt leaned inward and reached a hand across the table toward Alex. Before he realized what he was doing, Alex pulled away. His heart beat wildly in his chest, the simple gesture like dynamite to an ember. If Matt was offended, he was a master of disguise. "Don't dwell on them suspecting you. Just because we know the fire was arson doesn't prove you did it."

"Wait, so it *was* arson?"

Matt leaned back. "Oh, yeah. Sorry. I shouldn't have said anything."

"I won't tell." Alex forced a smile but his insides were the complete opposite. He was a wound-up ball of nerves over the fact he could be thrown in jail for a crime he didn't commit. At the same time, he was on edge because someone *had* burned down his store. *On purpose.*

"I appreciate that," Matt said. "But seriously, don't get worked up over this. You have a lawyer, right?" Alex nodded. "Good. Call him in the morning and give him a heads up."

Alex looked up at him. "But you just said—"

Matt shook his head. "I know. But you still need to tell your attorney so he can be prepared. Just in case Gregson pushes this on you."

"Oh. Okay." Alex sighed. "Listen, I want to thank you for...well, for easing up on me. And for taking a second to find out for yourself I'm nothing like my mother. Hopefully."

Matt smiled. "Don't mention it. And no, you're not. Like your mother, I mean." The waitress returned with two bottles of beer and Alex's patty melt. Matt grabbed one of the bottles and had the top popped before Alex could even pick his up. He took a long pull from the bottle, the muscles of his neck moving and flexing and his sexy Adam's apple bobbing up and down as he drank.

"So, I...I have to ask..." Alex took a much smaller sip from his own beer, the ice-cold liquid searing his throat on its way down. "Do you think I did this?"

Matt took several seconds to either consider his answer or decide whether or not to be brutally honest before saying, "No, I don't."

Alex sat back in awe. The statement took him by surprise. Given how hostile they were to each other when they'd first met, he'd been sure the sergeant would've been happy to pin the fire on him.

"Thank you," Alex said after a few seconds, taking another drink. "That means a lot."

"You're welcome."

They spent the next half hour eating and drinking and talking about nothing and everything. Alex learned Matt was originally from Seattle but had moved to Bangor after his mother's death, and Alex freely shared the fact he had just gotten out of a long relationship and was enjoying being single. After they went Dutch on the bill—which took some convincing on Matt's part, who said he should have paid given he had invited Alex to join him—they left the now-uncrowded diner and braved the dropping temperatures outside.

"Damn," Matt said, zipping up his coat. "You'd think I'd be used to this cold by now."

"Nothing like a New England winter," Alex said, wrapping his own jacket tightly around him, wishing he had worn something a bit thicker than a T-shirt.

"Winter? Hell, it's barely fall!" Matt furiously rubbed his hands together and blew into them, and Alex's dick twitched watching Matt's lips pucker. God, he couldn't help but think how good they would taste—or look, wrapped around his cock. The mere thought had his heart racing and his head spinning.

Oh yes, *definitely* time to call it a night.

"Well, thank you again for the company," he said, taking a step away from Matt and toward his car.

"Yeah, you, too," Matt said. "And don't forget to call your lawyer in the morning."

Alex saluted. "Will do, *Sergeant*." Matt laughed and waved bye before turning toward the other side of the parking lot. Alex did the same, a smile on his face as he headed toward his car.

"Hey!" He turned when Matt called out to him.

"Yes?" He waited while Matt jogged over to him and fished something out of his coat pocket.

"Here's my card," he said, handing Alex the small white square. Their fingers touched for the briefest of moments, and a warm, intense surge of electricity shot up Alex's arm. Judging by the look on Matt's face, that same surge shot through him as well. "My, uh, my cell number's on there in case you need me for anything."

Alex looked down at the card then back up at Matt. "Thank you," he said with a smile. They stood there in the parking lot just staring at each other with an almost palpable intensity. Alex couldn't deny feeling the mounting sexual tension hanging in the air between them. The pressure was so thick, so present. God, he wanted to jump Matt right then, taste him, *have* him. But he restrained himself.

"Okay, I, uh, guess I'll let you go," Matt said after several long seconds of silence, an awkwardness behind his words. Alex noticed his flushed cheeks and wondered how much of their pink hue was due to the cold.

"Of course," he replied. "I should get home myself before all the beer I drank wears off and I fall asleep."

"Oh, wow, I can't believe I didn't even think—Are you okay to drive?" Matt reached out an arm and his hand fell on Alex's shoulder. Even through the fabric of his jacket and shirt, an intense heat licked at his skin, pulsating from Matt's large hand. A lump formed in his throat, and he thought he would pass out at any second.

"Oh, yeah, I'm totally good." Totally good? Did he really just say 'totally good'? God, he *was* drunk.

Matt laughed a little. "You sure?"

Alex nodded. "Yes, positive. Besides, I'm only a couple of miles from here. I'll be home in a flash."

Matt pulled his hand away. "Good. Okay then, guess...I'll see you?"

Alex smiled. "For sure." They parted ways again, and by the time he was safely in his car, his head was spinning.

He just couldn't be sure if his euphoria was from the beer or the man he found himself wanting.

Chapter Six

MATT COULDN'T STOP thinking about Alex as he poured over his notes from the fire the next morning to get ready for his meeting with Chief Stevens. Dwelling on a case until it was solved was pretty normal for him, but this was a hell of a lot more than not letting go. He wasn't focusing on the case—well, not *just* on the case—because he was too busy thinking about Alex and how he managed to get under Matt's skin since the second they'd met. And the fact he was fucking gorgeous.

Matt was lonely. Had been since Cameron.

Cameron had been the one. *The one.* From the second they'd met, Matt knew. The feelings he had, they were like nothing he had ever experienced before. An overwhelming need to be with someone. To love someone. Protect them. They were never apart after meeting, and things couldn't have been better. At least, at first. A couple years in their relationship started...*changing.* Distance grew between them. They argued more and more, the fights growing intense as they escalated. They would go days without speaking to each other over shit most people wouldn't have even batted an eye at. Then, one night after a hellish shift at the firehouse, when Matt was dog-ass tired and just wanted to crawl into bed, he had walked in on Cameron going down on another guy in their bedroom.

Neither Cameron nor the other guy even noticed him come in. Too preoccupied, Matt had thought. So, he just stood there in the doorway to their bedroom—*their* bedroom—his emotions igniting like embers in a wheat field as the man he loved did things he was only supposed to do for Matt. *To* Matt. Each time Cameron's hand touched the man, each time his mouth, his lips, his tongue licked and sucked and caressed him, knives ripped through Matt, tearing him to shreds. With each moan, each sigh, his heart broke over and over and over until there was nothing left but rage. He had rushed the two of them, grabbing Cameron and snatching him away, the man's cock sliding from Cameron's mouth with a loud *plop*. The guy, shocked and scared shitless, shot out of the room like a lightning bolt, leaving Cameron still on his knees at the foot of the bed, wide-eyed and shocked, drool on his chin.

They'd had the biggest fight of their four-year relationship that night. Screaming, crying, hurling things across every room of their apartment. They went way beyond ugly. Matt had told Cameron he didn't love him anymore—a total fucking lie—and kicked him out in the middle of the night. He then spent the next several hours crying his heart out while burying himself in the bottom of a bottle until he couldn't feel anything anymore. The next day, though, everything changed, and two months later he was living in Bangor, hoping the new chapter in his life would be a hell of a lot better than the last. Twenty-eight was way too young to give up on your dreams, he knew that. He'd forgotten for a bit, sure. Partly because Cameron became his focus. Partly because he was too scared to go for what he wanted. But the night of their fight had made him realize life didn't give a shit if you were too scared or too in love or just too damned stupid to go for what you wanted—it forged ahead regardless. So, he had decided to refocus, recommit to reaching his dream. And Matt's dream was a simple one: make the most of his career and find a man to enjoy his life with.

Simplicity was never his strong suit.

Matt pushed the painful memories out of his mind as he pulled up at the Cliffside Fire Department as a short, older round man was heading to his car. The man was lugging an overstuffed box and what looked like a venti-sized Starbucks knockoff and was clearly not gonna win carrying both. Matt approached him just in time.

"Hold this for me, would ya?" the man said as he shoved the Styrofoam cup into Matt's hand before Matt could say no. The man swung open the back door of his car and dropped the box of files onto the seat. "'Preciate ya." He took the coffee from Matt and opened the driver's door.

"Do you happen to know where I can find Chief Stevens?" Matt asked just as the man lifted a leg to climb into the car.

"You're lookin' at him," the man said, planting both feet back on the ground. He extended a hand and Matt shook it, noticing the clammy palm and sausage-like fingers. "And you are?"

"Sergeant Fields. From the Bangor Fire Marshal's Office? I'm here about the fire at the Book Nook."

Stevens laughed. "Lemme guess... Evelyn Porter told you to jump, and you asked how high, right?"

"No, no. She asked my boss if he could spare an investigator to look into the fire at her son's business. I...volunteered."

"Volunteered? That what they're calling it nowadays?" More laughter. "With all due respect, Sergeant, I've been around a while. I know all about the politics in this town."

Matt smiled. "Yeah, well, this is all pretty new to me, so—"

"—so you still have time to jump ship, kid. Get out while you can." Stevens smiled as he eyed Matt. "But I'm guessing you're in for the long haul, huh?"

Matt gave a slight nod. "Guess so."

"Well, good on you. We can always use dedicated folks in this line of work. What can I do for you?"

"I did my preliminary investigation of the fire yesterday and wanted to go over what I found. If you have the time?"

"Shoot."

"Well..." Matt opened the accordion file he had tucked under his arm when Stevens shoved his coffee cup at him and pulled a typed form from the mass of papers inside, handing the paper to Stevens as he said, "The fire was clearly arson, no doubt about it. There's an obvious pattern, strike point, and use of accelerant." Stevens looked over the report as Matt continued.

"I'm confident the fire started in the basement near the furnace. The pour pattern climbed the basement stairs and led straight out the front door. There's also evidence of additional patterns breaking off the main one, leading to the office and restrooms. Obviously, someone wanted to make sure nothing was left standing. I'll have some pictures for you by this afternoon."

Stevens tossed the report into his car. "Nice work, Sergeant. Looks like you got everything under control on this one." He climbed into his car and pulled the door closed behind him. He lowered his window after a few impatient taps from Matt. "Yeah?"

"Uh, who will be taking over the investigation going forward, Chief?"

Stevens gave Matt a confused look before laughing again; Matt began to realize he didn't much like the man. "Seems like there's been some confusion, kid. Your office owns this one now. *You're* the investigator." Stevens closed the window and backed out of his designated parking spot, pulling out of the station before Matt had time to even register what he'd said.

MATT LEFT THE fire department two minutes after Stevens madder than he'd been when he'd gotten the call to drop his life and head to Cliffside. If he had known he would be stuck investigating the entire case with the help of what he imagined was a less than stellar police department, he would've fought his boss harder. Now it was too late.

Images of Alex sitting in the booth across from him last night flashed in his mind, and Matt smiled at the idea of being stuck in a town he had never even once thought about before today. His anger over the situation began to ebb, replaced with the possibility of getting to know Alex Porter better. Damn, what was it about this guy? Matt knew jack shit about him, other than he *had* to belong to the upper class; he was way too proper and polite not to. Although, he didn't really seem to fit in. At least in Matt's opinion. Alex came off as...average, for lack of a better word. Like everyone else, when it came to social status. But in the looks department, he was in a class by himself. He was just...beautiful. Beautiful was the only way Matt could describe him. At least on the outside. He hadn't gotten a chance yet to see what Alex was like as a person, other than at the bookstore and then at the diner. But a tiny part buried deep inside was more than interested in finding out.

A buzzing in his pants made him jump. He tried to calm down as he fished his cell phone out of his pocket and checked the screen. Cliffside area code, but otherwise he didn't know the number.

"Sergeant Fields." His voice was robotic. He had only given out his number to people he thought might need to reach him while he was in town—mainly, Chief Gregson— so he kept things professional just in case.

"Good morning, Sergeant. It's Alex Porter. From the bookstore?"

"Oh. Yeah. Mr. Porter. How...how'd you get this number?"

"Call me Alex, please," the sexy voice said. "And in case you hadn't noticed, this is a very small town. Word travels faster than anything."

Oh, Matt had noticed. He had also noticed the Porters pretty much ran the place and got whatever the hell they wanted.

"I was just wondering if there was any news on getting the investigation wrapped up?" Alex said.

"Um..."

"I know you can't really discuss details like you said yesterday, but...I'm kind of in a state of perpetual panic, waiting for the proverbial shoe to drop."

Matt could hear the tension behind Alex's words, no doubt the underlying fear that at any second they would haul him in and charge him with burning down his own business. He wished he could ease Alex's nerves, take away his fear and worry.

"I'm sorry Mr. Por—uh, Alex, but I can't comment on anything at this time. Not in an ongoing investigation."

"Please, Sergeant. I would greatly appreciate anything you can tell me."

Matt took a second to gather his thoughts—and focus on the actual case and not on Alex's sexy voice pouring through the phone—before saying, "Well, I *can* tell you this: no suspect has been named as of yet." Yeah, he knew giving the person who would most likely *become* the prime suspect a nugget of info could come back to bite him in the ass, but he couldn't stop himself. His heart broke for Alex. "And you can call me Matt. Again."

Alex huffed on the other end of the line. "Well, thank you, Matt, for sharing what I'm sure is privileged information." There was a long pause, followed by, "So...what happens now?"

Matt shook his head. "No. Don't ask me any more questions. I can't give away any more details to you. Or anyone. I'm gonna have my ass in a sling for this already."

"I'm terribly sorry to keep pushing, Sergeant. I just..." Matt could feel Alex's frustration through the phone. "Never mind. Sorry to have bothered you. Just wanted to get an update."

"You're no bother," Matt said.

"Listen, I..." Alex started, but his end of the line went dead. Matt thought he'd hung up or the call was dropped until Alex cleared his throat and said, "Never mind." His voice was soft, almost unsure.

"What?" Matt pressed. He knew if Alex asked him another case-related question, he would end up giving in. Which pissed him off. How the hell did a complete stranger have such a powerful hold over him?

A long pause followed before Alex spoke, an aggressive confidence back in his voice. "I was just wondering if you might like to get some lunch? Not to talk about the case or anything, so don't worry. I promise I won't pry any further. I just... I owe you an apology. For being such a jerk to you when we first met."

The way Alex talked, the confidence and phrasing he used—Matt found it incredibly sexy. "Hey, you were just giving what you were getting. I wasn't the nicest guy, either."

"Still, I unfortunately took out some of my personal issues on you, which was unfair. So please, allow me to make this up to you."

"Uh..."

"It's okay if you would rather not, or simply don't want to. I just thought—"

"—No, no, it's not that. I just...I think, well...maybe I should keep things professional. You understand, right?"

"Yes. Of course," Alex said. There was another long pause, then, "Well, then, how about some coffee? At least let me buy you a coffee. I could come to you, if it would be...more professional."

Matt could almost hear the laughter hiding beneath Alex's words. "Coffee sounds good. But I'll come to you."

"Great. I'm at the store just...looking around."

"On my way." Matt ended the call and buried his phone back in his pocket. Honestly, he was looking forward to seeing Alex again. Sure, their first meeting wasn't the impression he liked to give to someone—especially someone he just couldn't stop thinking about—but there was something to be said about the kind of confidence and expression Alex carried. He was...such a damn turn on.

Keeping it professional. Yeah, sure. Piece of cake.

Chapter Seven

ALEX SURPRISED HIMSELF. He had zero intention of being friendly with Sergeant Fields, let alone invite him out for lunch, but once they had started talking, something came over him. Something he couldn't explain, couldn't pinpoint. Whatever the something was, it allowed him to get over the fact the two of them didn't seem to get along. At first, anyway. Now, though, for some reason he *wanted* to get to know Matt Fields. Which was a good thing, since Matt was pulling up to the curb at that very moment.

He stood silent as Matt got out of his car and crossed the street, taken aback again by how sexy he was. Tall, lean, manly—traits that always got Alex right where it hurt in the best possible way. He fought the urge to jump him right there in the street and instead smiled and extended a hand as Matt approached.

"Good morning, Sergeant," he said, hoping he didn't sound too forced.

"Mr. Porter." Matt gave Alex's hand a firm but gentle squeeze, sending a shock through Alex's entire body.

"*Please call me Alex.*"

"Oh, yeah. Sorry, *Alex.* Don't know why the hell I keep forgetting. And please, drop the 'sergeant' and just call me Matt."

"Okay, *Matt.*" They both laughed a little, and Alex relaxed, the tension he had been holding onto falling away. The calm he felt was a far cry from the anger and frustration he had experienced when they first met.

Matt looked over Alex's shoulder and nodded. "Looks a lot worse in the daylight, huh?"

Alex spun around and took in the remains of the Book Nook. Of his life. His shoulders slumped in defeat. "Yes, unfortunately. Such a mess."

"Again, sorry for your loss."

"Thank you." He kept staring at the piles of debris and smoldering ash that were once a thriving business—*his* business. Seeing the charred remains instead of a bustling bookstore hurt his heart immensely. The site made him feel as if everything he had worked for in his life had been a complete waste of time.

"You okay?" Matt's voice was in his ear, closer than before.

Alex turned back around. Matt was only inches from him, a look of true concern peeking through his tough exterior. "Oh. Yes. I'm good, thank you for asking." Matt smiled, and a tiny sliver of Alex's anguish over the fire splintered and disappeared. "So, how about the coffee I owe you?"

Matt smiled. "Sounds good."

"There's a coffee shop just down the street I am obsessed with. Maggie's. Have you ever been there?"

"Oh, yeah, I love them. Their dark roast is out of this world."

Alex smiled, content with small talk for the first time in his life. Mindless conversation was one thing he never had in past relationships, the ability to talk about nothing in particular and be completely okay. Even with Brayden, who had been the only *true* relationship he'd ever had minus a few dates here and there, there was always the overwhelming need to fill awkward moments of silence with even more awkward conversation. But with Matt, things were easier somehow. As if they had been spending their days engaged in meaningless small talk for years. But they had only just met, which made the fact Alex was so comfortable around Matt all the more unusual.

They walked the few blocks down to Maggie's, and Alex went in to order their coffees—his a small cup of medium roast, extra cream and sugar; Matt's a large dark, black—while Matt took a seat at one of the small café tables littering the sidewalk out front. The line inside was relatively short given the late morning hour, so only a few minutes had passed before Alex was heading back outside.

But he stopped short when he noticed Matt talking with two uniformed officers who closely resembled the duo that took him to the station yesterday morning. His nerves were on edge by the time he reached them.

"Good morning, officers," he said, fear lacing his words.

The female officer took a step toward him. "Could you put your coffee down, please," she stated. Matt reached out and lifted the cups from Alex's hands. "Turn around, Mr. Porter."

"Wait, what's going on?" The fear lurking behind his words was now stuck in his chest, clawing desperately at his insides, frantic to escape.

This was it. It was happening.

"You're under arrest, Mr. Porter. For arson. Please place your hands behind your back." The female officer stepped up and aggressively spun Alex on his heels, her hands sliding down his arms. The cold steel of handcuffs encompassed his wrists, growing tight as they ratcheted closed. He could sense the eyes of the other customers on him, judging him. He looked to Matt.

"I'm sorry," Matt said. "I tried to get them to let me take you in."

"I can't...I can't believe this." His words were almost indiscernible, he was so overcome with emotion. First having to deal with losing his shop and now this; it was all too much.

"Don't panic, Alex. You're going to be okay." Matt's words fell on him like empty promises. No way could Matt know if he would, in fact, be okay, if everything was going to turn out fine. In that moment, Alex felt as though nothing would be okay ever again. He was being arrested for burning down his own store. The idea he could or would do such a thing sounded absurd. But here he was, in front of half the town, being placed in handcuffs. He was going to jail. And more than likely he would be standing in front of a judge and jury very soon, pleading his innocence. Jesus, how had things gotten so convoluted so fast?

"Will you call my mother?" he said to Matt as he was led to the waiting patrol car. As much as he hated to tell her, she had been right—he needed her again.

"Of course," Matt answered, following them out to the street. Alex locked eyes with Matt as the male officer pressed down on the top of his head and he slid into the back of the car, and he could see Matt's genuine concern. In that moment, he knew Matt pitied him. Which made the entire situation much more embarrassing and painful.

The backseat was extremely tight. His knees crushed into the rigid plastic back of the front seat, his shackled hands dug into his lower back, and heat poured from the dashboard vents right into his face, making him sweat. The interior smelled of cheap cologne and aged fabric, like his grandparents' house down in Virginia. God, he hated their place. But he would give anything to be there right then, instead of on his way to lock-up.

The door slammed shut, and for a fraction of a second he was alone in the car—which was more than enough time for him to feel the crushing weight of what was happening to him press down like a thousand bricks dumped onto his chest. His life was forever changed now. Not just because his shop burned down, but because no matter the outcome, whether the law found him guilty or innocent, the town would emblazon him with a big red "A" forever.

Arsonist.

Cliffside was a small town, and the one thing traveling faster through a small town than the wind is gossip. And once something has been said, there's no taking the words back. Once news got out he had been arrested for arson, he would be labeled an arsonist until the day he died. What the hell was he going to do?

THE POLICE STATION looked vastly different coming in the back entrance versus the front. Gone were the smiling faces, the friendly hellos, the deplorable attempt at décor. The back end of the building was cold and uninviting, a far cry from the warmer atmosphere of the main lobby. The walls were cinderblock, painted a dull, lifeless pale grey, oddly reminiscent of a funeral home. Which, Alex thought, was eerily fitting, given many viewed jail as a death sentence.

The officers Alex passed looked mad at the world, their faces stern, their bodies rigid and huffed up like they were about to be thrown in the ring and had to fight for their lives. The entire vibe was one of despair and judgment, and both were devouring Alex whole. Despair only outweighed the judgment emanating from those around him because of his loss. He had thought things couldn't get worse when he showed up to the fire the other night to witness his life in flames, but oh, how he had been wrong. This was much, much worse.

He was proud of how well he composed himself during the intake process. He was booked, fingerprinted, and searched, all the while holding back the tears he desperately wanted to shed. He even kept his emotions in check when they put him in the cell and the echo of metal slamming against metal reverberated around the building, an auditory seal on his fate. He lost his store and now his freedom; he would be damned if he lost what little dignity he had left.

"Hey." Matt's voice pulled Alex out of his self-loathing and he looked toward the wall of bars separating him and the world. Matt stood there, his face stern, emotionless. Even so, just seeing him made Alex feel the tiniest bit better.

"Hey," he said back, standing and crossing the tiny cell, stopping just short of the bars. "What...what are you doing here?"

"Chief Gregson called me after you were processed," he said. Alex nodded his understanding. "I wanted to make sure you were okay."

"You shouldn't be here. You're going to get in trouble, conversating with the accused."

Matt smiled. "Nah, I'm good. My part's done, anyway, now that they have...you."

Alex gave a half laugh. "Yes, I suppose they've done their job, haven't they? I figure they're all sitting around high-fiving and smoking cigars, talking about how they solved the case and now they rule the world."

"Damn, when's the last time you saw a cop show?" They both laughed, the sound calming Alex, making him feel somewhat better. Only a little, but nice nonetheless.

"I know I'm being dramatic. But not by much. Since they have who they think started the fire, they're done. The case is over. Right?" Matt didn't answer; he didn't have to.

Alex turned and walked back to the metal cot pushed against one cinderblock wall and slumped down onto the rough canvass. The weight of the world was crushing him, threatening to bury him alive. He had to focus on his breathing to keep from hyperventilating.

"Hey, don't think like that," Matt said. "They have some good police here. You gotta know they'll do the right thing."

"My point exactly. They think they already *have* done the right thing. They got the guy. They're done." Alex abruptly stood up and was gripping the bars between them in a second. "But I didn't do this. I swear, Matt. I— why would I? I loved my shop. I *built* my shop. Burning it down? Ridiculous."

Matt rubbed at the five o'clock shadow dusting his jawline and his eyes wandered the room behind him before landing back on Alex. He softly slid his hand over the top of Alex's, the warmth emanating from him simultaneously calming Alex and heightening his craving all at once.

"They know about the insurance policy, Alex," he said, his voice just above a whisper. "And they've already looked into the financials from the shop. The place was hemorrhaging money."

Alex stepped back as if he had been slapped and stumbled toward the cot. "Oh, God. They...they actually think I did this." Somehow, even though everything screamed the opposite, this hadn't seemed real until now. Up to this point, he had been holding out hope that his arrest, his booking, had all been a horrible mistake, a misunderstanding. But now...

"Things look bad, Alex. I'm not gonna lie. And I know I shouldn't even be talking to you about this, but..." Matt lowered his voice even more. "Look, I spoke to your mother. I believe she's on her way. And she's bringing your lawyer with her. So just...hang on, okay? They're coming to help."

Alex looked over at him. "Thank you," he whispered, his voice caught beneath a thick jumble of confusing emotions wedged in his throat. "Thank you for coming to see me."

He drew his legs up to his chest and fell back onto the thin, naked cot, rolled over and faced the wall, and shut his eyes. He mustered every ounce of strength he had left to hold back his tears as he battled the emotions rising inside him, praying he wouldn't lose his mind until this was all over.

But somehow, he knew it already was.

Chapter Eight

MATT LEFT THE holding area absolutely defeated. And really confused, because he couldn't understand why he seemed to care so much for Alex. But more than that, he just knew Alex was getting an unfair shake. Like because of his name, the Cliffside PD needed to make an example. Half-assed police work always set Matt off, and by the time he reached the front lobby, he was making a beeline for Chief Gregson's office. Sure, he was crossing a line by getting involved, but he would hate himself if he didn't.

"What can I do for you, Sergeant?" Chief Gregson asked once Matt dropped into one of two chairs opposite Gregson's high-back black one.

"Just following up on the fire on Shemwood. Wanted to make sure the investigators on the case are covering all bases." He was struggling to keep himself in check and not stir up a shit storm he wouldn't be able to get out of.

"My guys are top notch, Sergeant. Just like I'm sure yours are. Trust me, they're doing their job."

Matt picked up on Gregson's tone and shifted in his seat. "So, even though they have a suspect in custody, they're still looking at other possibilities, right?"

Gregson stared at him for a few seconds before speaking, no doubt trying to get a read on Matt and what he was really saying. "What's your interest in this, Fields? Why the concern? As far as you're concerned, it's case closed."

Matt wanted to tell Gregson to mind his own damn business, that he had every right to inquire as to the department's standards. Instead, he chose to keep things professional.

"I'm the lead fire investigator on this one," he stated. "So, I'd appreciate being kept in the loop on any developments. Professional courtesy and all."

Gregson nodded. "I see. Well..." He shuffled some papers on his desk, toyed with his computer's mouse— anything to look preoccupied. "I'll see if we can accommodate, *Sergeant*."

Matt rose from his seat, staring down at the captain, and said, "You do that," before turning and leaving the office.

THE ANGER MATT had over being ordered to Cliffside, having to drop an already overwhelming caseload to focus on Evelyn Porter's spoiled needs, and now the possibility Alex would go down for a crime Matt knew deep inside himself Alex didn't commit had him wound up like a snake ready to strike. He left the Cliffside PD and headed south down Main Street, toward a gym he had noticed when he first got to town. If he didn't get his aggression out, he was gonna hurt someone. He pulled into the parking lot, killed the engine, swiped his gym bag from the trunk, and headed inside.

Just stepping through the door calmed him. The place was so alive, pulsating all around him, tendrils of raw animalistic energy he could feel in his veins. He wasted no time hitting the locker room and changing into his typical workout gear: muscle shirt and nylon shorts. He headed straight for the bench press, piling on his max lift weight of two-hundred twenty pounds. Yeah, he knew he shouldn't, but he was stressed beyond stressed; no puny ass one-eighty norm was gonna make the cut.

He powered the heavy load up and down, over and over, paying no mind to the hot-as-hell employee who had slid over his head to serve as a spot. He didn't care about sex right then. All that mattered was shattering his bench record of twenty-four reps—and releasing his pent-up tension. He forged ahead, eighteen, nineteen, all the while thinking of Alex sitting in a damn jail cell, waiting to see if Cliffside PD was gonna fuck him over.

Twenty.

Twenty-one.

Fucking prick Gregson has it out for Alex, Matt thought as he ignored the muscles in his arms screaming for a break. He knew Gregson wouldn't play fair. Which meant Alex might go down for something he didn't do. Or at the very least, face a jury of his so-called peers.

Twenty-two.

Twenty-three.

Twenty-four.

Motherfuckers need to back off! His anger shot through his veins like the speed he'd taken on a dare back in college. Every vessel, every capillary, every nerve ending was alive, surging with fury and desire. He was so beyond pissed.

Twenty-five.

Twenty-six.

He bottomed out, dropping the bar. A large set of hands came out of nowhere and stepped in just before the weight crushed his sternum. The hands death-gripped the cold steel and Matt watched them carefully cradle it in the bench frame behind him.

"Damn, dude. You're intense." His spotter was smiling, impressed. Matt looked up at him, a perfect specimen of muscle, skin, and testosterone. His dick pulsed.

"That was nothing," Matt said, his breath ragged. His chest ached, and he knew he'd be hurting later, but right then, he didn't give a shit. He was still pissed off and needed to not be. He dropped his forearms onto the bar and leaned close to the guy. Sweat poured down his face already and he didn't care. He was in a zone, a blend of adrenaline and lust; the guy's worked-up appearance only added to the feeling. "I can show you intense."

Spotter Dude flashed a sexy crooked grin. "I bet you could." He looked around for a second and then added, "Follow me," before walking down a narrow hallway just to their left. Matt wasted no time, charging after him like a horned-up bull. Which, at the moment, he was. He had blinders on, his dick taking control. He didn't want to think of Alex, or the fire, or anything else. He needed to get off. Bad.

Two seconds after entering a small storage room at the end of the hall, Spotter Dude was against the wall, Matt's veiny forearm pressed against his throat. The guy was smiling as he gripped the muscle threatening to asphyxiate him and sucked in a deep breath, inhaling Matt's overbearing Alpha scent. The guy's obvious lust only fueled Matt's aggression—and his raging hard-on. He pulled his arm away long enough to spin the guy around, shoving him face-first into the sheetrock; he could feel the plaster give a little against the onslaught.

"This what you want?" he slurred into the guy's ear as he ground his steel cock against the muscular ass rutting against him. His mouth was pressed against the soft skin of the guy's neck, one hand around his throat, the other slipping around his waist to caress an impressive set of abs.

"Fuck yeah," the guy huffed, his voice trapped by Matt's grip on his throat. He ground his ass against Matt even harder, increasing Matt's sexual need to almost insurmountable levels. Jesus, he needed to get off so damn bad. "Fuck me, dude."

But as fast as the want, the need, had hit him, the feeling dissipated just as fast. Shit, he didn't even know this guy, this stranger he was currently manhandling in the backroom of a damn gym.

What the hell was wrong with him?

He let go of Spotter Guy and backed away, adjusting his aching cock. "I gotta go." He ignored the guy's protests as he made a beeline for the locker room and snatched up his gym bag, foregoing the showers. The sweat he had expelled—from overdoing himself on the bench and in the back room—had soaked his shirt and the top of his shorts, but he didn't care. He had to get the fuck out of there before he did something he would later regret.

But...why regret hooking up with some random guy? It wasn't like he hadn't in the past. Hell, before he had met Cameron, his norm was to go out, find a hot piece of ass, and get laid. But now, something was different. He was different.

Thoughts of Alex rushed his mind like water through a broken dam, and he had to take a beat once he was back in his car.

What the fuck?

What was the strange pull Alex had over him? Why was he so twisted up inside? He knew his damn postal clerk better than he knew Alex, yet here he was, sitting alone in his car thinking about him. Thinking about helping him get out of the mess he was in. Thinking about seeing him naked, touching him, tasting him, *having* him.

"Son of a bitch." Matt groaned and groped himself as he started up his SUV and sped toward his hotel room. He was rock hard by the time he closed the room door, and wasted no time stripping down and gripping his erection with viselike force.

He was spread-eagle on the hotel bed, naked except for his black no-show socks and underwear clinging to his sweaty calves, jackhammering his cock with a fury. His eyes were closed, visions of all the fun he and Alex could be having in his bed flooding his senses, and he was panting and grunting like an animal in heat. Which he was, one hundred percent. He jacked his cock with wild abandon, his groans of pleasure echoing around the small confines of the room. He began bucking his hips as he approached the edge, his body glistening with even more sweat, his heart threatening to explode from his chest. And as he came, Alex's face, Alex's body, filled his mind and took him further than he had been in a while.

His orgasm was massive, all-consuming. The release completely eviscerated him, left him spent, more tired than he'd been in a while. As he lay there covered in the remains of his pent-up stress, he realized several days had passed since he'd gotten off. Which was out of character for him, to say the least. Normally, regardless of what he had going on at the time, he made sure to get his release at least once a day. But...how many days now? Jesus, *eight*. Shit. No wonder he was so wound up, like he'd just run a marathon. Of course, meeting Alex had certainly amped up his sexual frustration too. Hell, Alex was the reason he had finally made the time to let go, to be honest.

He was just so fucking sexy. His smile, sweet but devilish at the same time. His delicious mop of curly black hair just begging to be wrapped around Matt's fingers. And Matt couldn't even think about Alex's ass. Jesus Christ, his ass...it drove him over the edge.

He lay there a few minutes until his breathing ebbed and returned to semi-normal before climbing off the bed, stripping off the few sweaty garments he still wore, and hitting the shower. The heat of the spray soothed his aching back and arms, trailing down his impressive glutes, thighs, and calves. Every inch of him was tingling after his amazing release, more so than he had experienced in a long time, and most of the anger he had earlier was gone. Now he was only left with concern for Alex. Genuine concern. Which totally freaked him out. He hadn't felt that way since Cameron, and certainly not over a guy he had seen all of three times. But still, he couldn't deny things anymore. He was worried about Alex, regardless of how insane his mind told him he was. The feeling was there, the worry, and there was no way, once he set his mind to something, he could ignore it. And right now, his mind was set on keeping Alex from becoming the scapegoat for an inept police captain who cared more about politics than justice.

Matt finished up his shower, toweled off, and got dressed. He opted for khakis and his department-issued white button-down, figuring a professional appearance would help get him in to see Alex, talk to him. Normally he didn't like using his position to get things he wanted, but he was more than ready to make an exception. Besides, sticking it to the Cliffside PD was kind of his newfound hobby. He planned to make damn sure they did their job and didn't let Alex take the fall. Yeah, he didn't *know* if Alex was innocent or not—not in his mind, at least. But the rest of him... Deep in his bones he knew Alex didn't do this. You know the feeling you get when you meet someone for the first time and instantly you're at ease, like you've known them your entire life? That's the only way he could describe the pull between him and Alex. And he knew there was no way someone with Alex's kind of energy could be a damn criminal.

The sun was just beginning to set, the sky streaked with golds and pinks and blues as Matt left the hotel parking lot and headed straight for the police station. He couldn't help but admire the beauty of the city as he drove. Small in comparison to Bangor, Cliffside had been taken care of well. Landscaping skirted every street. The city park didn't have a blade of overgrown grass. Even the trees were all equally proportioned. Everything reminded him a lot of the small town he grew up in, and he liked the old-time feel.

He pulled up at the station just as Gregson was leaving, and the anger he'd managed to tamp down earlier came rushing back. He crossed the lot and, being forever the professional, extended a hand to the captain, who gave him a death grip with his own.

"Good to see you again, Fields," the round man said. Even in the rapidly dropping early evening temperatures, Gregson's receding hairline carried a row of beaded sweat. Matt imagined his sweaty nature was a constant.

"You, too, Captain," Matt said. He flashed a fake smile and sidestepped Gregson, heading inside.

"Here on official business?" Gregson called out behind him.

He didn't even bother turning around. He simply said, "Yep," opened the door, and went inside, leaving Gregson with his mouth hanging open.

Chapter Nine

ALEX TUNED OUT the noise around him as he tried to get comfortable on the too-small cot. He instead focused on silence—the kind he had enjoyed every morning before opening up his shop. He would walk around the store, taking in the scent of all those bound pages, the heady aroma a natural relaxer for any stress he might have been facing at the time. Being in the Book Nook, organizing books or helping customers find the perfect read or even doing inventory, which would sometimes take days—this all was a part of him, as much as his lungs or limbs or heart. Nothing mattered to him more. God, what he would give to have a book right then. Just having the scent of the pages would calm him, help him realize even though things were bad, they were far from over.

He knew that wish was a futile one. The life he'd had was done. Over. This was it, he had nothing left. His store was gone. His freedom was gone. And he was left crumpled, broken, a damaged shell of his former self who couldn't be fixed again.

He leaned his head against the cinderblock wall behind him and closed his eyes. Controlled his breathing. Zeroed in on a tiny sliver of peacefulness buried deep in his mind. He forced his muscles to unwind and relax, his body going limp as his nerves eased. Gone were the noises sending him into a panic when they first hauled him in. He could no longer hear the shrill ringing of multiple phones, the echo of slamming doors, the muffled chatter about case after case after case. The world went silent, only his breathing filling the space.

The absence of sound was oddly nice.

"Wake up, Porter. You got a visitor." The baritone voice of the intake officer snatched Alex out of his meditative state and he jumped. He opened his eyes to find said officer standing in the doorway to his cell. "You deaf, kid? Get up." Alex wanted to tell the man to try being nice for once, see where kindness might get him in life. Instead he zipped his lip and did as he had been told. He followed the officer down a corridor, deeper into the station. His nerves ratcheted up a bit the further they walked, and he had to fight to keep them in check.

"In here," the officer said after unlocking a windowless door to their left. Alex bypassed the man and stepped over the threshold, every cell in his body on edge. His nervousness ebbed when he noticed Matt sitting at the table in the center of the cinderblock room.

"What—what are you doing here?" he asked once they were alone.

"I'm here to interview you," Matt answered. He fished a legal pad and a few papers out of a satchel on the far end of the table and pulled a pen from his shirt pocket.

"Interview? For what?"

Matt stared at him, his intense gaze drawing Alex in, making him feel for the first time things just might turn out okay. "I...I believe you," Matt finally said, and Alex could have cried. All he had wanted, all he needed, was for someone to trust him, to believe he was telling the truth, to know there was no way he could do something so horrible. His mother *said* she believed him, but Alex had difficulty believing her. But with Matt... An almost complete stranger had him convinced.

"God. Thank you. You have no idea..." Alex ran a hand through his hair and sighed with relief. He noticed Matt shift in his seat. "Um, if I may ask, Sergeant...what made you change your mind?"

"I didn't," Matt answered with a shake of his head. "I never thought you did this. You don't fit the profile."

"There's a profile for arson?"

Matt smiled. "There's a profile for everything in this line of work. And you aren't the type to burn things down for personal gain. So"—more paper shuffling, then—"I'm here to help you get out of here."

Alex slumped back in his seat. "I...I just..." He was smiling for the first time since the night of the fire, the fear and panic and worry that had seized him the second those cuffs went on his wrists now dissolving into nothing.

"What?"

Alex shook his head. "Nothing," he said. "I just... We didn't really seem to be getting along too well. I'm just surprised, that's all."

"Don't be. Regardless of personal feelings, I can't sit back and let an innocent man get railroaded."

Alex shot up in his seat. "Wait. What?"

Matt lowered his voice a bit, even though they were alone. "I don't trust Gregson. Or his department."

"You don't think they're up to something nefarious, do you?"

Matt shook his head. "No, no, I don't think so. I just don't believe they're...thorough in their police work. Gregson practically told me the case was closed. They got their guy." He lifted a hand toward Alex as he sat back in his chair. "I can't ethically stand for incompetence."

"But...isn't that how this all works? Police make an arrest and they're done?" Alex had believed all along he was doomed, headed for prison for something he didn't do. But now...

"Not always," Matt said. "Not when it's obvious the wrong person has been arrested. Hell, I don't even know you and I can see you're innocent. You have no motive. I know there's the insurance. But anybody would buy an insurance policy if they opened a new business. I mean, common sense, right? If I can see that, Gregson sure as hell should be able to. He should know better. But he's too fucking busy kissing ass to see what's right in front of him."

"I assume you are referring to my mother's ass."

Matt's features hardened. "What? Uh, no, not... I just meant he's too political to be a good cop. From my experience, anyway."

Alex huffed in frustration and plunked his elbows down onto the table. His mother would cringe if she caught him doing such a socially unacceptable thing. "This whole godforsaken city is nothing but a big political swamp. And if you're not careful, you will drown in the madness, Matt. Trust me."

Matt nodded. "Thanks for the warning, but I'll be fine. You're who I'm worried about. If we don't find who did this, you're gonna have a long road ahead of you."

"*We*? How in the world can I be any help?"

"Well, once we get you out of here, you can help me search the burn site—uh, I mean, the Book Nook—for clues as to who could've done this. I know, I know, I already did a search. But I wasn't looking for those types of things. My job was to determine cause. I thought the police would've done their damn job and investigated. My fault for assuming."

"Yes, well, you know what they say about assumptions." Alex was trying to lighten the mood but failed. Matt looked just as nervous as Alex imagined he was, which didn't help with the whole "save the day" campaign he was currently pushing. If anything, seeing Matt nervous made Alex feel worse, which he hadn't thought possible.

"Regardless, this is my fault. I should've been more thorough. Won't happen again." Alex could see anger swirling behind Matt's eyes and settling into the taut muscles lining his jaw. His rage was palpable. Alex just couldn't tell if he was mad at Gregson and the police, or himself.

"Don't blame yourself," Alex said softly. "This is no more your fault than mine. I'm so grateful to you for even offering to help."

"Well, you're welcome. But don't be yet. I still have to find a way to get you out of here."

"Already taken care of," Alex said. "My attorney showed, just like you said. No more than half an hour ago. He's filing paperwork to have me released as we speak. You most likely passed right by him when you came in."

Matt's shoulders visibly relaxed. "Finally some good news. Now we can focus on doing what the police won't—finding the real arsonist." He flipped through some notes he'd made on the pad while Alex sat in silence, watching. Alex was in awe over this man he didn't know, other than the arguments they'd had, yet was so eager to help him save his crumbling life. Not everyone would step up and help a stranger—even more so when said stranger was charged with a major crime. Alex smiled.

"What?" Matt asked when he caught site of Alex's wide grin.

"Nothing," Alex said. "I just...I don't know how I will ever be able to truly thank you." He did—God, thanking Matt had been all he could think about since they had met—but it would be extremely uncouth to admit so aloud.

"Like I said, don't. Not yet. Not until we clear your name."

"What are you hoping to find?" Alex asked after several seconds of silence as Matt dug through his notes.

"I don't know yet," Matt answered. "Something I think I found back at the site. Thought I'd made a note somewhere." He scanned a few more pages. "Guess not."

"Don't worry. Tomorrow we can revisit the crime scene, like you said." Alex had a renewed sense of hope, given the unexpected turn Matt just gave him. Like somehow they would fix this, the two of them, together. He never would have thought doing so possible given how they clashed, but now he was more than willing to give Matt the benefit of the doubt, to trust him. Besides, what did he have to lose?

"I need you to think," Matt said. "Is there anyone who would want to hurt you? Set you up even?"

Only one name came to Alex's mind. The same name he had been dwelling on since he found out the fire wasn't accidental. But he didn't want to believe his thoughts. He couldn't. Because doing so would mean the last few years of his life were for nothing. And he didn't feel that way. At least, he didn't *want* to feel that way. How could everything have been a waste? He didn't want to admit failure. And he most certainly didn't want to tell Matt yes, he did in fact know someone who might want to see him in pain—the same pain Alex had left them in just a few months ago.

But...did he have a choice? If he said nothing, how would he help his case? Help Matt *solve* the case? The choice in front of him seemed simple, yet was the exact opposite: save himself, or save...

"My ex." Alex blurted the words before he even realized, the weight of what he was doing settling heavily in his chest. "I think my ex... He could have done this."

No going back now.

MATT WAS WAITING outside the station when Alex and his attorney walked out. Alex was so glad his mother had decided to skip his release. She would no doubt have picked up on...whatever was sparking between him and Matt.

That spark was the craziest thing out of everything going on in his life. The fire, the arrest—nothing held a candle to the weird, unexplainable connection he had with Matt. He had noticed from the second his eyes found Matt across the police station the morning he was brought in for questioning, the morning after the fire. The energy between them was powerful, like an unseen force had latched onto him and was dragging him toward Matt. Up until this point, he had been fighting that force. Now, after Matt's offer to help absolve him of the charges... Maybe giving in and seeing what happened wouldn't be such a bad thing.

"Hey," Alex said after his lawyer said his good-byes and walked away, promising to be in touch very soon. "You didn't have to wait."

"I wanted to." Matt had been leaning against his SUV but stood up straight the second Alex was alone and walked over. "Besides, we have a lot of work to do. Starting with your ex."

God, Alex had almost forgotten their conversation, had all but blocked out the fact he was throwing Brayden under the bus.

"About what I said..." He wanted to take every word back. Take back blaming Bray for trying to destroy his life, have him arrested, make him suffer.

"What?" Matt raised a brow. "Second thoughts?"

Alex slumped. "I don't know. I just... don't know."

"Look, you were quick to throw out the fact your ex could've done this. He at least deserves checking out. Give me his name and address and I'll go talk to him first thing tomorrow, see if I can get a read on him."

"A read?"

"People tend to have tells," Matt explained. "Little things that give away when they're lying or holding back details. I'll have a conversation with the guy, see what I can see, and we'll go from there."

"So, we might destroy a man's future based on, what...a hunch you may or may not have after a five-minute conversation?"

Matt gave a short laugh. "It's a little more scientific than a hunch, but essentially, yeah. A very calculated, proven method of a hunch." Alex tilted his head. "Trust me, okay? I mean, I know we don't know each other too well—"

"—Or at all."

Matt smiled. "Either way, I know what I'm doing here. And I promised to help, so let me help. Let me do what I do."

So many things were barreling through Alex's mind he didn't know what the hell to do. On one hand, yes, of course he wanted Matt to find out who was trying to ruin him. He wanted his freedom. But on the other, he didn't know if he could potentially ruin Brayden's life if it turned out the man was innocent too.

But he had to take a leap of faith. He had to give Matt the benefit of the doubt, this man who was trying desperately to come through for him.

"Will you just... Don't mention my name, please? I don't..." God, if Brayden found out Alex was behind this— he didn't want to think about what his involvement could mean. Bray had a short fuse and would no doubt be set off by accusations this grandiose.

"He'll never know you pointed me to him, trust me."

"I'm trying my best," Alex said.

Matt gave a knowing nod. "I'll admit, that's partly my fault. I... I came into this whole thing with a chip on my shoulder. Toward the PD, toward your mother. And, yeah, toward you, too, if I'm being honest." He took a beat, then, "You didn't deserve my attitude. To be treated like you thought you were better than others. Sorry for making it hard for you to trust I'm on your side."

Alex stared at Matt, the intense magnetism between them growing stronger by the second. He resisted the urge to hug him.

"Thank you for your candor," Alex said. "But my trust issues are all my own. I was furious over the fire, so when you showed up with this macho attitude, you...I don't know, you set me off, I suppose. I was, well, more than just a little rude. I apologize."

"Totally understandable. I don't know if I would've acted any different."

Alex smiled and lowered his eyes. "Listen, could we maybe have a do-over on the whole 'grabbing some coffee' thing? The first time didn't go how I had hoped."

Matt laughed. "Talk about understatement. I don't typically get asked to coffee by guys who get arrested."

"Well, I do my best to stand out."

Matt's face grew serious. "I don't think you need any help there."

Alex cleared his throat. There was a stirring deep inside him, spreading over him fast. "So, uh...how about that coffee?"

"How about something a little more substantial than just coffee?" Matt asked, smiling. "How about dinner? We could go over the case. Maybe figure out a plan?"

Alex was taken aback. "Wait... You want me to feed you now?" he joked.

Matt's laughter filled Alex's ears and warmed him. "I think a meal is the least you could do for leaving me to pay for two very expensive cups of coffee that went straight in the trash."

"Well, I suppose you have me there, Sergeant. Okay, dinner over coffee. Tomorrow night?"

"Tomorrow night sounds good."

"Great, it's a date." Alex's cheeks flushed. "Uh, I mean, not a date. Dinner. Just dinner."

Matt smiled, the deep dimples of his cheeks sucking Alex in. "'Just dinner' works for me."

They stood there on the sidewalk staring at each other as if they both could feel the same things but neither wanted to admit it. Alex surely didn't. Not out loud, anyway. To himself, he could admit there was something happening, something he was scared to death of. But to Matt—or anyone else—he just couldn't vocalize the truth. And the truth was this man standing in front of him, extending an olive branch, was becoming so much more than a stranger.

Chapter Ten

MATT PARKED HIS SUV on the street across from Brayden Cooper's house on Brighton Street in the neighboring town of Emory. The drive only took a half-hour, just long enough for him to push his anger toward this possible criminal—and Alex's ex—under the surface, where he could use it if Brayden decided to play possum. He wanted to be on his game one hundred percent for this one; Alex's future depended on how good he was at his job.

This was the part of the job Matt loved. Getting to talk face to face with a suspect, find those tiny, unexpected clues telling if someone's lying or not. The very reason he wanted to be a cop when he was younger, so he could catch bad guys red-handed. But there was something about being a firefighter that caught his eye, and he never looked back. And now, being on the investigating side of the field, he could *play* cop and wrangle the bad guys. Which was exactly what he planned on doing with this Brayden guy.

"Brayden Cooper?" he called out after knocking on the front door and getting no answer. "Hello?" Several seconds of nothing passed, and he tensed up. He'd had people run in the past, sneak out the back or climb through a window, and he was always ready to take off after them—hell, the rush from an unexpected chase was fucking amazing. And this time would be no different if need be. He widened his stance and took several steps back until the side yard running the length of the house came into view. He'd already scanned the property on his approach, so he knew the long, narrow stretch of overgrown grass was the only way Cooper could run, unless he wanted to swim; a large lake butted up against the back.

Luckily, he wouldn't have to test his track skills today. Someone fumbled with the locks on the other side before the door swung open.

The man who answered was, for lack of a better word, jacked. Bulging muscles spanned his entire body—which was exposed except for a tiny towel hanging around his waist—and he was dripping wet.

Matt was caught off guard for a second. Hell, he'd had guys—and girls—answer the door buck ass naked; a towel was nothing.

"Brayden Cooper?"

The man seemed oblivious to the fact he was standing on his front porch basically naked in front of a stranger. "Yeah?" Brayden ran a large hand through his hair to keep water from his face. Matt noticed muscles he didn't even know people had rippling beneath the guy's skin and prayed like hell this asshole didn't try to run. Or worse, start swinging those massive arms.

"My name is Matt Fields. I'm an investigator with the Bangor Fire Marshal's Office. Do you have a minute to answer some questions?"

"About what?"

"Before we get into details, maybe you want to get dressed?"

"I'm fine." A tiny, mischievous smile spread across his face. "Unless I'm making you uncomfortable, Investigator?"

"I'm fine," Matt lied. Truth was, he kept picturing the stacked fucker pummeling him right there on the front porch. "I just thought you might want to avoid being carted off to jail in the nude." He had Brayden's attention now. He stiffened, which only made his muscles even more pronounced than before. He took a second to compose himself.

"What the hell is going on here?" Brayden asked, anger seething just beneath the surface. Matt could see it there, waiting to get out. He knew he'd gotten to him. Good.

"Where were you three nights ago, Mr. Cooper?" Matt asked.

"I don't see why my private life is any of yours or anybody else's business."

"If you'd rather answer my questions at the police station, I'm more than happy to give you a ride."

Brayden looked over Matt's head at the sky behind him and huffed. "I was home," he finally answered. "Alone."

Matt scribbled in his notepad. "Is there anyone who can verify this?"

"Well, since I was alone, I'd guess no."

Matt wrote that down, too, even though he'd only asked the question to piss the guy off. He eyed Cooper with a cool, collected stare, but inside he was cataloguing his features, his ticks, his unconscious tells. So far, nothing stood out as hidden guilt.

"Have you ever been to 1217 Shemwood Avenue in Cliffside?"

Confusion crossed Brayden's face. "Wait... Is this about Alex? Did something happen to him?"

"Why don't you leave the questions to me, Mr. Cooper."

"Is Alex okay?" Brayden pressed. He seemed jittery, nervous—worried.

As bad as he didn't want to—he didn't wanna give this prick anything—Matt gave in. "Mr. Porter is fine."

"Thank God." Brayden's death grip on the towel around his waist eased up a bit. He leaned against the doorjamb. "So, what happened then?"

The question brought Matt out of his stupor. "I ask the questions, remember?"

Brayden huffed. "Then ask already. Obviously, I was in the middle of something."

Matt tried to ignore the overwhelming urge to throw down his notepad and pistol-whip the bastard. "So, I'm guessing you *have* been to 1217 Shemwood then, yeah?"

"Duh."

Fucking punk. "Were you there three nights ago?"

"No." Brayden's mouth twitched, and Matt knew he was lying. He decided to push harder.

"You sure about that, Mr. Cooper?" Brayden stood motionless, his eyes boring into Matt's; he was trying to call Matt's bluff. "Mr. Cooper, if you refuse to answer my questions, I'll have no choice but to take you in."

"Like hell," Brayden said. "I'm not some thug or junkie, *Inspector*. I know my rights. I haven't done anything. You have no proof I was at Alex's store the other night. So, you can't take me anywhere."

Dammit. He was right, and he knew he was right. Matt couldn't take him in. So, this guy *wasn't* your average hot but dumb jock with more muscle than common sense. He was smart, knew about the law, what Matt could and couldn't do. Which told Matt plenty. Namely, Brayden Cooper had had some run-ins with police in the past. The average person didn't brush up on what they could and couldn't get away with when it came to law enforcement, they just did as they were told. But Cooper... Matt was itching to find out this guy's criminal history, see what skeletons he was hiding. And if any of them were fire-related.

Matt flashed a shit-eating grin and tucked his notepad back into the pocket of his shirt as he said, "Don't make any plans to leave town, Mr. Cooper. Understand?" before stepping off the porch headed back to his car.

"Whatever." Brayden stepped inside his house. "Hey?" he called, moving back out onto the porch. "What happened at Alex's shop?"

Matt stopped and turned to face the house. He didn't want to say anything—not when he believed this prick was responsible for the fire and was just fucking with him— but he did, anyway.

"Somebody burned it to the ground."

Brayden stepped down off the porch, gripping the towel struggling to break free from around his waist and crossed the lawn toward Matt. On instinct, Matt nudged back a bit. "Fuck," Brayden said, his free hand scrubbing against his five o'clock shadow. His gaze fell for a second before he homed in on Matt's face. "And... You think I... I could do something so fucked up to Alex? That's bullshit."

He didn't know why but hearing Alex's name coming from this guy's lips made Matt's skin crawl.

"Did you?" Matt asked the question knowing good and well what the answer would be.

"You know what. Fuck you. I give two shits what somebody like you thinks of me, but I would never do something like that." Brayden's words came out with such force, such conviction, Matt knew he was telling the truth. "His store means the world to Alex. I couldn't hurt him so bad. Not even if I wanted to."

"Wanna elaborate?" Matt asked. Something deep in his gut, way down where he almost didn't know existed, twisted with fear. He knew the words before Brayden even said them.

"Because I still love him."

Chapter Eleven

ALEX WAS SICK to his stomach by the time he pulled up at the Book Nook. He had no reason to go back there; he just wanted to. His mind was spinning with the fact Matt was currently at Brayden's house, questioning him as a suspect. All because Alex had to open his mouth about his suspicions and place Bray directly in the line of fire. Had he made a mistake doing so? Part of him knew he had. But a smaller, though equally as persuasive part was certain he did the right thing. Of course neither part mattered much now.

He pulled up to the curb in front of the Book Nook— which was still cordoned off with police tape and traffic cones—and killed the engine. He sat in his car way past exhausted. Not just from the events of the past few days, but also because he had was so stressed out over what might be happening between his ex-boyfriend and the guy who... To be honest, he had no clue what Matt was to him. In just a few hours, Alex would be having a "date/just dinner" with him. Given the two of them could somehow at least reach the point of being friends, of course.

If Alex were being honest with himself, he liked Matt, regardless of how things had started out between them. Matt was genuine. Honest. Alex didn't need more time to realize that. It was obvious already how much Matt prided himself on his word, on the job he did. His honesty and professionalism was incredibly enticing to Alex. He was also sexy and strong and masculine in an Alpha-male sort of way which always seemed to heighten Alex's attraction. Those were the reasons Alex found him so irresistible, why he had vivid thoughts of letting go and accosting Matt every time he was around him. But ever since Matt had stepped in when Alex needed someone most, Alex's overpowering lust began shifting into a desire to learn more. He wanted to get to know Matt past the physical draw between them.

He just hoped he had the strength to at least try to fix the mess he had already made. He had been so hostile toward Matt from the second they met. He would not have blamed Matt if he had told Alex where he could go. But he hadn't. Not yet, anyway. He was willing to be friendly, maybe even...more? God, what did "more" even mean? There was a question Alex wanted an answer to almost as much as finding out who set fire to his shop.

He pulled out his phone and keyed in Matt's number. The store—well, the piles of charred debris—could wait; Matt and his interrogation of Bray couldn't. Alex wished he could talk to Matt in person to find out if Brayden had any of the tells Matt had mentioned, to see with his own eyes if the man he had once loved was trying to tear his world apart.

Voicemail.

"Matt, this is Alex. I was just checking to see how things went this morning. Could you give me a call when you get this, please? I'm at the store. Thank you." He ended the call a little weary, his mind going over and over what could have happened.

Alex could already tell Matt was more than headstrong. And Bray was too. Perhaps even more so. Alex could remember fights they would have over the tiniest, most insignificant things like where to go for dinner or which movie to watch on TV. Trivial things most couples would have shrugged off or gotten past without a second thought. But not Brayden. No, he would explode, scream, sometimes even resort to throwing things to expel his anger. And in an effort to end the turmoil, Alex would always be the one to give in and apologize to help calm him back down.

But he wouldn't be there when and if Brayden blew up at Matt. He wouldn't be able to say he was sorry for accusing him, for disrupting his life. No, Bray would be on his own, free to become enraged and maybe even lash out. Alex could tell by looking at him how much Matt could hold his own, but with as much anger and hatred as Bray no doubt held, he wouldn't be able to hold back for long.

Alex paced the sidewalk in front of the Book Nook, nervous and on edge when his jeans began ringing. He pulled his phone from his back pocket and answered.

"Hi," he said, trying to sound calm even though he was a mess inside. "How did it go?"

"Oh, about as well as I expected," Matt said on the other end of the call. "He's...something else."

Alex sighed with relief, thankful Brayden hadn't started a fight and hurt Matt—or himself. "I'm sorry. He is a bit hard to take sometimes."

"My boss is calling, so I gotta go. We'll talk more about everything over dinner tonight. I think we may have something to help your case. See you soon." The call ended before Alex had a chance to say a word. He slipped the phone back into his pocket and, though the call had eased his worry, his nerves ratcheted up again. But this time, for an entirely different reason.

He was going on a date in just a few short hours.

MATT WAS AS nervous as a virgin on prom night when he pulled up to Alex's house. He'd never been there, number one, but also all these unexpected feelings bubbled up while he was getting ready. Up until now, he had looked at relationships like the damn plague. After Cameron, he was more than content with being single—at least for a while. But after meeting Alex... Damn, Alex was making him rethink things. Sure, he was attracted to him, and he hoped to see his ass up close and personal one day, but something more was brewing between them. He could feel as much. Which made no fucking sense. They had known each other a few days. How the hell could he be feeling *anything* in such a short amount of time?

He was lonely. Of course, that's all. Just loneliness. He was so fucking lonely. He missed Cameron, missed having someone in his life. And Alex was the first guy he had made any sort of connection with in the past few months, so it was only natural he was feeling whatever the hell he was feeling. He couldn't even describe what the feeling was, really. It was just...there. And he didn't even know if he was ready for more. After Cameron and all the fucked-up chaos their relationship brought him, was he ready to try again? That was the real question he didn't have an answer for. He wanted to think he was, but hell, he wouldn't know until the opportunity presented itself.

Had it already? With Alex? Was this the "more" he didn't even know he wanted?

Those and many more questions would just have to wait. Tonight, he wanted to have fun. He wanted to get to know Alex, see if they clicked, could become real friends. And maybe if things went how he hoped...

ALEX'S HOUSE WAS a cute Craftsman, a soft gray with rust-colored trim and stained-glass windows in the gabled roof. The house wasn't what he had imagined Alex would own, but somehow fit his personality—a proper, old-school home for a proper, old-school kind of guy. Clean, precise landscaping. A cute cobblestone walkway curving through the grass and up to the porch. An image flashed in Matt's mind of him and Alex enjoying lazy Saturdays in the swing hanging at the end of the porch, wrapped up in each other—which freaked him the fuck out. Jesus, he needed to rein himself in. He just learned Alex's name; picturing anything more than sex with him was ridiculous.

"Wow, you look... Wow." Matt was speechless when Alex opened the door. He always looked sexy as hell, but something was different tonight. He was more alive, electric, like he was pulsating with raw sexual energy. He was simply dressed, a black, tight-fitting T-shirt and even tighter jeans, but the confidence he held, the charisma oozing from him... Damn, Matt was taken aback.

Alex smiled, maybe blushed a bit. "Thank you. You look amazing too." Matt went for jeans instead of khakis, a sort of baggy pair he felt pretty good in, and a solid, maroon button-down. Yeah, he had a look, but he hoped dressing things up a bit helped. And judging by the look on Alex's face, he'd done a pretty good job. "Please, come in. If you'll excuse me for a minute?" Matt nodded once he was inside the house, and Alex disappeared down the hall to the right.

The interior was like a reflection of Alex. On the wall behind the couch—which looked like something out of one of those ritzy *Architectural Digest*-type magazines—hung three separate canvasses creating one big picture of what looked like the Roman Coliseum. Matt knew there was a name for the pictures, when one is cut up into more than one, but hell if he knew what that name was. He wasn't smart enough to remember something so formal. The image somehow matched Alex's strength and determination, like something Alex would love to see in real life.

On the opposite wall leading into the kitchen, there was an actual Samurai sword with a carved hilt and matching sheath hanging below. A full-blown fucking *sword*. That surprised Matt. Alex didn't seem like the type to want weapons in the house—or anywhere, really. He was too...kind, for violence. But then Matt noticed the razor-sharp blade and the intricate carvings, and they reminded him of Alex's razor-sharp wit and strong conviction.

He looked around the entire room, tiny spots screaming Alex jumping out at him: a haphazard stack of old books crammed anywhere they'd fit; a row of DVDs beneath the TV, none within the last few decades; a half-finished Rubik's cube on the coffee table. This place was the inanimate version of Alex, a perfect representation of his personality.

Matt was in awe.

"I apologize for leaving you alone. I'm normally not so rude." Alex crossed the room, and Matt couldn't help but catch a whiff of cologne when he walked by and snagged a set of keys from the bar around the corner. The scent was earthy, a masculine musk. The aroma tickled Matt's nose—and other parts of him too. God, he wanted to say fuck dinner and spend the night in bed.

No. He wouldn't give in to the urge, no matter how strong his need was. He wanted to get out, do something fun, get to know Alex as a person, not just a guy he wanted to screw. He shoved his wants to the back of his mind and let them simmer.

"No problem at all," Matt said with a smile. "You ready to go?"

"I'm beyond ready," Alex said, and Matt picked up on...something behind his words. "The question is, Sergeant, are you?" Alex had the sexy, almost irresistible form of teasing down to a fucking science. He really should add such a talent to his résumé.

Matt laughed. "You have no fucking idea. Lead the way."

Once they were on the road and headed downtown, Matt relaxed a bit. Back at the house, he was a bit overwhelmed seeing everything he liked about Alex in 3D, on display like little hints Alex could very well be a lot more than just a good friend. Somewhere, deep down, Matt kind of knew that already.

"So," Matt asked, stealing a glance over at Alex behind the wheel. "A dance club, huh?"

Alex smiled but didn't look at him, his cheeks turning pink. Alex blushing was just about the sexiest fucking thing Matt had ever seen. "Yes. And I apologize for changing the plans without running them by you first. But I figured, why waste tonight on just dinner? We both could use a little bit of fun." He looked over at Matt and smiled. "And this is not just any dance club," he added. "*Salsa* dancing." He had a mischievous smile again. "Very sexy."

Matt's dick pulsed.

"That's, uh, what I've heard," he said, solidifying the fact he had never even stepped foot in a salsa club. But he was eager to learn. More than ever, since his first time would be with Alex.

"Don't worry, Sergeant. I'm more than happy to show you how it's done." Alex smiled and bit at his bottom lip, and Matt's dick turned to stone.

God, how was he going to make it through the night?

Chapter Twelve

YUCA'S WAS THE hottest club in town when it came to Latin dancing. The most popular club in town period, as far as Alex knew. The place was overrun with patrons by the time he and Matt pulled into the parking lot adjacent to the expansive, illuminated building. He could feel the thump of the music as he parked the sedan.

"Wow, this place is insane," Matt said, ogling the massive line of partygoers wrapping the building, eagerly awaiting the opportunity to step foot inside and get lost on the dance floor. Though some had chosen *not* to wait, expressing themselves right there on the sidewalk. "Looks like we're gonna be waiting a while though. Crazy line."

"Don't you worry," Alex said once they were out of the car. He pressed the LOCK button on his key and the alarm beeped. "I happen to know a guy."

Matt gave him a questioning look. "You know a guy, huh?" Alex just smiled. He wanted to kiss Matt right then, taste the inside of his mouth, feel his tongue tangle with his own. He had decided before Matt even arrived at his house that he was done trying to fight the urges pushing him toward whatever this was festering between them. He was ready to embrace the sexual tension. Own it.

He chose to hold off on the kiss he so desperately craved, unsure if Matt would be comfortable with public displays of affection. Yes, Matt looked like a magazine model, incredibly handsome, but there was no true way

Alex could be sure if he preferred intimate moments to go unnoticed, or if a kiss on a crowded street was okay. And there were mobs of people in line to Yuca's. If Matt became offended or standoffish, their night could end before it even began.

"I'm very glad we're doing this," Alex said as they bypassed the line and skirted the rear of the building. "I think we'll have much more fun than sitting in a restaurant." He looked over at Matt and smiled. Oh, those eyes. He got lost in them every time he caught them with his own. Such a deep, rich brown, with the tiniest slivers of amber. If Matt's physique or evident masculine charm didn't pull you in, those eyes would absolutely seal the deal.

"Ditto."

"You did *not* just say ditto."

Matt laughed. "What? There's nothing wrong with ditto."

"Maybe if you're Demi Moore in *Ghost*."

"Oh, so you *have* seen a movie from the last twenty years. I was beginning to wonder after the old-timey collection I noticed at your house."

Alex feigned shock. "They were not 'old-timey,'" he said. "And were you checking up on me, Sergeant?"

Matt flashed a crooked grin. Alex's pulse quickened. "Maybe."

They both laughed, instantly putting Alex at ease, like they had known each other forever. Even though the reality was they didn't know each other at all, they were kindred spirits destined to be together. He was in awe at how strong his feelings for Matt had become in such a short time. He was taken by Matt. There was no denying anymore. He was genuinely kind, had a good sense of humor. And he obviously harbored similar feelings in return. Alex couldn't deny he enjoyed Matt's company since they each had apologized for being insufferable in the beginning. He enjoyed being around him, getting to know him better. But if he were being honest with himself, the feelings he had tried to ignore scared him a little. He didn't feel wholly ready for anything more than just a physical connection, regardless of the obvious deeper one growing between them. Anything more felt too soon, way too soon, since ending his relationship with Bray. But...he chose to have an open mind to the possibility.

"My apologies," Alex said with as much sarcasm as he could muster. "Please forgive me for not stocking my DVD cabinet with something as intellectually stimulating as...the *National Lampoon* collection."

"Ha. Ha," Matt said, throwing sarcasm back. "For your information, the *National Lampoon* movies are very smart. Tons of people love them."

"Hmm." Alex said with a smile.

"Well, we can't all be as cultured and refined as a bookstore owner." Matt instantly regretted his words. "Ah, damn...I'm sorry, Alex. I didn't mean to bring up what happened."

Alex waved off Matt's slip-up, trying to ignore the tiny pangs of hurt lingering in the recesses of his heart. "Don't be sorry. It is what it is, as they say." Yes, he missed the Book Nook. More than anything. But he had every intention to rebuild, recreate the life he had worked so hard to get. He didn't want to dwell on the loss, but instead look to what was to be.

"I promise you," Matt went on, "we're gonna catch the son of a bitch who took your shop from you. Trust me." Matt's body shifted, tension stiffening his previously lax demeanor. "I won't stop till I do."

There were so many things Alex wanted to ask—about Brayden, and if Matt believed he was behind the fire or if thinking so was just a hunch—but the last thing he wanted was to bring down the mood of the night. He wanted them to have fun, dance, and maybe end up bringing the sexual tension between them to another level.

"Well, I thank you, Sergeant. I do. But I don't want to talk about the case anymore. Not tonight." They reached a nondescript, almost unnoticeable door cut into the wall of the back of the expansive club. "Tonight, we're all about fun. Understood?"

"Yes, Sir." Matt saluted, and Alex couldn't decide if he wanted to laugh or punch him. "Hey!" He went with the latter.

"Oh, I'm sorry, Sergeant, did I hurt you?"

"Very funny."

"I thought you might enjoy it." Alex knocked loudly on the door. "You seem like the rough and tough type." The door swung open just as Matt was going to say something.

"Hey, Mr. Porter!" A tall, lively man wearing a T-shirt so tight every one of his muscles were on display flashed a brilliant smile at them. "Long time no see." He looked over to Matt. "Who's this?"

"Hi, Luis. This is my friend, Matt. Matt, this is Luis. He runs this place." The two men shook hands.

"Nice to meet you, Luis," Matt said.

"Same." Luis swung the door wide. "Get in here before we're mobbed by those fucking locos."

"Thank you." Alex clapped Luis on the shoulder as he and Matt passed, and he led the way through the dark back entryway until the front of the house offered enough light for them to see.

Yuca's was nothing like one would think a typical Latin dance club to be. Sure, there were lights and loud music, and the place was immensely overcrowded, but the atmosphere was very upscale. Like a high-end jazz club that happened to feature a massively large dance floor. Alex guided them through the maelstrom of dancers toward the lounge area on the far side of the expansive room where the music was a bit muted, toned down by the slotted walls cordoning off the area.

"This place is intense," Matt said once they found a tiny table and took their seats. A slender waitress in too-tight, skimpy clothing approached them right away. She took their drink orders—beers for them both—and disappeared with a smile and overdone sashay.

"I love this place." Alex had come alive for the first time since the fire. Partly because of Yuca's, but mostly because of Matt. Sitting across from him, Matt looked sinfully delicious in his maroon shirt, and Alex realized he was growing on him exponentially. They seemed to have a lot in common, given the short time they had known each other, a fact not lost on Alex. He needed someone in his life with shared interests. Commonality was one of many things missing between him and Brayden.

Though Alex had loved him, Brayden Cooper wasn't the type who liked being social. Unless "being social" involved a game of some sort. He was all about sports. Football, basketball, NASCAR; if tackling, fighting or crashing were involved, Bray was happy. While Alex enjoyed taking walks in the city park on Sundays, Bray wanted to simply hang out in front of the television and binge on ESPN. Bray's TV obsession wasn't the reason Alex left him, but it certainly didn't help.

Since meeting Matt, though, he now understood what people meant by "opposites attract." Even though the two of them couldn't be more different—a fire sergeant and a book aficionado tended to be opposites in every way— somehow, they seemed to click from the start. And even though he could tell Matt was more than a little frazzled by the vibe of the club and more than a little out of his comfort zone, he was at least willing to give a new experience a try.

Alex couldn't wait to thank him once they got back to his place.

"Let's down these and get out there," Alex said once the overly flirtatious waitress dropped off their beers. "Have a little bit of fun." He didn't wait for Matt, chugging half of his beer in one gulp.

"Damn." Matt tossed about a fourth of his back as well. "Impressive."

Alex was almost itching with anticipation as they stood from the table, and before he could stop himself, he was throwing himself at Matt, his tongue crashing into the man's mouth with undeniable desire.

The kiss was like an atomic bomb. The world around him exploded, and only he and Matt existed. His knees shook and he fought to stay standing as his tongue invaded Matt's mouth in a fit of lust, sweeping the warm cavern with ravenous hunger. His lips, soft and plump and on fire, were delicious, and Alex couldn't get enough of them. He nipped at the lower one like a starved animal, sucking the flesh into his mouth and reveling in delight. Matt groaned his approval and slid a hand around Alex's waist, drawing them closer together. Alex could feel Matt's massive erection pressed firmly against him and almost came in his own jeans. He knew he had to pull away before things got embarrassing.

"Jesus. Christ." He was panting once he and Matt separated, his skin on fire, his pulse skyrocketing. His head swam in a euphoric cloud. "Just... Wow."

"Yeah," Matt concurred, taking heaving breaths himself. His eyes were glazed, and the front of his pants was stretched tight. Alex couldn't help but smile.

"Okay," Alex said, brushing a finger over his still-tingling lips. "I take everything back. I take it all back."

Matt laughed. "Take what back?"

"What I said earlier. About you preferring to blend into the background and go unnoticed." Alex was having visible trouble forming coherent thoughts. "Believe me, I notice." He and Bray never shared a moment like that, not even in the beginning when everything was fresh and exciting and exhilarating. No, this kiss, this moment...was powerful.

"Ditto," Matt said, and Alex looked at him, really looked at him. His cheeks were flushed, his eyes erratic, lustful; he wanted more. Alex did too.

He slid a hand up Matt's arm and leaned in so he could whisper into his ear. "If you liked that the kiss, Sergeant, you haven't seen anything yet." He flashed the mischievous, crooked smile he already knew drove Matt over the edge and took the man's hand, leading them out onto the dance floor.

The music was thumping at just the right volume: loud enough to drown out ambient noise but not so much it verged on migraine territory. Alex wrapped himself around Matt's muscular body, using his hands to feel what he hoped to later see. He could feel the taut muscles of Matt's impressive back as he caressed him in time with the sexy Latin music. He fingered rugged, taut abs as Matt slid a hand behind his neck and drew their foreheads together. For a somewhat stoic man, Matt could move. Which only heightened Alex's erotic euphoria.

Alex had always dreamed of coming to this place with someone he was attracted to. Of course, there were hot guys just about everywhere you looked in Yuca's, but they were just eye candy; they were fun to dance with, but nothing was there. And Bray wouldn't have been caught dead in a place where his two left feet were put on display. Bray was sexy but utterly inept where rhythm was involved.

But Matt... Alex could *feel* the heat pulsating between them, almost reach out and touch it as they danced to song after song, each as fast and sexually charged as the one before. And Matt kept up with him as they were swept away by the music. The entire night had been spectacular.

For what seemed like hours, they writhed and spun and circled the dance floor, groping and rubbing and kissing each other as if nothing and no one else even existed, as if they were the only two beings on Earth. They gave in to the lust that had been building between them since laying eyes on each other, each succumbing to the pull, the connection. Alex couldn't help but think it was about time.

They salsa-ed and cha-cha-ed and rumba-ed all night, and by the time they left the dance floor, sweaty and so aroused they would have had sex right in front of everyone if it were legal, both of them were so beyond ready to be together. They made a beeline for Alex's sedan and, once inside the car, they couldn't keep their hands off each other, just like back in the club.

"My God, you smell so fucking good," Matt said as he nuzzled Alex's neck as he drove—which was no easy task with Matt's warm breath shocking his skin. "I want you so bad." Matt kept kissing and licking in all the right places, and several times Alex had to let off the accelerator to regain control of the vehicle.

"If you don't stop, I'm going to put us in the ditch." But Matt didn't. And Alex didn't want him to. He just did his best to focus on driving, on getting them to his house where they could do whatever they wanted to each other. About damn time.

"I've wanted you since the second I laid eyes on you," Matt whispered as he nibbled on Alex's ear. Sweet Jesus, he had an unbelievably precise control of his tongue. "I went straight to my hotel room and shot the biggest load of my life."

"Jesus." Alex swerved to avoid hitting a row of parked cars. "My God, why the hell can't this thing go any faster?"

Matt laughed into Alex's neck before pulling away just far enough to make eye contact. "You want me?"

Alex flip-flopped his attention between the road and Matt. "Are you kidding me? Since we first met. Just like you. God, you don't know what you do to me...*Sergeant*."

Matt made a sexy, animalistic rumble in his throat. "Fuck, I love it when you call me Sergeant." A large, muscular hand groped Alex's thigh, moving ever-so-deliberately upward. "Jesus," Matt whispered as he found what his fingers sought out, making contact with Alex's larger-than-ever rock-hard cock.

"Oh, my God, Matt. Please. Don't. You can't. Not yet. I'm going to crash." Alex was breathing heavier now, his eyes threatening to roll back in his head he was so turned on. "Please. Wait. We're almost there." Matt did as he asked, moving his hand down Alex's thigh off his dick. "Oh."

Matt leaned back in his seat but kept a hand on Alex's leg. "I can't believe how intense and...fucking *hot* that was," he said. "All the dancing and music and people. I've never experienced anything like that before."

Alex laughed. "So I'm guessing you had fun?"

"Are you kidding? Fucking amazing. And you..." Matt slid a hand around Alex's neck and wove his fingers through his thick hair. "You're an awesome, sexy dancer. You got some moves, mister."

"As do you," Alex said with a smirk.

"Oh no, I'm stiff as a board compared to you."

Alex pulled his eyes off the road long enough to glance down at Matt's crotch. "I would certainly say so."

Matt looked down too and smiled. "Look what you do to me. You get me so fucking hard. I just wanna..."

"What? What do you want to do?" Alex hoped with everything inside him they were on the same page. *He* wanted the two of them to bite the bullet and give in to the heat in every way possible. He only prayed Matt wanted the same.

Lust poured from Matt's eyes as he stared hard at Alex. His mouth lifted into a very sexy, mischievous grin and he said, "Oh, I think you know *exactly* what."

Yes, Alex believed he did.

Chapter Thirteen

MATT WAS LIKE a wild animal the second they stepped foot inside Alex's house. The door wasn't even closed before he was pushing Alex against the back, his hands groping at the waistband of his jeans, his tongue fighting for—and winning—entry into the warmth of his mouth. He couldn't think of anything other than having what he had wanted since the second they'd met.

"Jesus," Matt said amidst passionate, hungry kisses, "you are so...fucking...delicious." And Alex gave as good as he got, latching onto Matt's head with his hands and leading the hot-as-fuck make-out. He pushed Matt further into the house as they kissed, directing him down the dark hallway to a room at the end. Alex's bedroom. Once inside, Alex took half a second to flip on the bedside lamp, lighting up the room. Matt took advantage of the break to begin working on the buttons of his shirt. They'd had hours of intense foreplay; he was ready to be with Alex in every fucking conceivable way.

"Wait." Alex lifted a hand to Matt's when he reached the second button. His voice was raspy, deep, sexy. "Let me."

Oh, hell yeah.

Alex forcefully pushed Matt's hands away from his shirt, controlling the tempo of the moment. Everything slowed down—except Matt's desire, which was skyrocketing with every button. Alex kept his green eyes locked onto Matt's face, and Matt did the same. There was no denying what was going on between them, no denying this moment, right now, was where they both wanted to be. The sexual tension had been building and building between them and was, at last, coming to fruition, finally being fulfilled. Matt was buzzing with raw sexual energy.

Alex finished with the buttons of Matt's shirt and let it slide like water down his back.

He stared at Matt's chest, his eyes glazed over with want. "God, you're beautiful." Alex's hands were there seconds later, rubbing the overheated flesh, caressing the muscles of Matt's pecs. Matt's dick was fucking *screaming* for the same attention.

"Ditto," Matt whispered, and Alex gave him a sexy one-brow lift and sideways smirk. He laughed. "Hey, it's my thing. Just call me Demi, I guess."

"Maybe later." Alex slid his hands down Matt's chest, stopping on the button of his jeans. "Right now, I want this." His hand fell further until he was cupping Matt's throbbing cock. Alex gave Matt's bulge a squeeze and Matt bit his tongue and moaned.

"Fuck." He was falling over the edge, he knew it. Alex was driving him so fucking crazy. He pressed into Alex's hand, relishing the warmth pulsing into his dick. He forced his eyes open long enough to find the bottom of Alex's T-shirt. "My turn."

He lifted the fabric with ease, biting his lip when a sexy-as-fuck strip of muscle skirting the top of Alex's jeans was exposed. Damn, he couldn't wait to taste him there— and every other inch of Alex's incredibly perfect body. He peeled the shirt up and over his head, admiring every scintillating part as they were revealed: the abs; the perfect pecs; hell, even the sexy armpits. God, the man was beautiful.

"Next." Alex reached out and grabbed the front of Matt's jeans again. Matt almost came when heated fingers slipped behind the denim and brushed against his skin. He gripped Alex's muscular arms and brought him in for a kiss while Alex frantically undid Matt's jeans and pushed them down. Matt's underwear went next, freeing his strained, aching cock. The coolness of the air tickled him and set him on fire with lust all at once.

"Jesus," Alex whispered when he pulled away and stole a glance at Matt's erection. "Gorgeous." Matt blushed but didn't shy away. He wanted this. And seeing Alex's desire for him only made him want it more than ever.

He didn't say a word as he kissed Alex again and did the same with Alex's jeans and sexy black underwear. He kept his eyes locked on Alex as he lowered them all the way to the floor before stepping back for a look. He wanted a complete, unhindered image, because this first one would be forever engrained in his memory.

Seeing Alex nude, all hard and pulsating for him, almost sent Matt over the fucking edge. And Jesus, Mary, and Joseph, he had a dick piercing. A prince albert, Matt realized. God. *Beyond* hot. The metal there was a shock to see, but in some crazy way, fit Alex to a tee. The right amount of surprising edge. Just enough to amp up his sex appeal even higher. And that wasn't just because he wanted Alex so damn much. No, he meant every word. Perfect muscle tone, golden, sun-kissed skin, just the right amount of body hair to be sexy. Alex was almost too damn much. He smiled.

"Do you approve?" Alex asked after several seconds of enduring Matt's ogling.

"Better than I even imagined." And Alex was. Matt stepped out of the puddle of crumpled jeans and underwear pooled around his feet as Alex did the same. Once they were both free of the confines of clothing, there was no stopping them. Something else took over, something feral, primal. They lunged at each other like caged animals, groping and rubbing and kissing everything they could. Alex somehow managed to find every single erotic zone on Matt's upper body—earlobes, neck, nipples—while Matt explored with his tongue.

Son of a bitch, Alex tasted even better than he looked, which Matt thought would be impossible. But here he was, experiencing the most sensual, erotic moment of his life. He couldn't get enough of Alex as he licked down his chest, stopping to taste each nipple as Alex gripped his head and moaned. Alex's sounds of pleasure only fueled Matt's drive, made him more eager than ever to please him.

He licked each ab, his tongue dipping into the crevices made by the developed muscles.

"Oh, God." His tongue job was sending Alex into uncharted territory. Matt could tell, but he couldn't stop. An unknown force controlling him demanded he worship every fucking inch.

And who was he to say no?

Once his mouth made contact with the strip of Alex's stomach just above his groin and he tasted the salty, fire-hot skin there, Matt's entire body shivered. He was in pure heaven. If God himself were to call and say time to go, he would die a deliriously happy man.

But nothing compared to Alex's cock. Yeah, the rest of his body was fucking sexy as hell, something to truly behold, but this... This is what Matt had been wanting so fucking much. He wanted to feel Alex's manhood, touch him, taste him.

So, he did.

He wrapped a hand around the throbbing shaft of the engorged cock and Alex's body jerked. He sucked air in and began panting as Matt led him to the bed and pushed him onto the soft, plush mattress. Alex lay back, his stomach lifting and dropping in rapid succession as Matt squeezed and massaged his dick, flicking the prince albert with his forefinger. He had never seen one other than on the internet, and he was fascinated. The silver ball protruding from the slit in the head rolled beneath his finger, and he could see the affect his action was having on Alex; he was vibrating, he was so sexually charged.

"You like when I touch you there?" Matt asked with a wicked grin. He kept up his assault on the piercing, rolling both ends of the buried rod while simultaneously giving sporadic little tugs.

"Oh, God, yes." Alex's voice was just a step above a whisper, punctuated by his gasps. "You...have...no...idea."

Knowing he was making Alex feel so good only fueled Matt's desire for more. He was hot for Alex's cock, watching intensely as he lifted and pulled the skin of the shaft up and down. The head, all flared and thrumming under his touch, called out to him. Matt obliged, leaning in and flicking the bulbous flesh with his tongue.

"Jesus!" Alex arched his back off the bed as Matt licked and swirled his tongue around the top of his cock. He had to grip tightly to keep Alex's member from slipping away as Alex writhed in ecstasy on the bed. "Oh, God, Matt...please. Please suck me." Hearing those words from Alex, all raw and sexy and breathy, almost did Matt in. He reigned in his lust and did just as Alex asked.

With one fluid motion, he engulfed the rigid cock, right down to the base. Alex death-gripped the back of Matt's head and held him there, his cock filling his mouth in every way. Matt was having a fucking out-of-body experience, the taste and feel of Alex's cock taking him to a place he had never been before. He savored every second, loved the feel of Alex's hand on his head, keeping him locked in place; not that he would've dared move. No, he was enjoying the moment way too fucking much to move an inch.

Alex eased his grip a few seconds later, giving Matt the cue to work his cock even more. He lifted his head, letting his tongue taste every millimeter of the hard, hot skin of the shaft as he moved up. He stopped just shy of the head, keeping it nestled in the warmth of his mouth as he sucked. He tongued the piercing over and over, each flick of his tongue against the metal sending shockwaves over Alex. He bucked his hips in a frantic yet syncopated rhythm, sending more and more of his cock into Matt's throat with each thrust. God, Matt was so overwhelmed. So perfectly overwhelmed.

"Okay, you have to stop now, or I'm done," Alex pleaded, lifting his head to look down at Matt. "Oh, Jesus, you are so, so sexy." Matt opened his eyes and looked up at Alex, his face twisted with erotic pleasure.

Though he didn't want to, Matt let Alex's cock spring free of his mouth. "Are you sure you want me to?" He still held a tight grip, lapping at the underside with his tongue like a puppy to water, watching Alex react each time, his body tensing and lifting from the bed.

"You have to," Alex panted. "Because it's my turn."

Chapter Fourteen

ALEX COULDN'T WAIT one second longer before having Matt. He stood up from the bed, grabbing Matt's bulging biceps and lifting him from his knees. Without a word, he spun them around and aggressively tossed Matt onto the bed, his large muscular frame bouncing on the pillow top mattress. Alex paused a moment to take everything in. Here was this stunning, beautiful man lying stark naked on his bed, all muscles and golden skin and looking so incredibly delicious Alex thought he would die if he didn't have a taste right now.

Which is exactly what he did.

He took his time as he knelt in front of Matt, gliding his hands up his muscular legs, over his massive thighs, stopping only when he reached the mesmerizing erection between them. Matt groaned and his eyes closed, and Alex was floored with how sexy the entire scene was. Matt was beautiful, there was no denying the fact. But seeing him like this—vulnerable, exposed, lost in the euphoria of the moment—was overwhelming, to say the least. But Alex couldn't imagine the moment any other way. This was what he had been waiting for, longing for.

He put a tight grip around Matt's cock, the permeating heat sending shockwaves up his arm. Matt whispered "Fuck" as Alex slid his hand up the shaft toward the head, using his thumb to rub the precome pooling there. Matt bucked his hips and fisted the blanket in response, every muscle in his body seizing at once. Oh, was this a sight for Alex to behold. Just knowing he did such things to another man—*this* man—was spectacular.

He lowered his head and began kissing the area around the engorged member, the salty skin like a drug he couldn't get enough of. He tongued Matt's tattoo, a tiny infinity symbol just to the right of the sexy "V" of cut muscle leading down to his groin, and Matt dug his hand into Alex's hair. Alex slid his tongue farther inward until he could savor what he had wanted since he first laid eyes on Matt. And just as he knew without a doubt, the taste was beyond what he had hoped for.

Alex swirled his tongue around and around the head of Matt's cock while Matt groaned and whimpered and huffed like a madman. He licked up and down the throbbing shaft, savoring every second, every explosion of delight assaulting his senses. Once he reached the top again, he lowered his mouth all the way, engulfing every inch of the massive girth until he hit bottom.

"Oh my God, Alex. Don't stop. Please, don't... fucking...stop." Matt pleaded with him, and Alex aimed to please. He was way too far gone to even consider stopping. His desire for Matt was in control now, and he wanted nothing more than to experience Matt's orgasm up close and personal.

He increased the friction his mouth was creating, going up and down Matt's heated member faster and faster. Matt's hand dug deeper into Alex's hair, his fingers twisting and curling, guiding and forcing him toward the impending eruption.

"Oh, fuck." Matt was groaning a few seconds later, and Alex smiled around his cock, knowing he was about to get his reward. "Oh shit, fuck, don't... Oh, God. Alex.

Fuck!" Alex let Matt's cock spring free just as his orgasm blasted out with an intensity he had never before seen. Matt writhed and bucked and heaved into his hand as Alex jacked his cock. Alex was mesmerized by the pulsating stream shooting from the tip. After several intense seconds, Matt's seizing ceased, replaced by heavy, content breathing.

"Jesus. Christ," Matt whispered. His voice was hoarse and jagged, worn down by pleasure. Alex let go of his still-hard cock and climbed onto the bed, his own erection skirting Matt's muscular body, sending shockwaves through him. "That was...so..." Matt couldn't even finish the thought, he was so spent.

Alex laughed and nuzzled into his neck. "Perfect," he whispered, and Matt simply nodded. The two lay entwined for a moment before Matt lifted a hand and brought Alex's head toward him, guiding their mouths together, tasting himself there.

"God, I could kiss you all night." Matt gave Alex's lips one last flick of his tongue. "But there's something else I wanna taste." He smiled wickedly as he slid down Alex's body and onto the floor, his head hovering over Alex's massive erection.

Alex looked down at him. "You don't have to," he whispered.

"I *want* to," Matt replied, smiling before engulfing Alex's member all at once. Alex fell back onto the bed and closed his eyes, the suction from Matt's mouth taking control of his body. With each thrust, up and down, his hips were in sync, he and Matt working in harmony like a well-oiled machine. He was lost in a sea of euphoric bliss, his fast-approaching orgasm consuming him.

He grabbed the back of Matt's head and pushed him even farther down onto him. Matt took the force with ease, his mouth stretching around Alex's cock as if it were made to be there. Up and down Matt went, furious, determined—just like Alex felt. Alex was hot for Matt, plain and simple, and nothing in the world mattered right then other than letting himself fall over the cliff he was teetering on.

His mind succumbed to Matt's friction, blasts of psychedelic colors and stars filling the space where thoughts of the fire and Bray and secrets once sat. Now he could only see Matt, pleasuring him with such intensity the entire experience proved too much to take.

"Oh, God, I...I'm coming!" And he did. He exploded like a thousand atomic bombs, his orgasm bursting free with thunderous force. His body vibrated from head to toe, enveloping him in lustful heat. He had never been so present, so aware, as wave after wave crashed over him, consuming him, burying him in a sea of contentment.

After the euphoria passed, Alex stayed motionless except for the heavy breaths forcing their way out of his lungs. He couldn't move, his body far too gone to function. Matt climbed up to him, his warm hand gliding over Alex's stomach. Once Matt settled in next to him, his breath on his face, Alex took his time opening his eyes.

"You are amazing," he said, and Matt laughed.

Matt stroked Alex's cheek. "You're not so bad yourself."

"No, I mean ...that was the best blowjob I've ever had. *Ever.*" Matt laughed again and rolled over onto his back. Alex curled into him. "I mean, Jesus. Wow."

"Same here." Matt stroked Alex's hair with such tenderness, such warmth, making the moment even more perfect. Those strange yet familiar feelings Alex had earlier resurfaced now that the sexual tension between them had been quelled, and a nugget of fear came up with them. He was afraid he may be powerless to stop whatever was transpiring.

No. He couldn't ruin whatever was happening between them. He wouldn't let feelings he had no business feeling destroy the intense physical connection he and Matt shared. So he forced them out, made them retreat into the deepest, darkest, most obscure corners of his mind. If he couldn't get rid of them altogether, he at least would make sure they stayed hidden.

"Hey, what happened to you?" Matt's voice pulled Alex's mind back to the present. He pulled away and leaned against the headboard of his bed.

"What do you mean?"

Matt copied his posture. "You. Just now. You went somewhere else." He stared intently at Alex. "What's going on?"

God, he wanted to tell Matt the truth. Somehow he was starting to have...feelings for him. But he was scared. Scared if he did he would alienate him, send him running in the opposite direction.

"Nothing's going on. I'm good. Great, actually." He leaned in and gave Matt a kiss. "You were incredible."

"You too." Matt kissed him back. "But nice try if you think I buy your bull."

"What?"

"Tell me what's on your mind. I know something's up."

"And how do you know? Because you're an investigator for a living, you're also psychic too?" Alex shifted uncomfortably, knowing full well if Matt kept prying he was going to give in and let his secrets out. And what had just started between them would be done and over with.

Matt smirked. "You're funny. No, I'm not psychic. I can just see something is bothering you. And I think since we just did...what we did, we can probably talk about normal stuff too. You know, like adults."

Alex rolled his eyes. "Don't start acting your age now."

Matt pinched his nipple, and Alex yelped. "Watch the 'old' comments. I'm twenty-eight, not a hundred."

"Close enough."

"Deflection, huh? Must be big."

"What are you talking about?" Alex got out of bed and slipped his underwear on before heading to the bathroom.

Matt spoke louder so Alex could hear him. "Well, whatever is on your mind must be important since you changed the subject, that's all. You can talk to me, you know. I'm more than just a boy toy."

Alex was smiling when he came back into the room. "Boy toy? Don't you have to be, well, a bit younger to carry such a title?"

"Deflecting again."

Alex rolled his eyes. "I'm not deflecting anything, I just..." *Just tell him, Alex. Tell him how you feel.* "This...you and me...I..."

"I know," Matt said. He got out of bed and put his underwear on, too, before crossing the room and slipping his arms around Alex's waist. "I feel it too."

Matt's hands on his skin were so good, so right. The swelling in his chest was oddly right too. "You do?"

Matt nodded. "Yeah. Crazy, right? We just met. But...damn, I don't know." He pulled away and sat on the edge of the bed. "I feel like I've known you—"

"—Forever?" Alex sensed the same feeling too, like he had known Matt his entire life and not just a few days.

"Yeah. Which doesn't make sense to me." Matt stood up and took Alex in his arms again. "But at the same time, it feels too fucking good *not* to make sense, you know?"

Alex nodded. "I know."

"So, what do we do now?"

God, if only he could answer that question. Alex had no idea where to go next or what to do. On one hand, he wanted to move forward and see where whatever was rapidly building between them took him. On the other, he wanted to cowardly retreat back to when he was alone and had the Book Nook and life was simple, safe, uncomplicated. He decided to go with what his gut was telling him to do in the moment.

"Right now, we get some sleep."

Chapter Fifteen

"GOOD MORNING," MATT said when Alex finally opened his eyes. He had an arm draped across Alex's chest, letting his fingers trail around the man's muscular pecs.

Alex groaned. "Good morning, Sergeant. Sleep well?"

"Best in my fucking life. I think you might have helped out a little bit, though." He leaned in and gave Alex a kiss.

"Do you now?" Alex slid up and leaned back against the headboard. "Looks like I may have tired you out."

Matt laughed. "Oh you definitely did, but that's not what I meant, you tease. I just..." He locked eyes with Alex, finally able to admit to himself he felt...*something* for him. "Falling asleep next to you. Waking up next to you. It's just... Nice. Very nice."

Expressing himself in such a way was a whole new experience for Matt. He had always been a guarded man when feelings were involved. Hell, he couldn't even remember the last time his dad had said "I love you" to him, and his mother died when he was just a boy, so he hadn't grown up in a house where love and emotions were handed out like lunch sacks. He had been raised with the old-fashioned adage that men didn't cry, didn't hug, didn't *feel*.

But right now, he was a jumbled mess of raw emotions. But in the best fucking way. Because Alex had gotten to him, cut him open. The *new* feelings scared the shit out of him, yeah. But they were also freeing. He hadn't been so alive in...he couldn't remember how long.

"Wow." Alex reached up and brushed his cheek. Matt placed his hand over Alex's, relishing the warmth. He loved just touching him, feeling his hand on his skin, the warmth and security having Alex close to him provided. "No one has ever said anything like that to me before. I... Thank you."

He noticed Alex's eyes water and wanted more than anything to wipe away the tears pooling in them. He didn't like seeing him cry. Fucking *hated* seeing him cry, to be honest. He didn't want to embarrass him, though, so he kept his hand on his chest instead. But he could still feel the hurt in Alex's words, the surprise they carried. He no doubt meant what he's said. No one had ever told him how special he was. No one had ever made him feel safe, cared for him the way he deserved. Matt thought of that fucker Brayden Cooper then, and the fact he and Alex could have been in the exact place Matt and Alex were now. How could Brayden lie next to this man and not see how great he was, how much he deserved? Because he never truly loved Alex, Matt figured. That was the only possible way. Which told Matt the feelings he had for Alex, the fast-acting, overwhelmingly powerful feelings, were the real fucking deal.

"Just speaking the truth," Matt said back, getting lost in the brilliant jade of Alex's eyes. Sun peeking through the window over the bed lit them in the sexiest way, made them appear to glow intensely. He could have stared at them forever. "Like I said last night, I know this is crazy, but I can't deny what I'm feeling. Not anymore. When I'm around you, I'm like... I'm overwhelmed, you know? Like I can't think of anything else but you." He shook his head.

"Tell me I'm being a fucking idiot." Alex smiled, showing Matt he got it, he understood, he was right there with him. "I sound ridiculous, right? I mean, we just met. I know I'm crazy to feel this way... But I do."

Alex leaned into him, sliding an arm around his waist. He got lost in the feeling Alex's touch brought out in him.

"You may be crazy," Alex said with a crooked smile, his voice vibrating against Matt's neck that sent shivers straight down to Matt's cock, which pulsed with anticipation, "but you're crazy in the best possible way." Alex leaned back and looked up at him. "And who cares we don't know each other as much as some people do. Or as much as some people think we should. To me, the unknown is kind of what makes all of this so much more fun and exciting, you know? And as long as you and I are in the same place, on the same page, then, well...to hell with everyone else." Alex made a dramatic swoosh of his arm for effect and Matt laughed.

"I love when you get all riled up and talk street." Matt laughed more. "Just fucking with ya. But seriously... Knowing you feel the same way makes this so much better." God, what if Alex hadn't? Matt would have made an ass of himself for nothing.

"Of course I do." Matt heard the sincerity in Alex's words, as if there was never an answer he was more sure of. "I told you last night...I feel whatever this is too. And maybe *I'm* the one insane, or maybe this is 'socially unacceptable,' going for something like this with someone I just met, but..." He paused long enough to roll Matt onto his back and climb onto his hips. Matt's cock went rock hard the instant Alex's bare flesh made contact. "Whatever this is, I like it. A lot." He kissed Matt with such passion, such force, he took Matt's breath away.

The connection Matt had— sparked the second he laid eyes on Alex that night at the police station and had been growing at breakneck speed ever since—somehow strengthened and intensified even more. The overwhelming sensation was almost too much for him to handle.

He took measured breaths in between Alex's erotic kisses, returning Alex's passion and heat tenfold.

"And judging by this"—Alex said with his trademark mischievous smile as he reached between Matt's legs and gave his throbbing erection a squeeze—"somebody likes it too."

"Fuck, yeah," Matt managed to eke out, given Alex was basically jerking him off while straddling him. "So fucking much." He took control this time, flipping Alex onto his back so fast Alex didn't have time to react. Matt slid in between his opened legs, their hard cocks pressing together. "And some*thing* likes you too." He pressed hard against Alex, rubbing his cock up and down. Alex moaned and bit his bottom lip.

"I love whatever this is, too," Alex whimpered. "Oh man, do I love it." He reached back and gripped Matt's muscular ass, pulling Matt even tighter against him. He brought his hips up over and over against Matt's, and Matt returned the thrusting, his arousal reaching epic proportions. He leaned down and parted Alex's lips with his tongue, scoring the inside of his mouth with greed. Alex's hands left Matt's impressive glutes and crawled up his back and over his shoulders, brushing his pecs before trailing down his tensed abs and landing on his cock.

"I want you." His eyes burned with lust as they bore into Matt's. "I want you...inside me." He squeezed Matt's dick hard enough to elicit a grunt from Matt. "Fuck me, Matt. Please."

Jesus H. Christ. Hearing Alex speak that way, so out of character for him, drove Matt fucking insane. He couldn't have ignored the request even if he'd wanted to. His body had long since taken control, kicking out any lingering doubts about how deeply he was falling over the edge for this guy. He wanted Alex so bad. He was so desperate to have him he could think of nothing else. His job, his family, his friends—nothing mattered in this moment but giving Alex what he wanted, what he himself wanted.

He kissed Alex harder than he had ever kissed him, or anyone, before. The kiss was wild, animalistic in nature, and Alex went along in perfect stride. Their tongues dueled for control as he lifted himself from Alex's body and ran his hands down his thighs. He spread Alex's legs and ran his fingers up toward the one spot he had been dreaming of having.

Alex moaned and arched his back off the bed.

Son of a bitch, that reaction was like Heaven. "You want me there?" Matt's voice was breathy, totally lost in the euphoria of Alex's responses to his touch. Alex didn't say a word, but the depth and intention behind his moans said yes. "Right here?" His fingers found Alex's hole and rested there. "You want me here?"

Alex's entire body trembled and writhed with ecstasy, and Matt almost came watching him react to his touch. Damn, Alex was pure sex right then, and Matt wanted all of him.

He removed his fingers, certain he caught a whimper from Alex when he did, and used his hands to lift Alex's legs into the air. Alex's eyes fluttered open and he looked at Matt, sexual heat and desire and *need* all over his face.

"God, you're so fucking beautiful," Matt said, adjusting his position on the bed, placing his head level with Alex's groin. He lowered his gaze, his eyes working their way back up at a snail's pace. "So fucking beautiful." He blew a gentle breath on Alex's exposed hole, and Alex came unglued.

"Oh, God!" Alex screamed, arching his back again. "Matt. Please."

Matt teased, blowing again. "You want me to stop?"

"Oh, God, no...don't...stop." Matt smiled, but he did stop.

But only to replace his breath with his tongue.

The second he flicked Alex's hole with his tongue, both men transformed into wild beasts, ravenous, consumed with raw sexual desire. He tongued Alex with a frenzy, and Alex bucked beneath him with equal force. A perfect pair.

"I can't wait one second longer," Matt said after coming up for air. He was panting, and his body was covered in a light sheen of sweat.

"Fuck me." Alex was all but begging, he wanted Matt so much. "Right now." He gripped his legs and held himself open for Matt, who wasted no time grabbing a condom from the top of the nightstand by the bed. He tore into the shiny gold wrapper with his teeth and sheathed his rock-hard cock in record time. He kept his eyes glued to Alex's face as he worked to get prepared, his eyes pleading with him to get inside. Matt wanted nothing more.

Once he was ready, he slid between Alex's legs again and leaned over him, flicking his tongue against Alex's plump, suckable lips.

"God, you're so fucking hot." He found Alex's hole with his cock and pushed inside, slow but firm. Alex winced and Matt froze. "Are you okay?" Concern halted their dual desire. The last thing he wanted to do was hurt Alex.

"Oh yes,, I'm good. *So* good." Alex let his right leg rest against Matt's shoulder as he slid a hand around his neck. Such a simple touch sent shockwaves through Matt's cock. "Please, don't stop."

Though he was a bit apprehensive, he trusted Alex wouldn't lie to him, or do something he didn't want to. So he began kissing him again as he pushed forward, more of his cock sliding inside Alex's hole.

"Oh, God, yes." Alex was grunting and moaning, his face twisting with pain and pleasure; immense pleasure, if Matt's skills of deduction were accurate—which he would swear to right then given how worked up Alex was.

He kept inching forward at a firm, steady pace, Alex's warmth and tightness sending him inches from the edge. He focused on tasting the inside of Alex's mouth instead of the mind-blowing pleasure his cock was experiencing, because if he didn't, he would come way too soon.

Once he was all the way inside, Alex sighed.

"This feels amazing," Alex said. "So damn amazing."

Matt couldn't speak, but he agreed one hundred percent. Damn, did he agree. Nothing had ever been so fucking perfect. He felt like Alex was made for him, two halves of a whole, apart for so long but now put back together. And he was going to do whatever it took to make sure they stayed together.

"Fuck me, Matt." Alex stared deeply into his eyes. "Now."

And Matt did.

He pulled back until just the head of his cock was inside Alex before thrusting back in. Less than two seconds and they had created the perfect rhythm, back and forth, thrust and release. Over and over, Matt rocked into Alex, his cock squeezed tight by Alex's hole. He knew it wouldn't be much longer before he erupted.

Both men were lost in ecstasy, sweat covering their bodies, skin sliding against skin. Matt lowered his chest onto Alex's and slid his arms around his back, squeezing the two of them tightly together as he pounded Alex's hole over and over. Within seconds his orgasm climbed upward, desperate to release.

"Oh, God. Fuck, Alex, I'm so close." He was struggling to hold back his orgasm, waiting for Alex to join him. "You gonna come with me, baby?"

"Already there," Alex panted. His words were all Matt needed. His thrusting intensified to epic levels, and he held tightly to Alex, moaning and shouting as his orgasm ripped through him. Alex yelled out, too, as he came all over them both.

Matt couldn't move for a few seconds, his body in shock, his muscles seized in pleasure. His breathing was deep, rapid, heavy. He was, for lack of a better word, spent.

Alex whispered into Matt's ear before kissing him there. "My god, Matt, you are so exhilarating. I want us to be just like this all day, every day."

Matt laughed. "I don't think that'd be very healthy. You'd drain me dry."

"I would give you recovery time in between. You're a young, healthy man. You would be more than okay."

"Ha. Ha." Matt somehow found the strength to pull himself off—and out—of Alex, rolling onto his back. Alex curled into him, running a hand up and down his sweat-soaked chest and abs.

"I don't know what to call whatever is happening between us, Matt, but I don't want it to end." Alex's voice was somewhat distant, as if he had, all of a sudden, shifted gears. Matt leaned over so he could look into Alex's face. He couldn't ignore the seriousness there, the underlying fear that the joy they shared wouldn't last. Matt recognized that fear because he held tight to the same thing.

"We won't let that happen," Matt said back. Fear tried to consume him, eat him whole from the inside out, but he fought hard. Was Alex rethinking things, changing his mind about what he'd said?

"You promise?" Alex asked. His voice wavered, his eyes scared, vulnerable.

Though he couldn't explain where the words came from, Matt said, "I promise," and pulled Alex closer to him.

That was a promise Matt would fight like hell to keep.

Chapter Sixteen

ALEX HATED WATCHING Matt leave; he wholeheartedly meant what he had said, that he never wanted their moment to end. His unexplainable feelings for Matt were both exciting and overwhelming all at once, but he wouldn't fight them anymore. Fighting would be worse than the fear of opening himself up to the possibility. Matt had promised they wouldn't let this end, and Alex trusted him. Putting so much faith in someone he knew so little about was insane, he knew, but an unseen force was guiding him, pushing him toward Matt in the best possible way. And though he was scared to death of the unknown, he was ready for whatever was next for him. For them. He hoped Matt wanted the same.

He hopped in the shower and threw on a pair of torn, stained jeans and an old flannel button-down, trying to ignore the nagging feeling in the back of his mind how things were seemingly too perfect. Sure, he had lost his shop, but he had gained Matt in the process. And that win was more than worth the loss. But the feeling this might just be too soon, too fast, too easy to disappear, weighed heavily on him.

He pushed the thoughts from his mind and focused on controlling what he could in his life. Namely, getting the mess at what was left of his shop cleaned up so he could start moving forward. The police had released the property back to him, claiming to be done with searching the debris for their investigation, and he was eager to get moving with rebuilding. He grabbed some tools from the garage—a shovel, gloves, a box of industrial-strength garbage bags—and loaded them in the trunk of his sedan. Once he was on the road and headed toward the Book Nook, those feelings of unease he had been having faded away, replaced with a sense of purpose. He was going to get his life back in order. And now since maybe Matt was going to be a part of said life, things would be better than before.

HE PARKED AS close as he could to the burn site to save time when carting supplies. He intended to save whatever was salvageable, books or paperwork or any of the dozens of photos and mementos he had tucked all over the store. He hadn't been exaggerating when he said the store was his life. Nearly every inch of space inside the walls of the Book Nook carried some piece of him, and the lives of those he loved, on display. The first book he ever owned, a copy of *Windmills of the Gods* by Sidney Sheldon his grandmother bought for him at a tag sale, was the most prized piece of his past, so he made a beeline for the secret hiding spot the second he stepped over the threshold.

He had quite a bit of digging to do since the LGBT section of the bookstore—the largest, and the one he was most proud of—was now covering the hidden compartment in a massive heap of rubble and burned books, but he was able to dig his way down to the floorboards and pried them loose. He fished the fire safe out and grabbed the key from his back pocket.

"Thank God," he said out loud after he opened the charred black box and found the book was in pristine condition—well, as pristine as a used book bought from someone's front lawn ten years ago could be. But the condition of the book, or the monetary value, weren't what held importance for him. The most important page was the first one, and the message written there by his grandmother:

> *To My Darling Alex,*
>
> *I know this will be the first of many.*
>
> *Love,*
>
> *Grandma*

Alex hugged the book tightly against ˙his chest, memories of his grandmother flooding his mind.

He used to spend every summer there as a child, going home a week before school started only because his parents demanded. He doubted living with their grandparents for two months every year was at the top of most children's bucket lists, but for Alex, that time was priceless. Between scouring nearby towns for antiques with his grandmother to feeding the fish in the family pond at the back of their property with his grandfather, his summers were always full. Of things to do, yes, but also of love. His grandparents showered him with love, given he was an only child and their only grandchild, and he returned their affections wholeheartedly. When his grandmother had given him the book and he'd read the inscription, the two shared the best hug he could ever remember having. With the mother he had, the love from his grandmother was doubly special.

And Alex knew without a doubt his grandmother would have been proud of the Book Nook and of him. She always knew he would make something of himself, of the life he had been given. Just was one of the many reasons losing the place crushed him so. He feared he was letting her down.

He wiped tears from his cheeks and returned the book to the fire safe, determining the heirloom was safest inside the protective metal given the layers upon layers of filth all around him. He locked the box securely and made his way back toward the front of the store.

"Hey." Hearing the voice caught him by surprise. Seeing the man the voice came from made him drop the box. Right onto his foot.

"Dammit!" he yelled out, thankful the adjacent buildings were empty because he tried to remain couth when at the shop. He dropped to the floor and applied pressure to his foot. Once he was sure nothing was broken, he stood and tried to walk off the searing pain.

"Are you okay?"

"I'm fine. What are you doing here, Bray?" Brayden Cooper stood stoic, though Alex could tell he wanted to help.

"I just... I wanted to see you." Bray gave him a smile. "I've missed you."

Jesus, not again. Brayden had done the same thing right after he and Alex broke up a few months back, showing up at the Book Nook when Alex was hosting a local author's book signing. The place hadn't been super packed, but there was quite a crowd milling around, and Alex had been embarrassed and extremely upset over Bray's complete lack of manners. He had excused himself from the group—who was enjoying a reading from *His Only Love*, a western romance featuring two cowboys who found a life together—and dragged Bray to his office in the back. He promptly told Bray to stay away from him in the nicest way possible and returned to the party.

Apparently, Bray had to be told twice.

"I told you the last time you were here, I didn't want to see you, Bray. Why can't you listen?" Alex scooped up the fire safe again, carrying the box closer to his stomach this time as he stepped around Brayden and headed out to his car. He stumbled halfway there, and Brayden was grabbing his elbow before he could stop him.

"Be careful. You're gonna break something."

Alex snatched his arm from his ex and proceeded to his car. "I don't need your help." Yes, he knew he was being overly expressive. But Bray kind of deserved the cold shoulder.

"Look, Alex, I'm sorry...for what happened. Sorrier than you realize." Brayden stood next to Alex's open trunk as Alex secured the box inside. "I messed up. Big time. I lost you. I know that. I just—"

"—Just what, Bray? You just thought you would come here and beg for forgiveness for the millionth time and I would be willing to listen? I would say even though you cheated on me I'll happily take you back?" Alex slammed the trunk, the tiny *ping* of the force ringing in his ears. "I'm sorry, but us together again is never going to happen. So, why don't you save yourself some embarrassment and just leave."

Brayden didn't move. He lowered his eyes, shame drenching his features. He was sincerely sorry, Alex could tell; the gesture was far too late though.

"I don't want to get back with you, Bray," Alex went on. "I...I've found someone else." He hadn't intended on telling Brayden about Matt—not that he and Matt would be classified as a couple—but something inside him kept urging him to. Maybe the culprit was spite. Or the desire to see Brayden hurt, even just a little. Alex didn't know.

But once he had started, he couldn't stop. "His name is Matt. And he's amazing. He's kind, sincere. I...I really like him." Matt had said he liked Alex, too, but those words were fueled by a surreal night. And morning. Could he be sure once reality settled back in Matt would feel the same way? He held to the half-truth all the same.

Brayden looked as though he had just been kicked between the legs. His face curled into a jumble of wrinkled skin and strained muscle, and Alex couldn't help but notice his chest heaving a bit. He was mad—which made Alex happy. He was glad Bray was feeling even the tiniest fraction of how he had the night he walked in and caught Bray and a mutual friend in bed together.

"So, you're giving up on us, just like that?" Bray's teeth were clenched so tight the words sounded choppy and ragged. "After only a few months apart, you're...just done?"

Alex had to bite his tongue to keep from laughing. Was he serious? "Yes, Brayden, I'm just done." He hadn't called him by his full first name in so long, the sound was foreign to his ears. He had always used Bray, or Baby Bray—a nickname Brayden hated but tolerated, because they had loved each other once, in the beginning. But their love was long gone now. At least as far as Alex was concerned.

Brayden huffed for a few seconds, something he had always done whenever he was overly agitated, then headed back toward his car. Alex didn't turn to watch him leave—he never even wanted to see him again—until Brayden spoke.

"I get you're mad at me," he said. "But being pissed off doesn't give you the right to sic your fire-sergeant-or-whatever-the-hell-he-is boyfriend on me and accuse me of something I didn't do. Something I would never do. That's low, Alex."

"I..." He didn't know what to say. What *could* he say? He had done exactly what Brayden said. He had put Matt on to Brayden by opening his mouth. "I'm sorry, I just..."

"I love you, Alex. I would never hurt you. Even though you hurt me."

"What? Are you serious? *I* hurt *you*? You cheated on me!"

"And you left me. The night you...saw what happened, I begged you to talk to me. But you said no."

"Oh," Alex said, anger fueling him. "You mean the night before our *wedding*? Is that the night you mean?"

"Don't be nasty," Bray said. "Don't throw what happened in my face, Alex. I've said I'm sorry a thousand times. You just never cared to listen. You were just...done with me. With us. Without even talking about...anything, you left. You don't think that hurts?"

"Oh my God, I can't believe this." Frustration crawled Alex's skin. "You need to leave, Bray. Now."

Brayden stood there on the sidewalk for a few more seconds just staring at Alex before turning and walking away. "You know something," Brayden said once he reached his car and opened the door. "You're gonna regret this." He slid behind the wheel and fired up the engine, the silver Dodge Charger roaring to life. "One day, you're gonna regret ignoring me." He floored the gas, and the car shot forward in a rush of squealing tires and smoke.

Alex didn't want to admit it, but Bray's words, the look in his eyes... If Alex didn't know him better, he would have sworn he meant what he said as a threat.

Chapter Seventeen

MATT SPENT HIS morning looking into Brayden Cooper, but his brain was basically mush after the night and morning he'd had with Alex. Damn, Alex was fucking *insanely* good in bed. The fact he killed in the sex department made Matt like him even more.

Those were words he never thought he'd be thinking again. And he sure as hell never expected to *say* them to anyone. But there he was, sitting at his desk daydreaming like a kid with a crush. He was in all the way, no doubt. But his confidence didn't stop the fear from crawling in and taking root. Fear he was moving too fast. Fear he would somehow fuck things up.

Just like before.

He hadn't always been the way he was now. He used to be the wear-his-heart-on-his-sleeve kind of guy—despite his dad's attempts to "harden" him—letting his emotions run his life. He thought with his heart most of the time back then, letting what he wanted most dictate his actions, who he spent his time with, where he went. Being cavalier with his emotions was how he'd met Cameron.

Matt had moved to Seattle because of a guy he thought he loved, but once there, he realized the "love" he had was only infatuation. So, when his soon-to-be-ex was gone to work one day, he began removing his things from their shared apartment, carting them down the three flights of stairs to a moving truck he'd pre-rented. When he tried to manage the dresser on his own, a drop-dead-gorgeous guy showed up out of nowhere and offered to help.

That guy was Cameron. After loading his things into the truck, Matt offered to buy Cameron a beer to thank him, not taking no for an answer. The two were never apart from then on.

Not until the night of the accident.

Matt tried to ward off the memories he never revisited, but they barreled forward like a runaway freight train, smashing into the walls his mind had built to protect him and unleashing his past like water through a dam.

Matt and Cameron had their fights, just like any couple, but never about anything too serious. What to watch on TV, whose team was best, where to go for dinner—stupid, silly things was about the gist of their arguments the entire span of their relationship. But when Matt got a job with the Seattle Fire Marshal's Office the same time Cameron was let go from his position as head of marketing at a local research firm, tension reared its ugly head. Their perfect life began to turn sour, unravel. Nights spent curled against each other watching a movie or football game, or going out to dinner with friends, or passionate, hours-long fuck sessions instead turned to sleeping in separate rooms, canceling on friends so often the friends stopped asking, and a life void of sex. Arguing became their new norm, both always on edge with each other, always eager to show the other up, be right all the time regardless of the consequences.

The night they had their biggest argument, the night Matt caught Cameron with another guy, the fight ended with Matt telling Cameron he fucking hated him, and he wished they had never met that day in the stairwell. He could see the hurt on Cameron's face, but he'd been so fucking enraged he couldn't stop. He told Cameron how all the good in their relationship had been washed away by the fighting and Cameron's jealousy, to the point Matt couldn't even remember being happy with him anymore. Cameron had begged Matt to calm down, to forgive him, but Matt was too pissed, too hurt to listen. So, Cameron left the apartment. Matt was hurt, but glad the tumultuous relationship was finally over.

Unfortunately, he'd been right.

Early the next morning he received a phone call from his boss informing him Cameron's car had hit another vehicle head on, and neither Cameron nor the other driver survived. Matt's world was completely shattered, obliterated, and he had sworn right there in his kitchen, curled into a ball on the floor in unthinkable agony, he would never let himself love again.

Yet there he was, a year later, with a new life in Maine, a life with a future, with promise. And now, he was starting to have some pretty intense feelings for another man. Matt hadn't thought it possible to feel such a connection with someone again after losing Cameron. He had given up, even after the initial shock had worn off and the vow he'd made while on his kitchen floor faded away. He believed God was punishing him for forcing Cameron into his car, onto that road, when he was so pissed off. Cameron's death was his fault, and his punishment was a lifetime alone.

But now he thought maybe what he'd believed all this time wasn't true. Maybe what was happening between him and Alex meant he had been forgiven. He still didn't feel like he deserved to be happy, still held onto a tiny sliver of guilt over Cameron and knew he always would, but for the first time since his boyfriend's death, Matt had hope.

After pushing memories of his past out of his mind and reaching a stopping point on his research, Matt headed toward the Book Nook to meet Alex. Alex had told him before he left that morning he'd be there all day cleaning up, and Matt wanted to surprise him with lunch. Not a big surprise, yeah, but he was still in such a giddy, new and fresh mode despite his unwanted trip down Memory Lane, so the idea of sharing a surprise lunch break with Alex made him happy inside. Damn, he was like a love-struck teenager.

He parked down the street from the burned-out bookstore and collected the bags of sandwiches and chips from the passenger seat. After balancing them in his hands so he wouldn't lose anything, he got out and headed up the sidewalk. Alex was standing at the trunk of his car, the cool autumn breeze picking up and tossing those sexy curls of his, and Matt's heart raced. Jesus, just looking at Alex gave him fucking chills.

Alex seemed distracted, though, staring off down the street in the opposite direction. As he got closer, Matt could see he was upset, an unsettling mix of anger and fear on his face.

"What's wrong?" Matt asked when he was within earshot of Alex. Alex turned to look at him. Seeing him head-on, Matt noticed the fear outweighing his anger. "Alex? What happened?" He set the food down on the trunk of the car and was by Alex's side in half a second.

"Oh, nothing," Alex said, trying to play off his uneasiness with a wave of his hand. "I'm fine."

"No, you're not. Tell me what got you so upset."

Alex was quiet for a few seconds before looking him in the eye. "Promise me you won't do anything imprudent."

Oh, hell.

"No way." Matt shook his head. "Fuck that. If somebody did something to you—"

"—No one did anything to me," Alex interrupted. "Not...really."

Heat rushed up Matt's neck to his face. "Tell me." He could see Alex didn't want to say anything else, but he wasn't letting this one go. Not a chance in hell. "Alex, tell me *now*."

"Calm down, Matt. As I said, nothing happened. Just... Brayden was here."

The heat flooding Matt's entire body turned to rage. What the fuck was Alex's ex doing here? Cooper had some nerve.

"Son of a bitch." He turned away from Alex and started pacing, his mind going in every direction. Part of him wanted to go arrest the bastard on principle. The other part, the much larger and infinitely madder part, wanted to rip his head off his fucking neck.

"Calm down, please." Alex slid a hand up Matt's back. His simple touch cooled Matt a bit, but not enough to stop him. "It was nothing, I promise. He stopped by, I asked him to leave, he left. That was all."

Matt just shook his head, Alex's words not meshing with the way he looked. No one got so freaked out just because their ex showed up unexpectedly.

"You're this scared just because he stopped by for a fucking visit?" Doubt dripped from his words.

"I'm not scared." Alex tried to sound assertive, his hand falling from Matt's back. "I'm just... I don't know."

"What are you not telling me?"

"I don't know," Alex said. "I told you I thought Brayden might have started the fire and all I did was cause him unnecessary trouble. I don't want to overstep again."

"So, what, you're worried about the guy's feelings? That's insane." Matt didn't want to think it, but what if Alex still had feelings for Brayden? What if, for fuck's sake, he still loved the guy? A heavy lump formed in his throat.

"What? No, of course not. I'm not lying when I say I can't stand him anymore. Even so, I don't want him to get in trouble for something he may not have done." Alex glared at Matt. "Or worse."

Matt's brow rose. "Worse? What do you think I'm gonna do, beat the living shit out of him? Fucking *kill* him?" He wanted to—God did he want to—but his life was way too important to him to risk everything. But damn, if he didn't enjoy entertaining the thought.

"I don't know," Alex said with as much honesty as possible. "Look how mad you are just knowing he was here."

"Of course, I'm mad. I'm fucking pissed! He obviously said or did something to upset you, Alex. And you're...covering for the prick." He clenched and unclenched his fists over and over, his anger reaching uncontrollable levels. If Cooper touched him...

"Matt..." Alex smiled and slid his arms around Matt's waist. "I'm not covering for anyone, I promise you. I'm only worried about you, nothing else. I don't want you doing something that will get you into trouble." Though he was still fighting mad, Matt wrapped his arms around Alex and held him close. He wanted to protect Alex, always. Realizing keeping an eye on Alex 24-7 wasn't realistic was hard to accept. "And even though I don't need you to protect me like some damsel in distress," Alex added, "thank you. For caring so much. But you can't do anything which could be construed as retaliatory, okay? Promise me." Alex nudged Matt in the gut, and he grunted but gave in.

"Fine, fine." He still clung tight to Alex. "I promise I won't get in any trouble. But you have *got* to tell me what happened. I can't stand not knowing."

Alex pulled away, somewhat reluctant to say anything. Once he realized Matt wasn't backing down, however, he gave in and said, "I think Brayden may have threatened me."

Chapter Eighteen

ALEX TRIED HIS best to convince Matt that staying put after they finished eating the sandwiches he had brought for lunch was the wisest decision he could make, but Matt was stubborn if nothing else. He insisted he had a lot of work to do on the case and needed to go. After Matt promised yet again to avoid Brayden, Alex gave him a hug and kiss, lingering a bit longer than he should have because he had a tiny shard of worry in the back of his mind something bad was going to happen, then let him go.

After Matt was gone, Alex went back to trying to clean up some of the mess left behind by the fire. He spent the afternoon and early evening shoveling burned and waterlogged books into garbage bags, piling them up on one side of the room. By the time the sun had all but set, he had made a rather impressive dent in the mounds of debris.

"Not bad," he said aloud, shucking his gloves and carting them and the shovel to his car. After covering his seat with a few of the garbage bags to keep from dirtying the fabric—he was covered in layers of sweat, ash, and mud—he headed home.

To say he was exhausted would have been an understatement. He left the tools in his car once he made it home, only carting the fire safe protecting the book from his grandmother inside. The rest would just have to wait until tomorrow.

After peeling off his filthy clothes—deciding the best thing for them was to leave them outside on his back porch instead of putrefying the entire house—and taking a much need hot shower, he went straight to bed. Thoughts of Matt and Brayden and what could be happening to the latter by way of the former fought to keep him awake. Those thoughts lost the battle, however, and though he didn't feel sleepy, he quietly drifted off.

Dreams, followed by nightmares, kept him tossing and turning. First, there was Matt, beautiful, perfect Matt Alex was desperately starting to fall for. He had wonderful visions of the two of them reaching an unbelievable level of happy, having a nice home in a nondescript town much like Cliffside, spending their days laughing and loving, enriching each other's lives.

But those visions somehow melted and transformed into much darker ones. Matt coming home angry, picking fights with him, the two of them spending time apart, sleeping in separate beds, living in separate homes. Then came the images of Matt and Brayden fighting over him. Or, more accurately, Matt beating the hell out of Brayden, pummeling him to death. Then Matt being arrested for murder, hauled off to jail, sentenced to death.

He tried to fight off the images, the nightmares, but sleep held too tightly to him. He felt like he had been drugged, a foggy haze clouding his abilities, his senses, leaving him defenseless, powerless to the horror his mind was conjuring up.

Then Matt was there, not in jail, not dead by lethal injection. He was there, right there in his bedroom, lifting Alex from his bed, cradling him against his powerful, muscular chest.

Matt was shouting his name, but his voice was so far away he could barely hear. He wanted to respond, to ask him why he was calling for him when he was right there in his arms, but he just couldn't find his voice. The fog was there, too, in his throat, burying his words beneath cold, billowy tendrils.

Then they were outside, and Matt was taking extra care placing Alex on the lawn. Alex was cold, the northern nights not the place to be outside wearing nothing but a pair of boxer briefs, but there was nothing he could do about it. The relentless haze had complete and total control over him, keeping him trapped deep down in its drowsy depths. He grew tired of trying to fight, trying to push the overbearing fog away so he could be with Matt, who was now saying other words much too fast for him to make out. As Matt's voice began to fade, and sleep overpowered him, Alex wondered if the nightmare was finally ending.

ALEX WOKE UP in a stark-white room. At least, the room started out white. After several seconds, hazy images began to come into focus.

The room was...a hospital room? He noticed the flat-screen television affixed to the upper left corner of the wall. He could just make out the horribly tacky waiting-room-style chairs and ugly brown chunky end table against the wall facing the foot of his bed, which was large and had rails on both sides. Muted, syncopated beeping sounded in the background.

Yes. He was in the hospital.

But...why?

"Hey there." Matt's voice. It was soft, almost a whisper, and to his left. Alex fought tooth and nail to roll his head in the direction of the sound, but only managed a half-turn, his muscles spent. Thankfully Matt closed the distance and his beautiful face appeared before Alex's eyes. "Hey." Matt smiled, and Alex tried to smile back but didn't know if he had succeeded. "You scared the hell out of me, mister," Matt added, his hand brushing Alex's cheek. The warmth was soothing, calming him a bit. He was still panicked over being in the hospital and not knowing why, but having Matt there made his nerves somewhat bearable.

"I—" His voice was a rasp, his throat irritated and painful. He struggled to force out the words.

What the hell happened to him?

"Hey, take it easy." Matt sat on the edge of the bed, his hand never leaving Alex's face. "You've been through a lot. You need to rest."

But...why, he wondered. Why did he need to rest, when resting was all he had done for the last...he couldn't remember how long?

When did he get home from cleaning up at the shop? When did he go to sleep? How long had he been there, in the hospital?

The questions pounded in his head, as desperate as he was for answers. He winced and closed his eyes, trying to ward off their persistent invasion.

"Jesus, I thought I had lost you." Matt stroked his cheek over and over. "I've never been so fucking scared." He leaned down and planted a gentle but lingering kiss to Alex's lips. "You better think twice before trying to bail on me, you hear me?"

Though he was far too tired to speak, Alex smiled as he drifted back to sleep.

Chapter Nineteen

IT ONLY TOOK a fraction of a second for Matt's entire life to turn on its axis and inch toward destruction, just like with Cameron.

He had gone to Alex's house after returning to Cliffside from his second visit with Brayden Cooper—luckily for the bastard, he wasn't home—wanting to make sure Alex hadn't overdone things cleaning up at the Book Nook. After three full minutes of pounding on the front door and calling Alex's phone and getting nothing, he did his due diligence as an officer of the law and entered the house with reasonable suspicion. And he didn't give a shit if reasonable to him wasn't reasonable to somebody else; he was going in, and that was all there was to it. And thank God he did, because if he hadn't...

He didn't even want to *think* about what could've happened if he hadn't been there. If he hadn't found Alex unresponsive in his bed, hadn't gotten him out. He had been a crazy fucking ball of frantic nerves as he tried and failed to wake Alex up once he had gotten him out of the house. He hadn't been for sure, but he suspected carbon monoxide poisoning. And thankfully he had, the doctors had told him; his quick-thinking saved Alex's life.

Damn, just the thought of losing Alex—that scared the hell out of him. Which made the new and exciting and terrifying feelings he was having seem all the more real. Yeah, he was scared as shit to jump in feet first—but more scared not to now.

Knowing Alex was safe, was going to be okay, Matt was more determined than ever to find out what the hell was going on, who was out to get him. First, the intentional fire at the store, and now this.

Someone was trying to kill Alex. And he wouldn't stop until he found out who the fuck that someone was.

He sat back down in the chair beside the bed after Alex fell asleep but kept his hand in his. He just had to be touching him, had to know he was safe. From this moment forward, Matt made a personal vow to protect Alex at all costs. If doing so meant sacrificing his career, then he was more than prepared to give up being an investigator. Hell, he would give everything up, if doing so meant they would be together.

"Excuse me." A tiny wisp of a voice pulled Matt from his thoughts. He looked across the room to where a slender, familiar-looking woman in a light-green wool skirt and jacket was lingering in the doorway to Alex's room. She looked to be in her late fifties, maybe early sixties, with soft features and kind eyes. Matt let Alex's hand fall from his and stood.

"Um, hi," he said softly so he didn't wake Alex. He glanced down at Alex before turning his full attention to her. "What can I do for you?" He felt like a room attendant or waiter, asking such an odd question, but the woman wasn't too eager to explain why she was there, so he had no choice but to pry.

She took her time inching farther into the room, looking over at Alex and raising a hand to her chest. "Oh, dear." Her words were broken with emotion. "My poor, poor dear."

Realization hit Matt. "Oh. You're...Alex's mom." He hadn't met Alex's mom, only caught sight of her across the room at the police station on his first day in town.

Standing there now, in Alex's hospital room the morning after someone tried to kill him, she looked...different. Her hair, pulled tight into a bun at the back of her head the first time he'd seen her, was frayed around the edges. Her eyes were heavy, even a little puffy, like she'd been crying. Her color was off, pale. She looked like a mom with a broken heart. Matt knew Evelyn Porter was the reason he had to drop his life and come to Cliffside. He'd been mad as hell at her in the beginning, but now he could kiss her, because she ultimately brought him to Alex.

"Yes," she said softly, looking over to him. "I'm Evelyn Porter." She extended a hand toward him, and he had to move away from Alex's side to greet her.

"Nice to finally meet you, Mrs. Porter. I'm Matt Fields." His name didn't register on Evelyn's face, so he added, "I'm a sergeant with the Bangor Fire Marshal's Office. You, uh...you requested I come investigate the fire at the Book Nook."

"Oh, yes, of course." Her flair for the dramatic didn't go unnoticed. "Is there a need for a fire investigator in this matter?" she asked. "The doctors told me Alex was suffering from carbon monoxide poisoning. I assumed there was some sort of leak at his home. I swear, I don't know why he insisted on buying such a run-down hovel. But Alex has always been very independent, and the house was what he wanted, so I gave in." Evelyn's gaze roamed a bit until she found her train of thought again. "Do you believe something else happened last night, Sergeant Fields? Something other than an accidental gas poisoning?"

Matt was so taken aback by so many things—Evelyn Porter's clear misunderstanding of who her son really was, the fact she had no fucking clue who *Matt* really was—but somehow he managed to answer her.

"Well, maybe." He didn't want to scare the woman by telling her he was one hundred percent sure someone was trying to kill her son. "Given the fire at the bookstore, and now this at his home... It bears looking into." Matt caught the concern on her face and was quick to add, "But, please don't worry, Mrs. Porter. I'm sure neither I nor the police will find anything." A complete lie—he had no doubt the two things were connected—but he was trying to ease her nerves.

Evelyn composed herself and countered his bluff. "I highly doubt the local police or the fire marshal's office would spare someone for something they don't believe to be serious." Her tone and demeanor were stern, unflinching. Matt was beginning to understand why Alex had never introduced them.

"Mrs. Porter, I'm not here in a...professional capacity." What the hell was he doing? God, he had to stop.

Shut up, Matt. Just shut the fuck up.

He couldn't tell Alex's mother he and her son were...whatever they were. Her son's sex life wasn't his place to tell. To her or anybody else in Alex's family. Hell, he didn't know if she even knew her son was gay. And no way in hell was he about to open *that* can.

"Oh?" Evelyn held a lilt in her voice. Her next words almost put Matt in the bed next to Alex. "Are you his lover?"

He was speechless. Which wasn't something that happened often—hell, he couldn't even recall a time, to be honest—but right then, he was at a complete loss for words.

Evelyn smiled at his uncomfortableness. "Don't fret, young man. I've suspected for quite some time my son favored the *un*fairer sex. The old adage is no doubt true: a mother *does* always know." She made her way to Alex's bedside and brushed a rogue curl from his forehead. Matt stared at her intently, a little touched by her affection toward her son. But he hadn't forgotten about the intensity or the power she wielded too. Having her there made him want to protect Alex even more, knowing he grew up with such a ruling hand guiding him but still managed to turn out perfect.

"I'm so sorry, Mrs. Porter," he said, moving to the other side of Alex. "I had no idea..."

"It's quite all right." She held her hand against Alex's forehead while her eyes found Matt. "My son hasn't outright told me, true, but that doesn't change the fact." She looked down at Alex, her face softening again. "Do you love him?" she asked several seconds later, never pulling her eyes away from her son.

Wow. No way could Matt even begin to fucking answer her. He had no idea what you would call his feelings for Alex. Some might call them love. Others might say he was infatuated. Or lustful. Regardless of the term, Matt couldn't say anything out loud.

Evelyn lingered a few more seconds by her son's side before moving away from the bed. "I would bet you do," she said, making eye contact. "I can see so all over your face."

Matt smiled. "We just met."

She crossed the room and took Matt's hand into hers. "I met my husband only a few hours before I knew I would love him for the rest of my life. Don't focus on the how of things, just *enjoy* the fact you've found the best thing life has to offer. Having someone beside you in this life is what is most important."

God, she made the concept sound so...simple. Like loving somebody was the easiest fucking thing in the world. Unfortunately, Matt knew that in reality the truth was the polar opposite. Nothing was harder in life than allowing yourself to fall for another person. People weren't hardwired to set themselves up for pain. At least, he wasn't. Letting go and inviting pain in... He didn't know if he was ready to risk being hurt again.

"I promise you, I care about your son. A lot."

His words seemed to be enough for her. For now, anyway. "Then let me ask for another promise," she said with a halfhearted smile. "Perhaps one a bit more difficult." She let go of his hand. "Promise me...if you discover someone did this to my son, intentionally, you will find them and make sure they pay for what they've done."

Matt couldn't be sure, but he would almost swear he caught sight of what he was feeling mirrored in Evelyn Porter's eyes. The rage. The overwhelming determination to get justice for Alex, to protect him no matter what.

He assuredly made another promise he found easy to give. "I promise you, Mrs. Porter... I won't stop until I do."

Chapter Twenty

ALEX FELL INTO and out of sleep for the next several hours. His head was still groggy and his body ached like he had been in suspended animation, his muscles tired, weak, as though they hadn't been used in years. Voices faded in and out of the room, doctors and nurses talking about his heart rate, his blood pressure, his breathing. Matt, telling him he was there. Matt's voice was his favorite, the one he didn't think he would ever tire of hearing.

The late-afternoon sun peeked through the plastic vertical curtains of his hospital room window by the time he was strong enough to stay awake longer than a couple of minutes. He rapid-blinked for a few seconds to try to clear the sleep from his eyes and bring the room into focus. Things were quiet, the television muted on some cooking show, the only sound he could hear the incessant beeping of the heart monitor he had somehow grown used to since first waking up.

He yawned and stretched his arms and back as much as he could, given his position in the bed, thankful to at last be able to move. He had no clue how long he had been in the hospital, so having a little bit of feeling back in his arms and legs was wonderful.

"My son." The sound was barely a whisper from the corner of the room. His head rolled slowly in the direction and he could have passed out.

"Mother?" Evelyn Porter stood up from one of those ugly brown and orange chairs and crossed the room to stand by his bed. She smiled down at him, the calculated, precise smile she used when she was attempting to be empathetic, and he forced one as equally disdainful back. "What...what are you doing here?" The last person on earth he ever expected to see when he woke up was his mother. To say the two didn't have the best relationship was an understatement.

Charles and Evelyn Porter had never intended to have children. The night Charles won some humanitarian award Alex couldn't even remember the name of now, he spent the evening downing scotch and schmoozing with Maine's elite—and the night with Evelyn. Nine months later, Alex was born. The next eighteen years were filled with a cold distance between parents and child before Alex was old enough to venture out on his own. He never went back. Not even for a visit. Sure, he met up his parents from time to time, his mother more so after his father's death, but he never laid eyes on their house again, at least the inside.

"My child was injured. Where else would I be?" Evelyn was matter-of-fact, as if someone had just asked her what she was having for dinner.

Even in his current state, Alex could think of a dozen other places his mother could be—or where he wished she was. But he kept them to himself.

"It's...nice to see you." He prayed he sounded convincing. If Evelyn didn't buy his attempt at cordiality, she certainly didn't let anyone see, always the master of emotional secrecy.

"The doctors say you are going to be fine, make a full

recovery." She subtly changed the subject, as she always tended to do any time Alex threatened to get close to her. She had been standoffish as far back as he could remember. Even as a little boy, he never shared a bond with his mother. Or his father, for that matter, though their relationship was by far the strongest he held. He had to think long and hard to remember getting a genuine, heartfelt hug from either of them. But time brought indifference, and he had long since given up hope things would be any other way where his family was concerned.

"What happened to me?" It was the main question he needed answered. Yes, there were countless others, but why he was in a hospital bed far outweighed them.

Evelyn straightened her wool jacket—the same green one he remembered seeing her in on multiple occasions—and cleared her throat. "It was apparently carbon monoxide poisoning," she said, as if she were reading a menu or ingredients from a recipe.

"How long?" The second question burned through his thoughts. To him, he had been asleep for weeks but prayed he was wrong. "How long have I been in here?"

"Just since last night. But as I said, you will be fine. And they don't anticipate any lasting side effects."

He knew that was the piece his mother was most pleased to hear, because his full recovery meant she wouldn't have to visit more than once out of some sense of obligation or social acceptance. No, she could finish up visually doting on her son and get back to what was important in her life guilt free.

"Carbon monoxide? I... I don't understand."

"Yes, well, accidents typically are unexplainable, now, aren't they?"

He gave another forced smile. "I meant I don't

understand because I just had an inspection done on the house less than three months ago and everything was fine. I even had carbon monoxide detectors added. A free upgrade." Evelyn Porter was all about outward appearance to the rest of the world, so he cherished every chance he got to show his mother frugality.

She pondered his statement for a second, then said, "Perhaps this is information you should share with your...friend. Sergeant Fields?"

She had met Matt? Oh God. Those two coming face to face was something Alex had never wanted to happen. If left to him, Matt would have never even known his mother existed. What on earth had she said to him? Was she why he wasn't here, because she ran him off, scared him, *threatened* him? If she did anything to offend Matt, he would never forgive her.

"Mother," he started, but Evelyn, as she tended to do, interrupted him.

"He's quite a lovely young man." He could have sworn her smile was genuine—a fact which left him feeling more than a bit unsettled. "A handsome man, isn't he?"

"Yes, he is. *Very* handsome." He blamed his brazenness with his mother on the fog still clouding his brain. Or the drugs impairing his judgment. "And he's...more than a friend, Mother. But somehow, I think you already know that."

"I'm your mother, young man. Watch your tone with me." Evelyn adjusted her suit jacket for the tenth time and added, "But yes, I'm well aware of how...*close* you and Mr. Fields have become." Then something flashed across his mother's face he couldn't remember ever seeing before:

Admiration.

"I...I'm sorry I never said anything, Mother." He was

at a loss for words, his mind spinning with the realization she of all people seemed to be proud of him. And with the fact he had basically just come out to her—though she admitted she already knew.

Evelyn shook her head. "Don't be. It's not as if I gave you ample opportunity." She placed her hand on his, her skin warm...and oddly comforting. "I know I haven't been the best mother to you, Alexander. I...apologize if you didn't feel you could come to me with this."

He hadn't realized he was crying until her hand moved to his cheek to wipe his tears. So many emotions were rolling through him—fear, panic, hope, love—they were overwhelming to say the least.

"I wanted to," he finally said. "So many times, I wanted to. But..." He couldn't even finish the thought. His mother was connecting with him, after years of an unseen wall between them. He didn't want his words to ruin their moment.

"You could have." Evelyn's voice was soft, sincere. "I would not have judged you, or made you feel inferior for being...different."

"Gay, Mother. The word is 'gay.'"

Evelyn smiled, and he thought he caught the tiniest, briefest laugh. "I know the word, young man. And I know what you're thinking, but I am *not* afraid to say it." She didn't look uncomfortable, as far as he could tell, but she was an expert at hiding things. "My son is gay." She said the word with a conviction Alex had always feared; this time, though, he was grateful she had. She leaned down and gave him a kiss on the cheek. "And I'm so very proud of him."

THEY SAT TOGETHER for hours and talked about the past, and how Evelyn never learned how to connect with her son because he was so different from her. Where she was refined and closed-off, he was a free spirit, outgoing, socially adept. Evelyn enjoyed solitude, and silence, and organized function; Alex, the complete opposite. He thrived on being around others, causing a ruckus, a disheveled lifestyle—though he was always careful to rein himself in when in her presence. Seeing him in his hospital bed... Evelyn said the sight changed things for her. Suddenly, their differences weren't so important. Loving her son was. And she vowed to love him from then on.

"Thank you for being here, Mother," Alex whispered when Evelyn said she had to get going. "Having you here means a lot to me."

She wiped tears from his face again. "No more crying, my son." The stoic, rigid woman of his childhood was back, only this time softer, less cold. "You're a Porter. And Porters don't show emotion, remember?" He feared the past few hours had all been a dream until she tenderly laughed and bent down to give him a genuine, motherly hug.

"I love you."

"I love you, too, son." She turned to leave.

"Mother?"

"Yes, dear?" She turned back toward him.

"Did Matt...did he say when he would be back?"

"I don't recall." She appeared to be scouring her memory of meeting her son's boyfriend. "He said he was going to your house to have a look around, then he had to pay a visit to someone of particular interest in the fire at your shop. I assume he meant a suspect?"

Alex's skin flushed with fear. "Yes, he meant a suspect." He knew who the suspect was too.

Brayden.

Matt was going to Brayden's. Again.

He only hoped both men made it out alive.

Chapter Twenty-One

MATT LEFT ALEX'S hospital room more focused than he'd ever been. His only job was to find out what the fuck was going on, and who the hell was after Alex. And why.

He pulled up to the curb outside the house and killed the engine, sitting there in silence a minute to collect himself. He couldn't fail at this. There had been cases in the past he couldn't solve, couldn't piece enough of the clues together to get justice. Those cases drove him close to insanity. He couldn't let himself lose control with this one. Not with Alex. Matt had feelings for him. He couldn't let what happened to him go unpunished.

He got out and headed up the walk to the house. The place looked so different in the dark. Unlit, empty, abandoned. Alex cherished this place, Matt could tell, and he would make sure he got this and the rest of his life back.

Having gotten word from the fire department that the gas had been turned off, Matt opened the door with the key he had grabbed last night after the ambulance left with Alex and went inside. He had no idea what he was looking for, or even if there was anything to find. What happened to Alex very well could have been an accident, though every fiber in him screamed bullshit on that one— but he wouldn't be able to rest if he didn't treat this as an attempted murder case and something worse happened to Alex. God, just the thought made him sick. He pushed the notion out of his mind and walked the house.

Nothing seemed out of the ordinary, no signs of forced entry or foul play. But Matt had a clawing feeling in his gut, his inner voice urging him to keep looking, knowing something just wasn't right.

He checked upstairs, searching every room, every closet, even taking a peek in the attic. Again, nothing. The house looked exactly the same as the night he had met Alex here, their first date. Nothing out of place, nothing off. He didn't understand. How could things appear so normal, yet he feel so uneasy?

He headed back downstairs and straight to the basement. The large space was close to empty, only a few boxes stacked in one corner, a large furnace in the other. A long, casket-style freezer and old refrigerator filled the back wall behind the stairs, next to a storage closet he made sure was empty.

Frustration filled Matt's veins as he turned to head back upstairs. He glanced at the furnace as he put his hand on the railing of the staircase, the wheels of his brain starting to turn. Alex had suffered from carbon monoxide poisoning. Could the leak have come from the furnace?

He crossed the basement and gave the bulky appliance a once-over. The furnace was massive, likely bigger than necessary for this size house. The model looked like an older one, the kind in scary movies with the see-through door, decades of time turning the once metallic box to a more muted, rusty tone. He was no furnace expert, but he could see how something so old and outdated could've leaked deadly gas.

But still, the gnawing feeling in his gut was there, still pressing on him to not write this one off as accidental. He had practically predetermined the cause of the fire at the Book Nook, but it turned out he was wrong. He wouldn't make the same mistake again.

He fished his phone from his pocket and hit send, calling on the one person at the Cliffside Police Department he knew outside of this case. "Hey, Anna," he said, putting his phone on speaker while he continued to look around the basement. "This is Matt. How are you?"

"Hey, Fields," a strong, upbeat voice called back. "Good here. Can't complain."

"Glad to hear it. Listen, I was wondering if you could do me a favor. You know I'm in town about the fire on Shemwood, right?"

"I'd heard," Anna answered.

"Well, I need some fingerprinting done, maybe even fiber search. I know you're the best at forensics. Any way you could help me out?"

There was a millisecond pause, then, "You know I got you, Fields."

"Yeah? I appreciate that. Thanks a lot, Anna. You're a big help, believe me. The address is 254 Elm. A residence. Thanks again. I'll buy you a beer sometime."

"You know I'm holding you to your word, mister."

Matt gave a halfhearted laugh and ended the call, heading back upstairs. If Anna Colson didn't find anything, then he would think about letting his obsession go.

But if she did find something, *anything*, and it turned out someone *had* tampered with Alex's furnace and almost killed him, Matt would throw the bastard under the fucking jail.

MATT RECEIVED A call from Colson about ten minutes after he left. She was at Alex's house and found the key he left for her. He asked her to call him the second she found anything and hung up the phone. He wanted to stop by the hospital and see Alex, just to make sure he was okay, but he hadn't been by the fire station yet, so he took a right and headed in the opposite direction.

As he drove, he couldn't help but think how much his life had changed. Moving across the country, starting a new job...he had been scared, if he was being honest. But the decision turned out to be the best one he'd ever made. Because it brought him to Alex.

He had loved Cameron. Still did, in many ways. But Alex... There was something very different about the feelings he held for him. He couldn't explain why, but... There was an unseen force controlling him, keeping him tethered to Alex, making Alex his top priority.

Before moving to Maine, he imagined his life as much different than the direction it had suddenly taken. He pictured making sergeant, maybe even marshal, being a hundred percent focused on work, too busy to even think about another relationship. Cameron's death had been devastating for him, almost destroyed him. Even taking the chance to go through something as painful, as gut-wrenching again was no longer on his radar. He had wanted to start over, put his career first, forget about love.

But the universe had other plans. Namely, Alex. One look at Alex and Matt's entire plan to steer clear of dating and relationships became a thing of the past. After getting to know Alex, his idea of his future disintegrated, and he found himself wanting the life he used to dream about. And he was going to make damned sure he and Alex had everything.

Just as he made the turn onto Main Street, he caught sight of Brayden Cooper getting out of his car in front of the fire station. He couldn't believe the son of a bitch had the nerve to just stroll around town while Alex lay in a hospital bed. Yeah, he still hadn't found proof Brayden Cooper had anything to do with the bookstore fire, but he knew it in his gut the guy was involved. No doubt. Which to Matt meant Brayden was also tied to the carbon monoxide leak that almost did Alex in.

He ignored thoughts of losing Alex and parked across the street from the fire department. He got out and stayed as out of sight as he could while he kept an eye on Brayden, who was heading up the wide concrete drive. He walked with such confidence, like he didn't have a care in the world. Meanwhile, Matt was trying to focus on doing his job while not coming unglued over all Alex had been through. Son of a bitch.

He fished one of those free apartment hunter magazines from a rickety metal stand in front of a hair salon and pretended to be looking at the listings inside while he eyed Brayden. Brayden opened the door to the fire station and leaned in. He was obviously looking for somebody and, judging by how he kept glancing back over his shoulder, he didn't want anyone to know he was there. He closed the door and stepped back down the drive, and a short, fit woman dressed in standard fire department down-time attire joined him a second later.

She looked angry—much like Matt imagined he himself looked at the moment—as she crossed the concrete lining the front and side of the station. She and Brayden briefly hugged before getting into what looked like a pretty heated conversation.

Okay, what the hell? Who was this woman, and how did she know Brayden Cooper? And what the hell were they arguing about out in public?

More questions. Fuck. Something else he couldn't answer, couldn't explain, was the last thing Matt needed. He had plenty of those already. Answers were what was missing from the equation. And if he didn't start finding some soon, this case was going to get the best of him.

He turned his back to the station. He noticed Brayden and the woman saying their goodbyes using the large pane window of the hair salon as a makeshift mirror. His eyes were locked on them while pretending to read the paper as the woman headed back inside the station and Cooper got in his car and peeled out of there, speeding off down the street toward the highway.

He returned the paper to its rack with a mischievous smile, feeling better about his suspicions of Brayden Cooper than he had since finding out about him.

Even having to watch in the reflection of a window, there was no missing Brayden's pissed off attitude when he left the mystery woman and headed out of town.

Without a doubt, Matt just caught his first break. And there wasn't a fucking chance in hell he was going to let a step forward slip through his fingers.

Chapter Twenty-Two

ALEX WAS BORED. He had been stuck in a hospital bed for a full day, and his nerves were starting to fray. He had never been the type to lie around and do nothing, unless he was sprawled out on a beach somewhere enjoying the sun and whatever drink he could find. But on a normal day, he was always busy. Now, just lying there staring at the ceiling... The confinement was driving him insane.

He did regain some strength in his muscles after what felt like forever, and he wasn't feeling quite as sluggish as he had earlier in the morning. He managed to work his way over to the table beside his bed and grab the phone. He punched in Matt's number and held the receiver to his ear. After two rings, Matt's deep, sexy voice came on the line.

"Hello?"

"Hello, Sergeant." He was smiling ear to ear, just hearing Matt's voice enough to lift his spirits.

"Hey there," Matt said. Alex could hear tension behind his words.

"What's wrong?" he asked.

"What? Nothing's wrong. I promise. I just wish I was there with you, that's all."

Alex didn't buy his excuse for a second.

"Nice try, but I know missing me is not the only thing on your mind, I can tell. Spill. No secrets, remember?"

Matt huffed into the phone. "I'm just a little stressed out," he finally said. "But I promise, it's not a big deal. And I don't want you worrying over nothing."

"I want to worry. I *need* to worry. I'm going insane in this place."

Matt laughed. "Hell, enjoy all the free time you're getting. Because once you're out of there, I'm gonna have you so busy you'll be begging for a day to rest."

Alex felt a stirring in his groin at hearing those words. God, he wanted Matt. So badly. Right then. Right there in his hospital room.

"I can't wait."

"Me, either."

"Well...maybe we don't have to."

"Uh, what?"

"We could...you know..." Alex lowered his voice even though the door to his room was closed. "Have a little fun."

"Are you talking about... You wanna do *that*? In your room?"

"Yes. Yes, I do. But I'm here and you're...wherever you are. I was talking about a little phone fun, maybe?" Just the thought of getting off over the phone while Matt's irresistibly sexy voice filled his head sent shock waves through Alex's body, straight down to his cock, which was now rock hard and aching.

"Good Lord. You're a horny little shit, aren't ya?" Matt said with a laugh.

Alex laughed too. "Like you're not?"

"I am, but you take being horny to another level."

"Well, I can't help the fact I want to be with you. All the time."

"Ditto," Matt replied. "But unfortunately, I'm knee-deep in work right now. Afraid I don't have time to rub one out."

"Are you sure, Sergeant? I'm all alone in this bed. *Naked.* And so very hard." He was panting as he gripped his erection and squeezed. Pulses of electricity shot through him. "Please help me get off, Matt."

"Oh, my God." There was a slight pause, then, "Gimme two minutes."

Alex was smiling as he heard the car door slam, some rustling, and Matt's breathing kick up a notch. Knowing he got Matt worked up into a sexual frenzy only fueled his heat.

"Hurry, Sergeant." His own breathing was heavy, laced with impending sexual release. He wanted Matt—*needed* him—so much. Phone sex wasn't typical for him—he had never even attempted such a thing, to be honest, not even to one of those nine-hundred numbers—but an impromptu phone session would have to suffice if Matt couldn't be there physically. "Jesus, are you all right? What happened?" he asked after Matt started a coughing and hacking fit.

"Dammit! I'm okay, I'm okay. Took too big a gulp of water. My throat was dry as a fucking bone. Just got a little bit down the wrong pipe, that's all."

Alex laughed. "And which pipe do you mean?"

"Don't say shit like that." Matt groaned, and Alex took the sound as an invitation to do the complete opposite.

"Now, why wouldn't you want me to say such things? Aren't you horny, too? Don't you want me as much as I want you, Sergeant?"

He knew he was driving Matt over the edge. He didn't

have to see his face to know that. The connection they had, the unexplainable pull between them—that's how he knew. He could feel, even through the phone, Matt wanted this just as much as he wanted Matt.

"What are you doing right now?" Alex asked, his hand still tightly wrapped around his pulsing member. "Tell me, Matt. Describe every detail."

"I...I'm taking my clothes off," Matt said. His voice was just a whisper now, his need taking control. "Now I'm lying on the bed. I..." He stopped talking, and Alex could sense his apprehension.

"Don't be afraid or embarrassed," he offered. "We are in this together. One hundred percent. Just let go and have fun. Trust me, Matt. I'm right here with you, all the way."

Matt exhaled deeply. "Okay. God, I want you so fucking much, Alex. You have no idea what you do to me. Drives me fucking insane."

Alex was grinning ear to ear. "Are you fully naked?" he asked, guiding the conversation. He wanted to get off, plain and simple. His own animalistic instinct had taken over the second he touched himself, and its sole focus was release.

"I'm still wearing my boxers."

Alex was groaning this time. He loved Matt in boxers. The sight was erotic, all his muscle and bronzed skin sheathed only in thin plaid material. The mental image only added to his state of arousal.

"Now I'm pushing them down," Matt went on. "They're under my balls now."

"Are you hard?" Alex asked. Matt could only grunt in agreement, his heavy breathing reverberating through the phone. "Do you want to get off with me, Matt?" Alex was breathing fast and heavy as well, his voice forced out by a rush of air from his lungs. The excitement over this newfound form of expression was lighting up his senses in a way like he had never experienced. He was losing himself in the euphoria. "Get off with me. I'm so very ready." More primal grunting from Matt that made Alex's head spin with delight.

"Tell me," he pleaded once again. "Tell me what you're doing right now." He could hear Matt stroking, actually *hear* his hand furiously seizing his massive erection...but he wanted to hear the words, wanted to hear Matt describe exactly what he was doing to himself.

"I'm gripping it. Hard. So fucking hard."

"Oh, yes." Alex's breathing elevated more. "Does that feel good?" He already knew the answer; he was doing the exact same thing to himself. At the same moment. Though they couldn't be together right then, at least they could feel the same things simultaneously. The fact they were sharing such an intimate moment while so far apart from each other increased Alex's arousal tenfold.

"Fuck yeah."

"Tell me more," Alex begged, his voice hitched. "Describe it to me."

"The head is so flared," Matt whispered. "Looks twice as big. All purple and shiny. Burning up with heat. I'm rubbing my thumb back and forth, coating the skin with precome. God, this feels so fucking amazing."

"Jesus. Yes." Alex's voice was there but broken up by heaving breaths. The images his mind was conjuring were almost too much to bear. He could see Matt sprawled on his hotel room bed, his magnificent, muscular frame bucking and heaving as he carried himself to the threshold of release. "I wish I were there right now. I would pull your hand away and use mine to stroke you. I would grip you nice and tight, watch your cock swell and bulge beneath my fingers as I move up and down, up and down."

"Son of a bitch." He could sense Matt was on the edge, losing control, reaching his orgasm at super speed. "Fuck yeah, Alex. Stroke my dick."

"I would keep massaging, up and down, watching your head fall back, your eyes close, hearing you moan as I pull you closer and closer."

"God, yes...so close. So fucking close."

Alex had reached the point of no return, his hand creating intense friction on his cock as he imagined doing the same for Matt. Both men were too far gone now to even think of coming back. The need for release was so powerful, so overwhelming, completely consuming him—Matt, too, he could tell.

Matt's groans and grunts and panting only proved he was right there with Alex, right there on the precipice of orgasm. Alex knew he needed to finish, carry them over the edge.

"I would tighten my hand," he continued, "so tight around your pulsing shaft, as your balls tighten and lift and your legs tremble with anticipation. Then, just when you're ready to erupt, I would lean down and flick my tongue against your plump, warm head and—"

"Fuck! Fuck!" Matt screamed into the phone as his orgasm no doubt consumed him. Alex muffled his own cries of ecstasy as he exploded, covering his chest and abdomen and perhaps even the wall behind him, the eruption was so powerful. He struggled to regain control of his body. His chest thrummed, his core muscles aching from the exertion. He knew then he would be sore as hell tomorrow, but he couldn't care. The joy of the orgasm far outweighed physical side effects.

"Son of a bitch," Matt said after several seconds of primal grunts. "That was fucking amazing. I can't even... Alex...you're fucking awesome." He was still breathing deep and heavy, his voice labored and strained. "You still there?"

"Oh, I'm here," Alex answered, smiling. "And I would have to agree. Awesome is a fitting description." They both laughed.

"I was a little freaked out at first," Matt added. "But damn man, that was hot!" More laughter found its way into Alex's heart.

"I can one hundred percent say I have absolutely no idea what came over me. I was lying here thinking about you and how incredibly sexy you are, and before I knew what was happening, I was stroking myself and dialing your number."

"Jesus, Alex, you gotta stop. I don't have anything left in me to go another round." Matt laughed hard, and a twinge of something familiar rumbled deep inside Alex. To him, laughter was the absolute sexiest thing a man could do, and hearing Matt laugh always made him want more.

"Sorry, Sergeant. Don't arrest me for harassment."

"Shit, it'd be more like assault with a deadly weapon."

Alex smiled. "I'm miles away, in the privacy of my very own hospital room. I haven't touched you."

"You didn't have to," Matt threw back.

"Oh, really?" With the intensity of their phone fun, Alex could only imagine what would have happened had the two of them been lying beside each other. The mere thought sent shocks to his groin.

"Surprise, surprise, I was horny as hell today."

"Same here," Alex said, as if this were the most normal conversation in the world. He supposed it was more than normal to discuss states of arousal and the like with someone you just had phone sex with. "Well, I should let you get back to work, Sergeant. Besides, the nurses will no doubt be in soon, and I have...a bit of a mess to clean up."

"Jesus, Alex. You're killing me!" Matt groaned into the phone and Alex laughed.

"Sorry, I couldn't resist."

"You're such a damn tease, man."

"Oh, trust me, Sergeant. You haven't seen just how much of a tease I can be."

"Okay, I'm hanging up now."

"Forgive my language, but you suck."

Matt gave a little laugh. "But not as good as you."

Alex smiled. "Which is precisely why you need to get over here as soon as you can. So you can perfect your technique. I'm...so hard just thinking about you."

"Alex!"

Alex laughed. "Sorry again, Sergeant." He paused when Matt exhaled deeply. He loved the fact he could so easily get under Matt's skin. Talk about a huge turn-on. "I guess I'll let you get back to work. But promise you'll come see me soon. They said I can go home tomorrow, but I can't wait that long to see you again." He sounded like a child, he knew, but Matt brought those feelings out in him, the promise of tomorrow, the wonder of a brand-new life, just waiting to be explored.

"I promise I'll be there just as soon as I can."

"I plan to hold you to your word, Sergeant."

Matt gave a light chuckle. "I know you will." The line

was quiet for a few seconds until Matt added, "I..."

Alex's gut twisted, like Matt wanted to share something. Something undoubtedly bad.

"What?" he asked timidly. "What are you not telling me? Something's going on, I can tell."

"I... I have a lead. Nothing else so don't worry, it's just a lead. I didn't want to say anything because I didn't want to get your hopes up. But damn, I can't keep anything from you."

"And I'm very grateful you can't. I don't want you to keep anything from me, Matt. Ever. No matter how painful or scary, I don't want us keeping secrets. Not knowing what's going on with you, with the case, would only make me worry more. I can't help I'm a worrier. Worrying is what I do best. And I can also tell when something is on your mind, so I would have pulled the truth out of you eventually. So thank you for keeping me up-to-date instead of leaving me alone here, thinking you're getting into trouble." He waited for Matt to respond, then added, "You're not, right?"

"What, getting into trouble? Of course not. I'm just gonna see if anything pans out with this lead. And then I promise I'll come see you. I hate not being there. I just...I need to follow up on this."

"I want to see you, too, but I understand. I'll let you go. Just be careful, okay?"

"Aye, aye, cap'n."

Alex could picture Matt saluting. "Funny. Okay, bye."

After they ended the call, Alex couldn't help but feel that Matt, though he denied it, wasn't just following up on a lead but was about to get into something he might not be able to get out of. Namely, confronting Brayden again.

Brayden already knew he was a suspect in the fire—

the *main* suspect, as far as Alex and Matt were concerned—so he shouldn't be surprised if Matt showed up again with more questions. But Alex still worried Matt's anger over what happened, coupled with the possible intentional carbon monoxide poisoning... He was afraid Matt wouldn't be able to stop himself from letting his frustrations out on Brayden in a physical way.

All of a sudden, the images he'd had in his monoxide-induced sleep of Matt being hauled off to jail became much more of a real possibility for their future.

God, he desperately needed to get out of the hospital before everything fell apart.

Chapter Twenty-Three

MATT PULLED INTO the Cliffside PD parking lot like a man on a mission. Thoughts of Alex lying in a hospital bed, all hard and wanting him so much, had Matt fucking itching for release again as he headed inside. He was already wound up from catching a tiny glimpse of Brayden Cooper's true nature out on the street. Having Alex on the brain, too? He was fucking driving himself mad.

He sat down at the desk Gregson had emptied for him and pulled up the city of Cliffside website on the computer. He wanted to find out who the woman was he'd seen Cooper talking to. What was their connection?

He located the city's fire department listing and opened the page. A standard, generic picture of the station filled the top half of the screen with a couple of paragraphs describing the city's promise to protect and serve, yada yada. He scrolled down until he found the link to Employee Listing and poured over the pictures popping up on his screen.

She wasn't on the website. Maybe the mystery woman really was a mystery. Which didn't make any damn sense. How was she working there and not on the site?

He had an idea and did a search for the Bangor Fire Marshal's website next. The setup looked a lot like the Cliffside one complete with similar paragraphs of text beneath an equally unimpressive picture. He scrolled to the bottom and clicked on Employee Listing.

Just what he thought.

His picture wasn't there, either. Well, not the one he took when he got promoted to sergeant. He was still listed as an inspector. Obviously city organizations didn't think updating their websites was a priority, since he'd been promoted over two months ago.

Which meant the mystery woman was new, too, and most likely started working at the fire department sometime after he was promoted with the marshal's office.

Matt wasn't the type of guy who believed in coincidences. The fact she was new to the FD and seemed pretty well acquainted with his prime suspect had his wheels spinning.

There was a connection, he knew. He could fucking *feel* it. He just had to find out what that connection was. He had to know what the hell Brayden Cooper was up to and how the firefighter played into the plan.

He closed the window on the computer, locking the screen so no prying eyes could see what he'd been up to and left the station. He was speeding pretty much the entire drive out to Emory, whipping in between cars, not using his turn signal when switching lanes or passing, totally counting on professional courtesy if a county cop or, God forbid, a state trooper clocked him. Luckily though, he made it without incident, slowing down only once he was turning onto Brayden Cooper's street.

He killed the engine and just sat there. He had to get his shit together. Last time he was out here, Cooper had basically called his bluff. No fucking chance he was letting that happen again. He was going to prove the bastard was behind the fire. *And* the "accidental" poisoning.

"Don't fuck this up." He stared at himself in the rearview mirror. "Don't let this piece of shit get away with what he's done." His eyes were tired, heavy, the bags beneath them more pronounced and darker than usual. The stress of...well, everything was getting to him. The case, Alex—everything was teetering on a cliff. If he didn't fix things, his life would plummet over the edge and explode.

He got out of the car and crossed the street toward Cooper's house. Things looked no different than last time, but he noticed a car parked out front he hadn't seen when he was here before. He already knew what Cooper drove— silver Dodge Charger, which was parked in the drive on the left side of the house—and this ordinary looking four- cylinder pick-up was definitely not a Dodge Charger. He gave the truck a quick peek inside as he walked past the driver's side. Empty, no surprise, except for a Red Bull can in the cupholder. He noticed the driver's seat was up a little close to the steering wheel though, not what you'd expect from a guy as tall as Cooper. Someone either fished something from the back or the driver was short.

He made his mental notes and headed up the sidewalk. He had just reached the porch steps when the front door swung open. But Brayden Cooper didn't come out to greet him.

The mystery woman did.

Son of a bitch.

"Can I help you?" she asked, attitude pouring off of her. He was taken by surprise. What the hell was she doing at Brayden's house? He had just seen her at the fire station *with* Brayden, and now she was here. He was more confused than before on how these two knew each other, but he kept his cool and didn't let his surprise show. The last thing he wanted was the woman to suspect he knew about her.

"I'm Sergeant Matt Fields from the Bangor Fire Marshal's office." He kept his voice calm, seemingly unaffected by the whirlwind going on inside his head. "I'm looking for Brayden Cooper."

"Bangor?" the woman asked. "Long way from your jurisdiction."

He stared her down for a few seconds before offering a fake smile and saying, "Well, my office is over the entire southern district of Maine." He wanted to wipe the smug look off of her face. He could see the anger skitter across her features. No doubt she had planned on stopping him before he even got started.

"So," he said again with a calm, carefree demeanor. "Is Mr. Cooper home?"

The woman just stood there staring him down for so long he didn't think she was going to cooperate. Which would've made his day, because he was itching to haul her ass in on obstruction charges—or at least make her think he would.

"Bray!" she yelled over her shoulder, never taking her eyes off of Matt. The wiry muscles running along her jawline rolled and flexed.

Matt held back a smile.

Brayden Cooper stumbled out onto the porch, looking like he'd just woken up from a three-day bender—which was impossible given the fact Matt had seen him only a couple of hours earlier and he looked fine. Now, giving the woman next to him a dirty look and white-knuckling the porch railing, he looked like hell.

"Mr. Cooper?" Matt's hatred for him showed through his words. "You okay, Mr. Cooper?" Brayden looked at him through bloodshot eyes and wiped his nose.

He wasn't drunk.

He'd been crying.

"I'm fine." Brayden leaned against the porch column at the top of the steps and crossed his arms. "What the hell do you want, Sergeant? I thought you and I said our piece the other day."

"You two know each other?" The woman looked from Matt to Brayden, who was a step up behind her.

"Yeah, we go way back." Brayden sniffled. "He thinks I started the fire at Alex's."

The woman stared at Brayden, her eyes wide.

Huh, maybe Brayden Cooper *didn't* burn down Alex's store. Or if he did, this woman had no clue.

She turned back to Matt. "I was there that night, Sergeant. At the Shemwood fire. I'm a firefighter with the Cliffside department. And I have to say, it didn't look like arson to me."

So you're a fire inspector, too?, is what Matt wanted to say. But he decided honey was better than vinegar—and bluffing was even better. "Yeah, to me, either. I was prepared to rule the fire accidental."

He caught Brayden in his peripheral. The man stood tall, almost proud, like he'd gotten away with his plan. Fat fucking chance, if Matt had his way.

"So, what changed your mind?" the woman asked.

"Your chief." He made sure to lock eyes with her. She didn't flinch, didn't even look the least bit surprised. Either she wasn't, since she knew good and damn well arson was at the top of the list, or she was one hell of a poker player. "His initial report listed cause of fire as suspected arson. My department has opened an investigation."

"And you think Brayden was behind it." The woman was matter-of-fact in her tone, like Matt looking at Cooper for the crime was no surprise.

"I'm following up on all leads." A textbook answer. Something told him she wasn't the type to accept textbook answers.

"Oh yeah?" She smirked. "And how many of those you got?"

"I'm not at liberty to discuss an ongoing investigation." His anger toward this woman was mounting by the second. She was ballsy, for sure. But she was out of her fucking mind if she thought she would intimidate him. If anything, she was confirming his suspicions that Brayden Cooper was guilty—and she was somehow involved.

"Of course not," she said with a smirk and a tiny laugh. "Well, I'd be happy to share *my* report with you, Sergeant, since I was lead on the call. You'll see we determined the fire started approximately fifteen to twenty minutes before we were called and another six before we got there. And Brayden was home the entire time, drunk off his ass."

He tried not to let the woman's holier-than-thou, firefighters-rule attitude get under his skin as he turned his attention to Brayden. "Why didn't you mention this to me the last time we met, Mr. Cooper?" He did his best to stay professional, to not let on the fact he knew the two people standing in front of him were behind everything.

"Like she said, I was drunk. Don't remember much about anything."

"So, you can't remember where you were?" Matt was jotting everything down in the notepad he'd pulled from his pocket the second the woman intercepted him.

"He was home," she answered. "I stuck him in a cab myself. So drunk he couldn't even stand up on his own. There's no chance he was there."

"Huh." Matt's mind was spinning like a top. "So, if you put Mr. Cooper into a cab and *he* was intoxicated—"

"—Don't even think it," she interrupted. "No, I wasn't drinking. I was on duty." She glanced over her shoulder at Brayden, who looked ready to vomit at any second. "I got a call from a friend telling me this one was stumbling drunk. I took my lunch and headed over to get him. I gave the cab driver his address and sixty bucks to bring him all the way out here. Then I went back to work."

She was being very forthcoming—which made him think she was a little too ready with her answers.

"And this friend's name? I'd like to verify Mr. Cooper's alibi." He had already made a mental note to contact the cab company to see if anyone made a drive to Emory the night of the fire, which would have helped with Brayden's alibi. But he just couldn't resist the chance to get to her.

"*I'm* verifying his alibi," she said with force. Yeah, he got to her.

"Sorry, but I'm afraid that's good enough, Miss...?"

"So, what, the fire marshal's office don't extend professional courtesy?" She ignored him asking about her name. Didn't matter; he'd find out on his own the second he headed home.

"I'm not a firefighter."

"No shit." She shook her head with a surprising laugh. "Tell you what. Since you don't have a warrant or any *real* reason to be here other than to jerk us around, why don't you hop back in your little SUV and get the hell out of here. We're done." She turned and headed for the door, grabbing Brayden by the arm and pulling him with her.

"Be safe, *Sergeant*," she added as she opened the door and went inside. The way she said "sergeant" turned Matt's stomach; he only wanted Alex calling him Sergeant. She made the word sound gross, which pissed him off. He also picked up on her not-so-subtle threat, but nothing couldn't kill the surge of self-assuredness currently pumping through his veins.

"I'll be in touch," he called after them.

He was smiling ear to ear by the time he got to his car, because he was surer than ever that Brayden Cooper was his arsonist.

Chapter Twenty-Four

MATT BYPASSED THE hospital once he got back to Cliffside. It was killing him not to stop and see Alex, to make sure he was as okay as he'd sounded on the phone, but the little exchange he'd just had with Brayden Cooper and his mystery friend was gnawing at him like a pack of rabid rats. If he didn't dig further to find out what was going on with those two, he wouldn't be able to focus on jack shit otherwise. And being distracted wouldn't be fair to Alex. He deserved Matt's undivided attention. And Matt planned to give him that once this case was over. Which, if he was dead-on with his suspicion of Cooper, wouldn't be long.

He called Alex on the drive through town to tell him he would be by shortly—almost turning his car around and heading to the hospital when Alex started begging— and made a beeline for the fire station. The woman hadn't looked to be leaving Brayden's house anytime soon, so this was his prime chance to find out just who the hell she was.

He didn't bother trying to hide the fact he was there as he pulled right up the drive to the station, parking in front of one of the large, open bay doors. A young, attractive guy dressed in similar standard-issue attire he had seen the mystery woman in earlier exited the oversized garage and greeted him.

"Hey, Sergeant." The man's instantly set Matt at ease.

"Am I that obvious?" Matt flashed a smile of his own as he shook the man's hand.

"Nah, I noticed your stripes." Matt glanced at his sleeve. Yeah, once he paid attention to his uniform shirt, they did kind of stick out, especially to those in the field.

"Can't believe I never even noticed them before," he replied.

The fireman was about Matt's height, maybe a little shorter, with tanned skin and dark, close-cropped hair, a Hollywood-style swish in the front. Bright blue eyes contrasted nicely against the darkness of his features. Dimples pocked his cheeks when he spoke.

"So, what can I do you for?" the guy asked.

"I'm Sergeant Fields, with the Bangor Fire Marshal's office. But call me Matt." He extended a hand, and the man gave it a firm shake.

"Nice to meet you, Matt. I'm Lieutenant Cruz. But you can call me Diego."

He was Latin. His dark features were a dead giveaway—and the fact he oozed sexual energy. Not to mention the tiny hint of an accent Matt had no doubt made people melt. Yeah, Matt was a hundred percent into Alex, but he wasn't blind.

"Nice to meet you, too, Diego. I was wondering if I could ask you a few questions?"

"Shoot."

"There's a female firefighter who works here—" he started.

"Oh yeah, Gina Stanton," Diego interrupted. "One of a kind, that one."

"Oh yeah?" Matt's curiosity was piqued. Sounded like he wasn't the only one who was rubbed the wrong way by the mystery woman—Gina.

"Yeah, she's a tough one. Real chip on her shoulder. Had some trouble at her old station from what I've heard."

"What kind of trouble?"

"The word is she had a run-in with a fellow battalion member from a neighboring house. Things got physical, apparently."

"You mean...he assaulted her?" Matt was a little shocked. He hadn't pegged Gina as the victim type.

Diego laughed. "The opposite if you can believe it. The prick tried to pick her up at a bar. She turned him down, he got a little rough, and she laid him out."

"Wow." There was the woman he'd met—tough as shit and itching to fight.

"Yeah, caused quite a stir, according to the guys at her old house. The dude wanted to press charges, but his chief talked him down. But only if Stanton was transferred. So, now we got her." Diego didn't seem too excited about his firehouse getting another station's sloppy seconds., Matt wanted to know why.

"So, you get stuck with the problem child. Gotta be tough."

"Eh, is what it is, you know? I do an okay job keeping her in line."

"So, how long has Miss Stanton worked here?"

"She's a Mrs., I think," Diego said. "From what I can tell, she's married. But to answer your question, she's been here about two months or so. A little less, maybe."

There was something Matt didn't pick up on earlier, the fact Gina Stanton might have a husband. He jotted the info down in the notepad he'd fished from his pocket. He also made a mental note that Gina had, in fact, started with the Cliffside Fire Department around the time he thought.

"What makes you think she's married?"

"Uh, just talk, I guess. She's mentioned her ex a few times, how big of a dick he is, that the usual cock and bull. Could be an ex-boyfriend, I guess. But something just made me think husband. I dunno."

He made notes as Diego talked, making sure not to miss anything. He wanted to be damn sure he knew all there was to know about Brayden Cooper's new friend.

Hell...could Cooper be Gina's ex? He was supposedly gay, but sexual preference didn't mean shit nowadays. Married guys played for both teams all the time.

"Was her ex who she was talking to this morning? I drove by and noticed them out front." He hoped like hell Diego would say yes, Brayden was Gina's husband/ex. Their relationship would explain Gina's overprotective nature when it came to Cooper.

"Sorry, Sergeant, I just came on shift half an hour ago, so I wasn't here when she was. But I could ask around, if you want?"

"Thanks, I'd appreciate it. And please, call me Matt."

"Sorry. Matt." Diego flashed a smile again with just the right amount of crookedness to be sexy. "Give me your number and I'll let you know what I find out."

"Oh, yeah, of course." Matt was admittedly flustered a bit because he missed Alex. *Bad.* Diego's good looks only made him ache worse. Matt needed to see Alex, as soon as possible. He fished his card from his shirt pocket and held it between two fingers.

"Call anytime," he added after Diego plucked the card from his hand, then turned to leave.

"Will do," Diego said. "Hey, Matt?" Matt turned back around. "You, uh...maybe wanna get a drink sometime?"

Holy hell. The guy was asking him out. Damn. Sure was gonna hurt to turn him down.

"Uh..."

"Hey, sorry, Sergeant. I overstepped. Your rank is well above mine, I get it. All good here." Diego held out his hands and backed up a step. "Stupid of me to assume. I just...you're *really* good-looking, and I thought maybe... Damn. Just ignore me, okay?" Diego smiled, his entire face turning a deep, bloody red. Matt was extremely flattered.

"Hey, don't be embarrassed. Really." He stepped closer to Diego. Close enough to get a big whiff of cologne, only adding to Diego's appeal. "I'm flattered. Honest. I just...I'm kind of with someone."

"Kind of?"

Matt smiled. "I'm *with* someone. Not kind of." Hell, he was just gonna bite the bullet and admit he wanted to be with Alex and nobody else. Even a guy as good-looking as Diego.

Diego smiled. "Hey man, glad to hear it. Whoever they are, they're very lucky." Damn, hot *and* nice—a combo you didn't see too often anymore. Then again, Matt had his own nice, sexy-as-hell guy waiting on him to wise the hell up and put him first. And he was gonna do just that.

"I'm the lucky one." He was grateful to be talking about something other than the case. Of course, the fire— and proving Brayden Cooper was his arsonist—was his top priority, but that didn't mean he wasn't an average guy at the same time. "He's the catch, not me."

Diego's face lit up. "Don't sell yourself short, Sergeant." The way Diego said Sergeant reminded Matt of Alex's sexy, playful use of the nickname.

His cheeks burned crimson. "Thanks, I appreciate that. And...back at ya...Mr. Fireman." He almost said "ditto" but stopped himself. He'd keep ditto for Alex only.

Diego laughed. "Mr. Fireman? Really?"

Matt laughed too. "Sorry. You try coming up with a nickname on the spot." They both laughed.

"True, true," Diego said, and a moment of silence fell between them. But Matt noticed he was oddly comfortable like he had known Diego a lot longer than the few minutes they'd been standing there talking. Matt could see Diego becoming a friend one day, which wouldn't be such a bad thing. And he knew Alex would like him too. Matt had a nice thought of how cool it would be to have a mutual friend he and Alex could both hang out with.

The image of them hanging out with Diego, laughing and having a ball over some beers down at the beach on a warm summer day was the first time he had imagined a future with Alex, the first time he had actually pictured the two of them doing things together, having the same friends. The possibility felt amazing.

"Hey, how about you, Alex, and I get together sometime? Go out for a beer? We might even find you a guy." Damn...did he really just say that? "Sorry, man. I don't know why that came out. I don't even know you. I just... Sometimes I stick my big foot in my mouth."

Diego laughed again and waved off Matt's fuck-up. "Don't sweat it. Hell, I'll take whatever help I can get. Finding decent guys in this town is close to impossible. Present company excluded, of course."

"Of course."

"And thanks for the offer. I might take all you guys up to hang out one day."

Matt smiled. "I hope you do." He pointed to his business card Diego was still holding in his hand. "My cell is on the back. Call me, we'll set something up."

Diego glanced down at the card, flipping the matte white square of paper over in his hand. "I definitely will. Oh, and I'll check with the others about Stanton. Find out if the guy you said she was with is her ex or whatever. Talk soon?"

"Sounds good. Thanks for your help. And nice to meet you."

"You too. Take it easy out there." Matt nodded and smiled as Diego headed back inside, tucking the business card in the back pocket of his jeans. Matt hopped in his car and left the fire station, heading straight for the hospital.

He needed his Alex fix, fast.

Chapter Twenty-Five

"GOD, AM I glad to see you." Alex was grinning like a kid on his birthday when Matt stepped into his hospital room. He had missed him more than he thought. "Get over here and kiss me, please."

Matt obliged, crossing the room and leaning down toward him. He cupped Alex's head in his hand and Alex fell into their kiss, getting lost in the familiar and very welcome taste of Matt's perfect mouth. Their tongues dueled for control. Their breathing accelerated to rocket speed. Alex kissed with a fury, desperate to meld together with Matt.

Matt broke their kiss. "I so needed that." His voice was breathy, his eyes glazed over. Seeing Matt so into making out made Alex's cock grow harder than ever.

"I need this." He reached out and gripped the front of Matt's khakis. Matt's throbbing erection pulsed in his hand.

"Fuuuck." Matt's entire body twitched, and he clamped his eyes shut. Alex groped and rubbed Matt's cock, and Matt bit at his lower lip. Alex had him right where he wanted him. Well, for the moment. He planned on tasting what he was currently massaging before Matt left for the night.

"We can't—gotta stop." Matt opened his eyes and looked down at him. "We can't do this here."

"Do you *want* me to stop, Sergeant?" Alex grinned like a mischievous child who just got caught with his hand in the cookie jar and was trying to charm his way out of trouble. He knew what Matt wanted. He could feel it, right between his legs. And the last thing he could tell Matt wanted was for him to stop.

"God." Matt gripped Alex's wrist. "No, I don't. But...we can't do this here."

"Yes, we can." He leaned forward and pulled Matt down to him. He wrapped his arms around Matt's neck and kissed him again, aggressively, passionately. "Please, I *need* you. So much." He kept kissing Matt, and Matt gave as good as he got.

"Fuck, I want you, too," Matt said between passionate kisses. "But we can't. Not yet." Alex could feel Matt's reluctance as he pulled away from him and stepped away from the bed. Matt adjusted himself and Alex smiled.

"You are so unbelievably sexy right now." Alex reached beneath the thin blanket draped over his lower half and rubbed his own massive erection. "See what you do to me?" He threw the blanket off to the side and gripped his cock through the uncomfortable hospital gown he was wearing.

"Fuck. *Stop it.*" Matt was smiling. A delicious, genuine smile, which drove Alex mad. "What if somebody walks in?"

"Oh, you don't have to worry about someone catching us. I told my nurse Nancy she would be best served staying away when you showed up." Matt's eyes grew so wide Alex thought they were going to pop out of his head, which made Alex laugh hard. "Calm down, I'm just toying with you. You are so gullible sometimes."

"Funny." Matt grabbed one of the chairs against the wall and brought it up to the head of the bed, sitting down before Alex had the chance to go for his groin again. "Seriously, though," he said, and Alex noted the change in his tone. His sexy, lustful demeanor shifted to a darker one. Matt slid his hand on top of Alex's and dragged his thumb back and forth of Alex's knuckles. "Are you okay?"

Alex rolled his eyes. "Please, not you too. I've already had a lecture from my mother. Don't give me one, too, okay. *I'm fine.*"

"Your mom?"

"Yes." He pulled his hand from beneath Matt's and adjusted his blanket. He was still hard, which was no surprise when Matt was close by. "And I have to tell you, she had plenty to say about you."

"Oh? What, uh...what did she say?" Seeing Matt all nervous and antsy like a little kid, worried if he impressed Alex's mother, sent Alex's libido into overdrive.

"I was going to drag on and on and make you think she didn't like you..." He locked eyes with Matt. "But you're so cute when you're nervous, I just couldn't be so mean to you."

Matt let out a deep rush of air from his lungs and flopped back down in his chair. "You ass. That was... You've got a mean side, huh?"

"Not mean. Just fun."

"Yeah, fun. Sure." Matt rolled his eyes. "But what did she say, for real?"

"She was impressed. Which I already knew she would be."

Matt sighed with relief. "Thank God. Your mom liking me will make our life a hell of a lot easier."

"*Our* life?" That was the first time Matt had said the word "our" or mentioned the future—*their* future—in any way. He would have cried had he not still been so painfully horny for Matt, who was currently roping him in in ways he didn't even realize.

"Uh, yeah. *Our* life." Matt pulled his chair closer to the bed and reached up, taking Alex's face in his hands. "I realized something today. Something that took me by surprise. I don't...I don't want just *my* life anymore, Alex. My life *has* to have you in it. It can't be just me anymore. Not after you. Not possible."

God, Matt was pushing Alex so far over the cliff he couldn't even see the edge anymore. His heart swelled, his eyes filling with tears.

"Hey, don't cry." Matt brushed them away when they started to fall from Alex's cheeks. "I'm sorry I made you cry."

"Don't be. This is a good cry, I promise. The best cry." Alex brought Matt's up to his face, relishing the warmth of their touch. "I just...I never thought I would have this again, you know? I never thought I would find a man as amazing as you. This is just a little overwhelming, to say the least."

"Yeah, for me too." Matt kissed him. A soft, gentle kiss which held more passion than any of the kisses they had shared before. The moment was magical, lifting Alex and holding him safely. "But...man, I wouldn't change a damn thing," Matt added after he pulled out of the kiss.

"No? So, you don't think the way we met could have been, I don't know...a little less dramatic?"

Matt laughed and shook his head. "No way. Even the fire was perfect."

"Well, thank you for *that*." Alex playfully shoved Matt, who sat down again.

"No, goofball, I don't mean what you think. It's just, if the fire never happened, odds are we never would've met. And not meeting you, not getting to know you, would really fucking suck. So, yeah, to me the fire was kind of perfect."

Alex smiled wide. "I think maybe coffee or even a fender bender would have been a bit easier to stomach, but yes, I guess I understand what you mean."

THE TWO TALKED for hours. Matt told Alex everything about his relationship with Cameron, his death, and how losing Cameron in such a horrible way had all but obliterated his spirit. Alex's heart warmed learning Matt gave his all when in a relationship.

Alex recounted his relationship with Brayden, and how he never would have imagined someone he once loved so fully could in any way try to ruin him. Matt was visibly disturbed at hearing Alex reminisce about someone who he strongly believed was the guilty party, but he held himself together well.

Matt filled Alex in on his second visit to Brayden's house, his surprise houseguest Gina, and even meeting Diego.

"So," Alex said, raising an eyebrow. "Do you have plans to dump me for the hot, Latin fireman?"

"Not a fucking chance."

Alex smiled. "Has he contacted you yet?" He was thankful to have something other than himself and what happened to him to talk about. And even though he still didn't think Brayden was capable of arson—and for sure not attempted murder if his carbon monoxide overdose turned out to be no accident—he had to admit he was a bit intrigued by this Gina person. He and Bray hadn't been apart very long. Had Bray known Gina while he and Alex were together? Was she someone new in his life? Questions piled high on top of the already almost insurmountable list he had tallied since the fire.

"Nothing yet," Matt said. "I know this is gonna sound crazy, but I can *feel* it." He held his thumb and forefinger millimeters apart as he added, "I'm this fucking close to catching him."

"Well, you know what I think. But you're the fire expert, not me. And if you have a gut feeling, I suppose you have to follow wherever your intuition takes you."

Matt stared hard at him for several tense seconds before saying, "You sure?"

Alex nodded. "Yes, I really do. I just can't believe Bray would do something like this. Or the fire. I'll admit he's a complete asshole and moron, but arson? Attempted murder? I just don't see him in that light. I can't. But, I trust you. So, if you think he did, then I stand by you. And I hope you get him."

"Thanks for trusting me. And I'm sorry you have to go through this. The fire, the attempt on your life, all of this—" Matt swept a hand around the hospital room "—and the fact Brayden is probably the one behind everything. It's not fair to you."

"Don't be sorry. Neither you nor I have control over any of this. Carrying around guilt for something you had nothing to do with isn't fair to you. It wouldn't be fair to anyone. Sometimes things just...happen."

"I know, I know. But, it's you. And I..." Matt started to say something but stopped. He locked eyes with Alex. "I...really like you. And the fact I've let this happen—"

"—No," Alex stopped him. "You didn't let anything happen. You didn't even know me when this nightmare started."

"I knew you when you were almost killed. And I wasn't there to protect you."

"First," Alex said, his words sharp, "I don't need protecting, thank you. And second, you don't know if someone tried to kill me." Matt cut his eyes at Alex. "Okay, you don't have *proof* someone tried to kill me. I won't let you blame yourself. Even if what I think was an accident turns out not to be, that is still not your fault. Or anything you should have or could have stopped. It just..."

"God, please don't say is what it is." Matt ran a hand through his hair. "That's shit you say if you get cancer or break your arm. Not when somebody is trying to kill you."

"Will you stop? No one is trying to kill me. I'm nobody special. Why would anyone waste their time?"

"*You* stop." Matt shook his head. "Don't sell yourself short to try to make me feel better."

Alex smiled to defuse the tension he could feel building between them. He didn't want to fight. But he also wouldn't stand by and let Matt shoulder any blame for the horrible things happening to him. "Well, what *would* work?" he asked, lifting an eyebrow. "Because my job from now on is to make you feel better."

His words seemed to do the trick. He caught a tiny smile slide across Matt's face. "Nice try. And believe me, when this is all over, you can make me feel better as much as you want."

"Wait, what? When this is all over? I hope you don't think I'm waiting for you to solve this case before something happens. Because that just isn't possible." Matt couldn't hold back his laugh. "Wait, were you...?"

Alex tossed a pillow at Matt. "You are just a bad, bad man."

Matt threw the pillow back. "That's for making me think your mom doesn't like me."

"I said I was *going* to make you think she doesn't like you. I didn't actually do it!"

They both laughed, and Alex was relieved the tension had eased. The happy-go-lucky vibe they normally had was coming back.

"Okay, I guess I better get out of here before they come in and kick me out." Matt stood and came up to the bed. "And you need to get some sleep."

Alex grabbed Matt's hand. "Don't go. Please. Stay the night with me."

"Um, probably not the best idea." Matt leaned down and gave Alex another heated kiss, making Alex's pulse race. "As bad as I want you right now, we would no doubt get in trouble."

"Jesus." Alex's cock stiffened again. "*That's* how you intend to leave me?"

"No." Matt slid his hand to Alex's groin and gave his erection a squeeze. "This is." He parted Alex's lips with his tongue and swept inside his mouth, all the while rubbing Alex's cock. Alex could do nothing but moan and kiss him back.

"You are mean, Sergeant," Alex said after Matt let go and stepped away.

Matt smiled. "Get some sleep. I'll be here first thing in the morning." He made his way over to the door before turning back. "By the way," he said, pulling the door open, "I'm moving in with you until I nail that bastard Brayden to the wall." He was gone before Alex had the chance to protest.

Alex had no intention of saying a word.

Chapter Twenty-Six

MATT DID AS he said he would, showing up at the hospital first thing the next morning. He checked his car in with the valet so he could call to have it pulled up to the door before he and Alex came down. He didn't want Alex having to walk more than necessary. Yeah, he knew he was okay, deep down, but he still wanted to make sure Alex didn't overdo himself—in any shape or form. Which he knew wasn't going to go over well come bedtime.

"You ready?" he called as he stepped into Alex's room just as Alex dropped to the floor.

"Ow!" Alex leaned back against the side of the bed as Matt rushed to his side.

"Son of a bitch, Alex." Matt knelt down and cradled Alex's neck in his hand. "Are you okay?"

"I'm fine. My legs have been giving me fits all morning." Alex gave his right thigh a hard punch. "They just went out on me."

"Here." He slid his hands under Alex's arms and helped him back onto the bed. He brushed his face to make sure he hadn't hurt himself. "Is... this normal?" God, he hoped so. He couldn't fucking take something else going on with Alex.

"I suppose so," Alex said, and Matt sighed with relief. "The doctor said one of the possible long-term side effects is sudden loss of muscle control. I guess I'll have to do a lot of physical therapy to strengthen the muscles. There was a lot of other things he said, too, but I was too angry to listen."

"Why? Taking it easy doesn't sound too bad. You'll do the physical therapy and be back to a hundred percent in no time." He was trying to make things sound better than they were. In truth, the situation sucked.

"Because I run," Alex answered. "Every day. That's my escape. My *me* time. Now, after all this...who knows if I will ever get to again? And that...really sucks."

"Two things..." Matt sat down on the bed beside Alex and slid an arm around his shoulders, pulling him close. "First of all, don't start saying shit like that. What happened isn't gonna stop you from doing anything you wanna do. I won't let it."

"Like you can prevent the effects of what happened to me."

"I can," Matt stated matter-of-factly. "I'm like Superman."

Alex laughed. "So, what's second, Superman?"

"I didn't know you like to run."

"There's a lot about me you don't know. Yet."

Matt raised an eyebrow and smiled. "Ditto."

MATT WANTED TO carry Alex into his house once they made it home, but he held back. The last thing he wanted was to make Alex feel inferior or helpless. He wanted Alex to remain independent but be there ready to catch him if he fell. Literally. Seeing Alex drop to the floor back at the hospital had scared the shit out of him. He wasn't letting something so scary happen again.

Anna Colson had in fact determined the furnace at Alex's house had been tampered with, so Matt made sure to have the ancient beast replaced with a state-of-the-art one, at his expense, before he brought Alex home. He also had the CO_2 detectors replaced, even though Alex had said they were relatively new. He wanted to make damn sure the place was one hundred percent safe before Alex slept another night there.

"I feel like I've been gone a month," Alex said as he slumped onto the couch in the living room. "I am so glad to be home."

Matt sat down beside him. "And I'm so glad this mess is over."

"It's not, though, right?" Alex looked over at him, concern in his eyes. "You're not going to let this all go, are you?"

Matt sighed with frustration. "I can't. I'm sorry. I know you want me to. And I know you don't think Brayden is to blame. But I have to do what I think is right." He took Alex's hand in his. "The man tried to kill you. I can't let him get away with this."

"*Allegedly*," Alex corrected. "He allegedly tried to kill me. And technically *someone* allegedly tried to kill me. The person responsible might not have been Brayden. But I understand. Like I said last night, you have to do what your gut tells you to do. I just...I want my life to go back to the way things were. Before the stupid fire."

"Hey, before the 'stupid fire' I wasn't even here. And I kind of like being here."

Alex rolled his eyes. "You know what I mean."

Matt leaned into him. "Yeah, I know. And I'm working on giving you what you want. I promise."

"You could start right now." Alex slid a hand into Matt's lap and gave his cock a squeeze. Matt's member grew to life in record time.

Matt groaned. "Dammit." He wanted to pick Alex up, take him to the bedroom, and have wild, mind-numbing sex. Hell, he wanted to be with Alex more than anything.

But Alex's health outweighed Matt's wants. And after watching Alex fall in the hospital, seeing him in pain... He couldn't risk something worse happening.

"You know I want to." He slipped his hand around Alex's wrist to stop the extremely pleasant caressing. "God, I want to. More than you could ever fucking know. But...we can't."

Alex pulled his hand away and leaned back. "So...what? You're not attracted to me anymore? Over the novelty already?"

"What? Are you fucking crazy? Jesus, Alex. You just had your hand on my dick. I think you can see how much you turn me on. Hell, I stay hard most of the day just thinking about you. Touching you. Kissing you."

"Then...why don't you want me right now?" He could see tears threating Alex's eyes and the sight damn near broke his heart. Knowing he was causing Alex more pain— that was almost as bad as the actual pain Alex's ex had caused him.

"Oh, God, Alex. Please don't feel that's what's going on here." He shifted so he was facing Alex on the couch and took hold of both his hands. "I want to be with you. All the time. If I could quit my job and spend my days just *being* with you, I would." Alex's face softened a bit. Some of what Matt was saying seemed to be getting through the hurt, the embarrassment. "But after this morning, seeing you on the floor..." He shook his head, unable to finish, his words choked by emotion.

"*That's* what this is? You're worried...you'll hurt me?"

Matt half laughed. "Not like you think, but, yeah. I'm worried it'll be too much, too soon. You almost died the other night. If I hadn't come by—"

"—But you did come by," Alex interrupted. "You were here, and you saved me. And now, I'm fine. I promise." Alex pulled a hand free from Matt's grip and crossed his heart, then held up three fingers. "Scout's salute."

He smiled and lifted an eyebrow. "You were a scout, too?"

Alex laughed a little. "No, but this is what people do when they want you to believe them, right?" They both smiled. "I promise, Matt, you don't have to worry about me all the time. I'm a big boy. I can take more than you think."

"I know you can." Matt shook his head, his own eyes watering a bit. "I just don't want you to have to."

Alex cupped Matt's face in his hands and lifted his head until their eyes met. "Your concern for me is one of the main reasons I...I think I might be falling for you. Because no one has ever cared so much about me or wanted to protect me as much as you do.

At first I told myself your overprotective nature was just part of your job. But now I know it is so much more. This is what you *have* to do, like it's a part of you, part of your DNA." Alex smiled, his genuine concern warming Matt's heart. "But you don't have to spend all of your time worrying about me. I love the fact you do, believe me, but I don't want you to stress out over things you can't control. And no matter what you think, you're not *actually* Superman."

Matt faked shock. "Hey there, mister."

Alex leaned in and kissed him. "You're Superman to me," he said. "A super man."

More than he thought possible, Matt was gone, completely taken by Alex. And he trusted him more than anyone. Even more than himself. If Alex said he would be okay, Matt *had* to believe him, had to give him a chance to *prove* he was okay. The thought scared the hell out of him, sure, letting go and giving up control of something as important as Alex's health. But if he didn't, if he didn't prove to Alex he was in their relationship all the way, they were doomed before they started.

"Thank you," he said. "For being so honest with me. I..." *Just say the damn words. Tell him, Matt.* "I think I'm falling for you too. It scares the shit out of me, but...I'm ready. Ready to see where this takes us."

Matt kissed Alex this time, his tongue dipping into the warmth of his perfect mouth. God, Matt would never, ever tire of the taste, the incredible fucking sensation. Kissing Alex was like the first time, every time.

"Why don't we go to bed," Matt whispered around his kisses. "So I can be your super man."

Alex tried to laugh but Matt's tongue went deep into his mouth, silencing him. Instead, he wrapped his arms around Matt's neck and kissed him back.

"Are you sure you're okay with this?" Alex asked after pulling away. "I don't want you doing anything just because I want you to."

Matt took one of Alex's hands from behind his neck and guided his fingers down his body, over his taut abs, and placed them on his throbbing erection. "Oh, I'd say I'm okay with it." Truth was, he was scared to fucking death. Scared he might take things too far once they got started. Scared Alex might have some sort of reaction to physical exertion and pass out...or worse. But those concerns took second chair to how much he wanted Alex right then. And when Alex smiled and started jacking him off through his pants, those concerns all but disappeared, and Matt couldn't think of anything but being inside Alex.

"Finally." Alex released his grip on Matt's cock and jumped up from the couch. He held tight to Matt's hand, pulling him up and to him. "Don't worry, Sergeant, I'll go easy on you." Alex took a cue from Matt and slipped his tongue into Matt's mouth. Matt groaned and slid an arm around Alex's waist.

"God, please don't," Matt said, his body electric with lustful want as he followed Alex to the bedroom.

Chapter Twenty-Seven

ONCE ALEX GOT Matt into the bedroom, his need took complete control. He was on Matt in half a second, making out with him as he frantically unbuttoned his shirt. He loved Matt in those button-downs, but oh, did he love him more *out* of them.

He pushed the shirt down Matt's back and let it pool on the floor, a frantic heat surging through him once those golden pecs were in his face. Like a kitten to milk, he lapped at Matt's perfect nipples, slipping each one into his mouth and massaging them with his tongue. Matt's head lolled back and he moaned as he lifted a hand to Alex's head. Alex smiled as he bit and nipped.

"Do you like that, baby?" He used his tongue to steal a taste of each muscular orb. Matt didn't answer with words, only grunts and more pressure on Alex's head. He obliged his man's wants, working each nipple with expert skill and greed.

He headed down Matt's torso, making sure to pay special attention to each defined muscle, letting his tongue roll over each ab, tasting Matt's unique scent in every crevice. He tasted like honey and sweat and the intoxicating scent that was his and his alone—and the combination was driving Alex mad. He felt as though his tongue wasn't big enough, fast enough, to taste Matt the way he wanted, the way he *needed* to.

He went even lower, until his lips brushed the delicious black trail of hair disappearing into the top of Matt's pants. He could have stayed right there, all day, tasting; there was heaven. Pure. Insatiable. Heaven. He groaned as he licked the sexy strip of fur-covered skin, relishing in the pleasure he knew he was giving Matt.

"Fuck, Alex...please don't stop." Matt's body was vibrating under his tongue, his skin on fire, heat pulsating off of him. The manly pheromone he was releasing was driving Alex, sending him into orbit. The entire house could have burned down around them and he wouldn't have stopped worshipping Matt.

"Oh, I won't." He unbuttoned Matt's pants as he kept up his tongue work. Once he had the zipper down, he slipped a hand inside and groped Matt's throbbing cock through his underwear.

"Oh, Jesus." Matt's voice was shaky as he brought a hand to Alex's head and pulled Alex against himself. Alex moaned into Matt's groin, his tongue moving up and down the shaft of his cock, soaking the throbbing erection through his briefs. He slipped his fingers behind the band of Matt's underwear and lowered them and his khakis, lust overpowering him at the sight of Matt's impressive cock springing forward.

"Wow. I will never tire of this," Alex said. "You're so beautiful." He didn't waste a second more on talking. He gripped Matt's dick and took the length into his mouth, lowering to the base in one swift motion.

"Fuck!" Matt almost came unglued. He writhed and bucked beneath Alex's mouth, and Alex responded with the most intense sucking he had ever done. He inhaled Matt's cock, burying the entire length deep in his throat with each thrust. Matt's hips fell in time with his movements, until they were in perfect sync, moving as one.

After a lifetime of perfect syncopation, Alex released his hold on Matt's cock and stood. "I want you." He cupped Matt's face and pulled him close. "All of you."

"God, yes," Matt said, sucking Alex's tongue between his lips. "Fuck me, Alex. I want you inside me."

Those words were what Alex had hoped to hear. He took Matt's hand and led him to the bed, both of them falling onto the mattress in a tangle of arms and legs. He wasted no time in pulling Matt's pants and underwear from around his feet, kissing Matt's muscular legs as he worked his way up. Matt moaned and breathed heavily as Alex licked and kissed each inner thigh, then opened his legs wide when Alex's tongue brushed his balls.

"Oh, fuck yeah. That feels so fucking good."

He responded to Matt's encouragement by sucking each massive orb into his mouth and rolling them around with his tongue. Matt wriggled and bucked his hips as Alex extended his tongue outward and hit the spot just under Matt's sac.

"Oh, fuck, fuck, fuck." He let Matt's balls slide from his mouth so he could go after what he had been wanting since day one. He pushed up on his thighs and Matt lifted his legs, his ass rolling up and into Alex's sightline.

God, Alex was overwhelmed with want. A force took control of him, his desire mounting to uncontrollable levels. His need to taste every inch of Matt had him diving in like an Olympic swimmer, greedily tonguing Matt's hole with a frenzy. As Matt thrust forward, trying to get more of Alex inside him, Alex worked Matt's ass with every ounce of energy he had, the taste, the heat, consuming him. After several long, wonderful minutes he pulled away, his lungs tight in his chest, his breaths coming out ragged and short.

"Alex?" Matt asked, noticing Alex's labored breathing. "Are you okay?" Matt was breathing heavy, too, which made Alex smile.

"I'm far better than okay. Now..." He gripped Matt's hips and death-rolled him onto his stomach. "Give me this sexy ass."

Matt's concern disappeared. "All yours," he said, burying his head into the pillows and lifting his ass into the air in such a perfect way Alex had to use every ounce of self-control he could conjure up not to come.

"Jesus." Alex snagged a condom from his nightstand and had his dick covered in less than a second, then positioned himself behind Matt. Just the sight of this macho, muscular man beneath him, ready for him, drove him wild. He gripped Matt's hips and, though he had every intention of moving slow to remember each delicious inch, he buried his pulsating erection deep in Matt's ass in one incredible thrust.

"Dammit!" Matt yelled out. Alex paused his thrust, worried he had gone too deep too fast. But Matt just backed up onto him and his ass muscles squeezed Alex's cock. "Fuck me," Matt moaned. "Fuck. Me."

And Alex did. He let his pent-up sexual frustration and anger over all the things that had happened to him unleash, pounding into Matt like a jackhammer. Matt met him thrust for thrust, his "yes" and "more" comments carrying Alex farther than he thought he would last.

But in only a few minutes he sensed the familiar stirring in his balls, the wonderful tightening signaling an impending release. He gripped Matt's hips tighter, thrust into him harder, deeper. He panted and grunted as every muscle in his sweat-soaked body tensed and his orgasm shot forward with the power of a tsunami, wave after wave crashing over him, enveloping him, consuming him.

Matt shouted his release, too, his hips bucking and his ass clamping down on Alex's cock like a vise. Once both of their orgasms had ebbed, Alex fell onto Matt's back, drenched in sweat and more than fulfilled.

"Sorry about your sheets," Matt said as he rolled onto his back, Alex's semi-erect dick slipping from inside him.

Alex shrugged. "They're just sheets."

Matt rolled onto his side and gave him a kiss. "Thank you," he said, taking Alex by surprise.

"For?"

"For everything you just did. And for not passing out on me."

He smacked Matt on the arm. "Seriously? You thought I would pass out?"

"Ow!" Matt rubbed his shoulder and smiled. "I don't know. Maybe. I just...If anything happened to you because of me..."

"If something had happened, it would have been because of *me*, not you. Understand?"

Matt held up his hands in surrender. "Yeah, yeah. I understand. Geez, calm down, mister."

"I'm sorry, but I don't like you blaming yourself for the problems in my life." Alex hated when Matt took everything onto his shoulders, like Alex himself held no blame. If things turned out Matt had been right all along and Bray was behind the fire and the poisoning, then Alex would have to accept that—and some of the responsibility for bringing Bray into his life. But Matt? He was blameless. "You are the only good thing going for me right now. I need you, yes, absolutely, but I can still fend for myself."

Matt lay there in silence for a while before saying, "Okay, I hear you." He got up from the bed and crossed the room, headed for the bathroom. He stopped once he got to the door and turned back to Alex. "You coming?" Alex smiled and jumped up from the bed, following him into the shower.

They spent the next half hour having some pretty intense shower sex, each getting off again before washing up and heading back to the bed.

"Hey, if you don't want me to stay in here, it's cool." Matt was standing at the foot of the bed, watching as Alex climbed naked under the covers. "I can take the couch."

Alex rolled his eyes. "Get your sexy ass in here." He flipped the covers back on the other side of the bed. "If you're staying in this house, you're sleeping in this bed."

Matt climbed into bed beside him, and Alex slid over next to him, resting his head on Matt's chest. He was so happy. He didn't believe he would be again but there he was. Sure, he had some things going on in his life he would describe as less than ideal, but right then, in this moment, he couldn't have been happier if he'd tried. He snuggled closer to Matt, who wrapped an arm around him, his fingers tracing up and down his spine.

"I'm glad you're here," Alex said, sleep gripping his words. "I feel safe with you." And he did. Not that he was scared *away* from Matt, he just... He couldn't properly put his thoughts into words. There was a feeling, an unseen force that swept over him. People often described it as a security blanket, wrapping you up and making you feel warm and protected. And he realized that was wholly accurate. He *was* warm and protected with Matt. And that was a wonderful feeling he never wanted to lose.

Matt kissed his forehead and sighed. "This is all I've ever wanted. I keep people safe every day. Yeah, it's my job. But I love being the one to protect others. I just wanna be able to do the same for you."

Right then, he understood where Matt had been coming from earlier. He knew Matt wasn't exactly scared of Alex getting hurt, or of hurting him. It was the fact he saw himself a failure if he couldn't do for Alex what he did for everyone else, for his community. He needed to keep Alex safe as some sort of validation he belonged there. Which made the feelings he had for Matt all the more powerful and real.

He let sleep take him as thoughts of Matt and the wonderfully dysfunctional life he was currently living filled his mind.

Chapter Twenty-Eight

MATT SLID OUT of Alex's bed the next morning just before sunrise. He slept well, better than he had in a long damn time—which was no doubt because he had Alex's warm body wrapped up next to him all night. Damn, did he love feeling Alex next to him. He loved last night, too, being with Alex again. He loved sleeping next to Alex, waking up next to him. But most of all, he loved that he could keep Alex safe.

After throwing on yesterday's clothes, he leaned down and gave Alex a gentle kiss.

"Sleep well." Alex rolled onto his side, dead to the world. Matt was glad, because he needed sleep. He knew Alex wasn't one hundred percent yet, and rest was no doubt the best thing for him. He planned to stop by and check on him just as soon as he could as he slipped out of the bedroom and bypassed the kitchen. Even though he wanted coffee so bad right then he would've sucked the juice straight from the beans if he could have, he would just have to grab some after he went back to his hotel room and showered and changed into some fresh clothes. Last fucking thing he needed was somebody commenting on the fact they'd seen him wearing the same shirt yesterday. He didn't really think anybody would notice— and he sure as shit didn't care, to be honest. Hell, plaid shirts all sort of looked the same after a while anyway.

He had just pulled away from the curb when his cell phone went off.

Who the hell's calling me this early?

He answered the call and held the phone to his ear.

"This is Fields," he said, turning down Main Street toward his hotel.

"Hey, Matt? This is Diego. From the fire station?" Matt didn't need the re-introduction. He recognized Diego's voice, with its deep, rich tone and just the faintest hint of an accent.

"Hey, Diego. What you up to this morning?"

"Just getting off work. Sorry to call so early, but I figured I better before I get home and crash."

"No problem, what's up?"

"I asked around about Stanton," Diego said. "Just wanted to let you know what I found out."

"Great." There was a familiar itch in Matt's gut and his top-priority case came rushing to mind—as if Alex and everything happening to him wasn't always there in some form or another. "Did anybody at the station know the guy she was talking to?"

"No, I don't think so," Diego said, and Matt's bubble burst. Fuck, he just knew somebody there was going to recognize Cooper, know how he was connected to Gina Stanton.

No such luck.

"Oh." Matt hadn't been expecting Diego's answer.

"Sorry, man. Wish I could be more help. But one of the guys here said they *do* know Gina is married. Or was, technically."

"Divorced?" He wished he had pulled off the road so he could jot down the information Diego was feeding him, but he didn't have the time. Instead, he focused on making sure his brain kept a running record so he could recall what he needed later.

"Widowed," Diego countered.

"Widowed? Really?" Another thing Matt didn't see coming. Gina Stanton was just full of surprises.

"From what I've gathered. Looks like her husband killed himself. About six months ago."

"Damn."

"Yeah. Kinda crazy."

Crazy didn't come close.

"Don't suppose you know what happened? Or maybe his name?" Matt could find out himself the details of the suicide if he could track down the man's last known address or place of death.

"Afraid not," Diego answered. "But supposedly it happened next door, in Emory."

Where Brayden Cooper lived. And where Matt had seen him and Gina Stanton all buddy-buddy on Cooper's front porch. The word "coincidence" was tickling Matt's mind but he forced the idea out. No chance all of this was coincidental. Those two lived in the same town and somehow knew each other.

"Thanks for this, Diego. This really helps."

"Happy to." He could hear pride in Diego's voice. "And don't forget, you owe me."

Matt laughed. "No worries. I never forget a favor."

Diego laughed this time. "Just messing with you, Sergeant. We're all good."

Matt shook his head though he was in the car by himself. "Nope. You're right, I *do* owe you. How about next weekend? You, me, Alex. And...maybe a friend, if you're game."

"A friend?"

"Don't worry," Matt said after he picked up on Diego's hesitation. "He's a good guy. A cop. And not as much of a dick as I am."

"Oh, well, in that case..."

Both men laughed and the tension always pressing down on his shoulders lately—except when he was with Alex—dissipated a bit. Matt liked Diego, and he was glad he had met somebody he could shoot the shit with and just be buddies. But he made a quick mental note to mention Diego to Alex before some gossip whoremonger in town did. Hell, they'd spin things so he and Diego were going at each other right in the middle of the fucking town. And the last thing Matt needed was more drama, for himself or Alex. Alex had suffered enough. From now on, he would stop at nothing to make sure Alex's life was as smooth as glass.

"Okay, so maybe it's just the three of us this weekend." Matt pulled up at Cliffside Inn and circled the parking lot to his room in the far back corner of the property. "Don't wanna scare you off."

"Hey, I'm game," Diego said. "Like I said, I need all the help I can get in the dating department."

"Okay, then. I'll invite him. Name's Sean. He's a great guy. Never-meets-a-stranger type. I think you two will get along great. How's a week from Saturday sound?" He fished his room key out of his pocket and let himself in.

"Sounds great, man. Thanks."

"Thank *you* for all your help. I'll text you the address later."

"Perfect." He was prepared to end the call before Diego added, "And hey, I'll see if I can find out anything else about Stanton. If it'll help."

"Anything would help. I appreciate the effort, Diego. Thanks." Matt was genuinely surprised and touched by the offer. Meeting somebody who actually enjoyed helping others was a rare trait. And he could tell Diego Cruz was one of those people. "But don't go to any trouble. I'm the one getting paid to solve this case, remember?" He held the phone against his ear with his shoulder as he kicked out of his shoes and pants.

"Has anyone ever told you not to look a gift horse in the mouth, Sergeant?" There it was again, the way Diego called him Sergeant, sounding so damn much like Alex, all sexy and playful.

Matt tried to ignore the innuendo he picked up on hidden behind the word, even though he knew Diego hadn't meant anything.

"Uh, not lately," Matt answered as he unbuttoned his shirt and peeled off the fabric, moving his phone from ear to ear as he did. "And for your information, I'm not biting the hand or staring down the gift horse or whatever. I'm just... I don't want you to feel like you have to do anything you don't want to, or don't feel safe doing, just because you offered and I accepted."

"I wouldn't have offered if I minded helping out. I want to."

"Okay, then...thanks again."

"No worries. I'll keep you posted. Oh, and glad to hear Alex is home from the hospital. Chief filled us in."

"Thanks, man. Me too."

MATT RELISHED IN the heat of the early morning shower, letting the hot water spray down his neck and back, relieving some of the tension in his muscles. He rubbed at his neck as the water blasted him, his skin tingling beneath the scalding spray. Man, he had such shit going on. He was almost frantic with anticipation of solving the fire at the Book Nook—he could just about taste how close he was—and was beside himself over the now-confirmed attempt on Alex's life. He was also desperate to find out who the hell Gina Stanton was and how she knew Brayden Cooper.

The overwhelming feeling he was having only increased as he hopped from the shower, threw on some clean clothes, and headed back to the police station. If he didn't take some of the things off his plate, he was going to explode.

HE HAD JUST sat down at his temporary desk when the sound of his name being yelled from behind him echoed across the room.

"Fields! Get in here!"

Captain Gregson.

Fuck.

Though he didn't want to, he got up and made the five-foot trek into Gregson's office. By the time he shut the door, his stomach was in his throat—and his anger was on a steady rise.

"Uh, yeah?" Matt stood behind one of two chairs on the opposite side of the large oak desk taking up way too much of Gregson's tiny office.

"Take a seat," Gregson snapped, stopping whatever he had been doing to glare at Matt.

Matt obliged, slithering into one of the chairs like a snake.

"Now," Gregson went on, "you mind filling me in on what the hell you were thinking when you decided to go *back* to Emory without asking me first?"

Matt's rage meter shot into stratosphere. "With all due respect, Captain, I don't need your permission to do my damn job."

Gregson interjected. "You could've run your plan by me first, Fields. Regardless of your position with the fire marshal's office, this is *my* town, my jurisdiction. I need to be in the loop on any and all investigations going on." Gregson linked his hands together on top of his desk. "I don't know how you folks handle things in Bangor, and frankly I don't give a shit. Here, under my watch, you don't go rogue and interrogate witnesses for investigations in my precinct unless I know ahead of time. Understood?"

Matt fake saluted as he stood up. "Yes, sir. Won't happen again, sir."

"Keep your smug attitude for your city friends, Fields. Just don't go off half-cocked again without running things by me first. One call to Teagues and your ass is outta here. To hell with what Evelyn Porter wants."

Just the idea of losing his job, having all the time in the world to spend every day in bed with Alex—damn, Matt was tempted to hop in his car and head to Emory right then.

"I'll do my best to accommodate, Captain." He wanted to tell the bastard to go fuck himself, but his professional ethics wouldn't allow him to.

"Just a minute," Gregson said, and Matt turned back toward him. "Since you went anyway... What'd you find out about the suspect? Braxton...?"

"Brayden," Matt corrected. "Cooper."

Gregson nodded and leaned back in his chair. "Get anything?"

Matt shook his head. "Got some theories, nothing concrete yet. But I'm working on the details."

Gregson sat quiet for a minute, mulling over the fact Matt didn't seem to know dick about being a detective, before saying, "We need something on this prick. Anything. I wanna nail somebody's balls to the wall on this one. I'm done getting phone calls from Evelyn Porter every time something goes down in this city she doesn't like."

"Why is she calling you?" Matt asked.

"She's called who-the-hell-knows how many times since the night of the fire, *demanding* I get to the bottom of what happened, and *insisting* I keep her informed about the case."

"Are you serious?" Matt couldn't believe Evelyn Porter thought she had the kind of power to sway a police captain. Then again, maybe she did. He didn't know the woman, other than their short but intense visit at the hospital. For all he knew, she ran Cliffside. Which would explain why Alex had such fucked up feelings about his mother.

"Dead serious. Which is why we need to bring somebody in on this. ASAP." Gregson turned his attention to the mounds of paperwork on his desk, which had seemed to at least double in size since the last time Matt had been in his office, inadvertently dismissing him.

"Oh, and Fields?" the captain called just as Matt made his way over to the door. Matt turned and raised an eyebrow.

"Yeah?"

"You've got free rein to come and go in Emory for as long as you need. Already cleared."

Like he needed clearance to visit anywhere in his own jurisdiction. But he kept quiet and let Gregson have his glory, responded with a nod, and left the office. He went back to his desk pretty much in shock. He just realized something. Even though he had a hell of a way of showing it, Captain Gregson somehow trusted him, his judgment. Matt wouldn't have believed gaining such a hothead's trust was possible had he not just witnessed the transformation first-hand.

For the rest of the morning he poured over his notes from the case, mad as hell because he hadn't been able to link Brayden Cooper to the fire or the attempt on Alex's life. He knew a connection was there, he just had to find one. And he knew he would. He always did. His ability to work a case like a puzzle was the main reason he got promoted to sergeant so fast. And this puzzle had so many pieces it was staggering.

Hours passed before he realized Alex hadn't called. He hadn't said he would check in, but Matt assumed he would. He took a break from pecking at his keyboard like a bird and gave Alex a call.

Voicemail.

He tried not to worry, assuming instead Alex must still be asleep, so he left a simple message asking Alex to give him a call if he got the chance. What he had wanted to do was yell into the fucking phone, *demanding* Alex call him back the second he got the message. But he didn't. No, he needed to keep fighting to build up the trust between them. He had learned the hard way how trust was the core of a good relationship—something he hadn't bothered to cement in his and Cameron's doomed relationship. Even though Cameron died, Matt now knew one of them no doubt would have ended things. And he

242 - | M.J. James

didn't want The End to happen to him and Alex. Not before their relationship even got off the ground.

He had just gotten his phone back into his pocket when it started ringing. He fished it back out and answered without hesitation.

"There you are," he said, his nerves calming. "I was wondering if I was gonna hear from you."

"Uh...Matt?"

He pulled the phone from his ear and checked the number.

"Oh, hey, Diego. I thought you were Alex."

"Sorry to bother you again, man."

"No problem at all, what's up?" He noticed Diego's voice sounded a bit rushed, frazzled, like he was nervous or on edge.

"I just thought you'd wanna know Gina Stanton quit her job."

"What? She quit?" Matt's mind started spinning.

"Yeah," Diego said, disbelief in his voice too. "Chief just came in and told us about ten minutes ago. He said she walked in this morning just after he got in and quit." There was a long pause before he added, "Weird, huh?"

Weird? A fucking understatement for sure.

Why the hell did Gina Stanton quit a job she just got a couple of months ago? And so fast, out of the blue?

What the hell was going on?

"No shit," Matt said, trying to lock the pieces together. First Gina and Brayden Cooper were arguing out on the street. Then he found them both at Brayden's house, as if the fight never happened. Now Gina up and quits her job? Nothing was making any fucking sense.

"Yeah, I thought so, too," Diego said. "Figured I'd call you. Maybe this means something?"

Oh, this *definitely* meant something. Matt just didn't have a damn clue what.

"Not sure what, but, hey, thanks a lot for letting me know. I really appreciate your help, man."

"Yeah, sure, no problem. Guess I'll let you go."

"Hey, before you do, quick question."

"Shoot."

"You don't happen to know where Gina lives, do you?"

"One sec." The sound of rustling paper filled the line before Diego's voice came back. "Looks like her last address is over in Emory. Wow, I didn't know she made such a commute every day."

Son of a bitch.

"Lemme guess," Matt said, already knowing the answer. "8466 Brighton."

"Uh, yeah. How did you—"

"—Lucky guess." Matt abruptly ended the call—he'd apologize to Diego later—and all but flew out the door to his SUV. He was peeling out of the parking lot in record time.

Now there was zero doubt in his mind Brayden Cooper and Gina Stanton were behind the fire at Alex's store, and most likely had tried to kill him too.

He didn't have proof yet, but he wasn't wasting any more time.

He was going to get a confession instead.

Chapter Twenty-Nine

THOUGH HE WANTED to go straight to Emory and muscle a confession out of Brayden and Gina, Matt *had* to check on Alex first. He tried calling him again while in the car, and again his phone rang and rang until the voicemail picked up. He didn't want to worry, but damn, he couldn't help himself. A tiny feeling in the pit of his stomach was telling him something was...off.

He pulled up to the curb outside Alex's house and jumped out, leaving the door open as he ran up the walk and banged on the front door.

Nothing.

Oh, God, not again.

What if Alex was unconscious, or had suffered some bizarre side effect from the poisoning? Or what if someone had tried to kill him again? And succeeded this time?

The questions fueled Matt's fear and pumped up his adrenaline to dangerous levels. Without even thinking, he kicked in the front door, no time to search for a possible hidden spare key. He tried Alex's cell again, caught off guard when the familiar ringtone bounced around the room. He found the phone underneath the sofa, and panic seized him, gripped his chest like a vise. Son of a bitch. Something happened. To Alex. Matt shot down the hall like a bullet, screaming Alex's name over and over as he headed to the bedroom.

Empty.

Fuck fuck fuck.

Where the hell was Alex?

He checked every room—bathroom, laundry room, even closets and the pantry—while he simultaneously called out for Alex and dialed the police on his cell. He ordered a unit to get their ass over there and hung up, frantic and freaking the hell out. After checking the back yard just in case Alex had decided to get some air or something and forgot his damn phone, he rushed back to the SUV and hopped in.

Son of a bitch, they had him, fucking Brayden and Gina had Alex. They had snatched him right out of his own damn house. Matt didn't have any proof, but fuck, he didn't need proof. *He* was the proof, because he was damned good at his job. He was never wrong when he listened to his gut. And right now, his gut was screaming at him how much he was right. Alex had been kidnapped by those two fucking psychos. He didn't wait for the patrol car to show up as he peeled out, headed for the freeway.

For Emory.

For that bastard, Brayden Cooper.

HE WAS SMART this time around, calling the Emory PD and having one of their units meet him at Brayden's house. He pulled up seconds before the uniforms, the pair blocking entry and exit to and from the street.

"Looks empty," one of the officers noted as the three of them, guns drawn, approached the front of the house. Matt didn't respond, even though he had the same feeling. He signaled for the officers to split up and circle to the back while he went for the front door. As the two uniforms disappeared around the side of the house, he tried to center himself and focus. If he found Alex inside, and he was hurt in any way... Jesus, he didn't know what the fuck he would do, how he would react. He couldn't be sure he could control himself. He was damn sure of one thing, though: If Alex was dead, Brayden and Gina were too. Fuck his badge.

After knocking and knocking and getting no answer— he hadn't expected to, really—he kicked the door in with the force of all his anger and rage behind him. Wood splintered and the door flew open, slamming hard into the wall of the kitchen, shattering whatever framed picture was hanging there. He entered gun first, skill taking over and guiding him.

He went through the entire procedure of checking the house, the officers from Emory joining him. But their effort was all for nothing. His initial feeling had been dead-on.

The place was empty.

They were gone.

THE AREA SURROUNDING Brayden Cooper's property was swarming with law enforcement within minutes. SWAT, Forensics, CSU—the place looked like a fucking war zone, everybody trying to find out what the hell had gone down in Cooper's house. Matt paced back and forth between his SUV and the Emory unit parked closest to the property, his mind fracturing with each passing minute.

How did he let this happen? How did he let Alex get hurt again? Keeping him safe was the one fucking thing he had promised Alex. And he'd failed. Miserably, horribly failed. Alex was gone, maybe forever, all because

Matt didn't try hard enough. He didn't dig deep enough, fast enough, and now Alex was paying the price for his screw up.

"Fields." Captain Gregson approached Matt, calmer than Matt had ever seen him. Gregson was high-strung on even the calmest day; how the hell he was so unimpressed with what was going down was beyond Matt.

"Any word?" Matt asked. He was wringing his hands and popping his knuckles over and over, something he *never* did. Damn, he was going fucking insane with worry. Fear had seized his entire body, controlling him, drawing him deeper and deeper into a black, bottomless hole he was afraid he would never be able to climb out of.

"Nothing yet. CSU is dusting every damn inch of the place. If they had Mr. Porter in there, we'll find something."

Matt started pacing again, going over and over in his mind what he could have done differently. "I know this is gonna sound crazy, but I *know* they have him. I can feel it."

"In your gut. I get it." Gregson patted his own large belly. "Gut feeling is a cop's best friend. And you're the closest thing to a cop I've ever seen. So use your gut. That intuition, that instinct, will always steer you in the right direction if you pay attention."

"Thanks for understanding." He kept up his pacing, thoughts of how he could have prevented this gnawing away at him.

He should have rode Brayden Cooper hard when he found him crying on his porch. He knew then, deep down, how Brayden was being eaten alive with guilt; he just chose to ignore what he saw, put proper procedure over gut instinct. His slip-up may have cost Alex his life. If that happened...

"Fields." Gregson's voice pulled Matt back to reality. He glanced over at Gregson. "Why do you have such a strong investment in this one? What is it about this case has got you so wired?"

He hadn't intended on telling Gregson he was with Alex, but the words fell out of him before he could stop them.

"I...I think I might love him." Three simple words had never held more meaning than in that moment. With all his being, Matt knew right then he was in love Alex. To the point he was willing to risk his career.

"I figured as much," Gregson said with a no-nonsense flair. "You spend way too much time worrying over Alex Porter just to solve a damn case."

Matt was in shock. No way he had heard right. No, his mind was playing tricks on him, worn out over worrying so damned much. "What?"

"Don't look so surprised, Fields. I may be old, but I ain't stupid." He gave Matt the tiniest hint of a smile so brief Matt couldn't be sure of what he had actually seen. Gregson moved closer to him, his voice lower when he spoke. "You be careful, Fields. Understood? Falling for a victim is never a good idea. And I can't imagine your commanding officer will like how this is playing out too much either."

"Alex isn't a victim." Just hearing those words pissed him off. "And with all due respect, Captain, I don't give a shit about my job right now."

Gregson nodded. "I hear you. Believe me, I do. Just be careful, like I said. You're too damn good at what you do to lose everything now."

Matt meant what he said. His job, and keeping his job, was so far out of the realm of his concern, he couldn't have cared any fucking less what happened to him. Alex mattered now. That was all. Getting Alex back. Keeping him safe.

"Thanks," he said, his voice calm even though he was raging inside. Gregson's little speech somehow diffused what could have become a very volatile situation. Gregson nodded and walked away.

Jesus, he needed to get ahold of himself. Not because he was surrounded by what were essentially his professional peers, but because he had to be razor-sharp focused if he ever hoped to get Alex back. Alive.

He went back to his car and climbed in, letting the silence consume him. He closed his eyes, trying to block out everything around him—the noise of the police chatter, the squawk of countless radios, the thudding of his heart. His heart. The one sound impossible to ignore was the rapid *thump thump thump* of his heart. The over-stressed muscle was beating wildly in his chest, the thrum reverberating in his ears. He took several slow, controlled breaths to try to calm himself down.

"He needs you. Alex. He needs you." He kept repeating the words over and over to himself, his voice breaking through the silence of the car's interior. If he said them enough, maybe they would get through the muck in his mind and help him focus.

He had almost calmed down enough to not hear his heartbeat anymore until the ear-piercing ring of his phone shattered the quiet. He snatched the phone from his pocket and turned on the speakerphone so no one would see him taking a call. Last thing he needed was an army of cops swarming him.

"Hey there, Sergeant." The voice on the other end of the call was disguised, muffled like someone was holding a towel over the mouthpiece, but he knew without a doubt who had called him.

"You're wasting your time trying to change your voice, Stanton. I'd recognize that shrill shit anywhere."

There was rustling on the line, then, "Watch yourself, Sergeant," Gina spat. "You piss me off enough, I might just have to hurt your little boy toy here." Alex cried out in the background, and every inch of Matt's body seized up.

"Touch him again and I will fucking end you." His fury was at a cosmic level, replacing the doubt and guilt and self-pity, until his anger was the only thing left. The kindness and loyalty and good-natured spirit he had worked so hard to build back up after Cameron died was now gone. He was pure raw rage.

Gina Stanton laughed into the phone. "Big words for somebody holding none of the cards."

"Why?" he asked. "What do you want with him?"

There was a long moment of silence—so long, Matt had to look down at his phone to make sure he hadn't lost the call—before Gina said, "Tell you what, sergeant. Why don't you start driving and I'll call you back in five and let you know where you can find me. I'd rather tell you in person why your friend here is so important."

"Matt, stay away! Please! Ow!" Alex again, telling Matt to not try to save him. Not a chance in hell that was gonna happen.

"What do you say, Fields?"

He bit his lower lip until he tasted blood. He wanted to see Gina pay for what she was doing but going in half-cocked would only get Alex killed. Matt had done enough to him. He wasn't going to be the reason Alex died.

"Talk to you in five." He ended the call and started the car. Gregson was knocking on his window before he threw the car in reverse.

"Where you headed?" Matt could see in Gregson's eyes; he knew.

"I gotta get out of here. I can't...I just can't be here right now." He hoped Gregson bought what he was selling, but somehow knew he didn't.

The captain took a deep breath and looked around before turning his attention back to Matt. "Okay," he said. "Go on. I'll let you know what we find out." Matt nodded and slipped the car into reverse. "And Fields?" Gregson said. Matt pumped the brakes looked up at him.

"Yeah?"

"Do as I said and be careful."

Chapter Thirty

MATT SAID A silent thank you Captain Gregson didn't call him on his bluff and demand he get the hell out of the car. He didn't have the time or energy to fight the entire Emory and Cliffside Police Departments right there on the street. But he would have. He would have fought every fucking officer there if they tried to stop him from finding Alex and saving him. They would've had to kill him first.

His phone rang and he answered with the button on his steering wheel, having connected to the car's Bluetooth the second he left Brayden's house.

"Where am I going?" he asked without even looking at the caller ID on the stereo's display screen.

"Head north, toward the mountains." Gina's voice poured from the SUV's speakers, softened by the soundproof interior. "I'll call you back in ten minutes." The line went dead.

"Fuck." Matt's voice was trapped in his throat, emotion coming into play since he was out of the chaos of the crime scene. Alone, the reality of what was happening was sinking in fast.

He was headed to what very well could be his death. But he didn't give a shit as long as Alex came out of this alive. He meant what he'd said: Alex was the most important thing. Matt would die for him. If he was about to prove that, so be it.

The ten minutes drive to reach the line between Cliffside and the neighboring Rockport just north of town stretched out like an eternity. He wanted so desperately to get there, find Alex, and get him out. After, he planned on killing Gina Stanton and Brayden Cooper. If murdering those pieces of shit led to him going to jail, or worse, he was fully prepared to face his fate.

"Enough with the cat and mouse," he said after answering the phone on the first ring. "Tell me where the hell you are so we can end this."

"Don't worry, Sergeant. Not much farther."

Matt huffed but gave in to the only option he had. "Where to?" He could almost feel Gina smile on the other end of the line.

"I know you're not from here, so it may take you a while to find this place."

"Just tell me. I'm good with directions."

"So far," Gina said. "Let's hope you stay that way."

His frustration with her and the whole situation was beginning to flare again. "Address?"

Gina laughed, and Matt wanted to rip her tongue from her mouth. "Get on 95. About fifteen miles up to exit forty. Turn right on Springwood. Another seven miles until you see a dirt road to your left. Drive until it dead ends." She stopped talking and he catalogued all she had said. "See you soon, *Sergeant*." Hearing Alex's nickname for him on her lips again turned his stomach.

Once the call ended, Matt stomped the gas pedal into the floor. The SUV shot forward like a rocket, reaching over a hundred miles per hour in seconds. He was super focused, eyes locked on the road, his mind trying to build a plan of attack once he reached Gina and Brayden. And Alex.

God, Alex.

He had to be so scared. Terrified. Thinking his life was all over. The thought got to Matt more than any other. Knowing Alex was suffering God only knew what at the hands of his ex, scared to death of what was going to happen next...

Matt was going to fucking rip Brayden Cooper apart with his bare hands. Gina Stanton, too.

He had never been much of a fighter. Hell, he never even punched a guy until after he graduated college, and only then because some drunk ass college punk thought Matt had been hitting on his girl in a bar. Matt had tried to defuse the situation by talking to the guy, but Mr. Frat wanted to be a badass. He swung at Matt, thankfully way too plastered to hit a target, and Matt laid him out before he even knew what the hell had happened. Luckily, the guy's drinking buddy was way more seasoned in the art of bar brawling than he had been at the time and got him the hell out of there before his life ended before it began. Since then, Matt had resisted getting physical any chance he could for fear he would strike without warning again.

But all bets were off the second he got one-up on Cooper. Or Stanton, if she came at him. He would tear them both to pieces if doing so meant saving Alex.

He sped up Interstate 95 like a NASCAR pro, praying he didn't get pulled over. If he did, he was done. He'd be hauled in like any Average Joe, professional courtesy be damned. But just like with Gregson and his job earlier, he didn't give a shit. If he got arrested, he'd simply find a way out. He'd find a way to get to Alex. To save him.

He reached exit forty in minutes, turning right on Springwood just like he was told to. Another minute or two before he spotted a narrow dirt road cut into the woods on his left. He slowed his cruiser just enough to take the turn sideways, barreling into the woods in a cloud of dust.

The road wound deep through the trees, the brush growing thicker the further he drove. By the time he reached the end, there was no more than two feet of clear space on either side of him. He knew, deep down, how the situation rapidly went from bad to worse, but what fucking choice did he have? He had to do what Gina told him to if he wanted to see Alex alive again.

Every fiber of his being was screaming at him to stop, turn around, protect himself as Matt got out of the car once the dirt road ended. He made sure his gun was secure in its holster and his backup was strapped to his back. He had a decoy on his ankle, and he hoped Gina and Brayden didn't search him, only ordered him to remove the two pieces cops typically wore. If he had to give up all of them, rescuing Alex would go from difficult to almost impossible.

His pocket started buzzing. He had muted his before getting out of the car so he wouldn't be found if they had to run once he got Alex out of there. He fished it out and answered.

"Walk forward." Gina's voice was stern, the playful, over-confident tone from earlier now gone. She was worried, Matt could tell. Now that he was there, the situation wasn't just talk anymore.

He kept the phone to his ear as he rounded the front of the SUV and crossed the dozen or so feet of remaining dirt road. He paused once he reached the thick, overgrown edge of the woods.

"Keep going." He did as instructed. The line went dead, so he slid the phone into his pocket. All of his nerves were on edge, sensing how bad of an idea this was to go in blind. He wanted to pull the gun from his back so he would at least have a fighting chance if Gina or Brayden decided to scrap whatever they were up to and open fire on him. But he kept the fraction of cool he had left and kept walking deeper into the woods.

"Far enough." Gina's voice came out of nowhere about a half second before the cold barrel of a gun pressed against the back of his head. He froze. "Get your hands up," she demanded, and he obeyed. He lifted his hands over his head and splayed out his fingers. He knew procedure here, all the right moves police demanded of suspects to ensure their safety. And he wanted Gina to think she was safe, to think he was here to do whatever she asked of him. The truth couldn't have been farther away.

She slid a hand to his side and lifted his gun from its holster. She tossed the weapon into the woods on his right, and Matt tried to focus on how far away it landed just in case he might need to hunt the piece down later. "Where's the other one?" she asked.

"There's not another one."

"Bullshit. Where is it?"

He played the game like a pro, huffing and slumping his shoulders like his plan had been found out. He started to bend down but Gina stopped him. Just like he knew she would.

"Don't fucking move." She circled him like a pack of starving vultures, gun held head-high, until she was facing him. She looked way beyond stressed, her eyes heavy and bloodshot. If he didn't know better, he'd swear she was high. And that thought scared the shit out of him. The last thing he needed was a strung-out junkie with a gun.

Gina kept her eyes locked on him as she knelt in front of him and lowered her free hand down to his ankle. She fumbled a bit before removing his gun, holster and all. She tossed them both in the same direction as his department-issued Glock, but he didn't dare look since her eyes were glued to his face.

"This way." She waved the gun in the direction she wanted him to go and stepped to the side, waiting for him to move first.

"You said you wanted to tell me face to face why Alex is important," he said as the two of them traversed a tiny, man-made path cut through the brush. "Here I am."

"We'll get to that, don't you worry, Sergeant. Plenty of time for catching up." She nudged him in the back with the gun. "You just keep moving."

Matt wanted to keep pushing to try to find out why she and Brayden took Alex, why they wanted to hurt him, but he could sense her patience was already paper-thin. He couldn't risk sending her over the edge.

So, he kept quiet as they walked. Sweat scored his back, soaking through his shirt—which was fucking crazy given the drop in temperature. But he was jacked up on so much adrenaline there was a furnace sitting in his damn chest. He wanted to wipe the sweat from his forehead but was afraid to make any sudden moves with a gun on him. Gina was beyond unstable; she just might shoot him by accident.

After what felt like two or three miles, the brush began to thin out, and they stepped into a small clearing, empty except for a tiny, run-down cabin tucked in the far back corner. He tensed up just knowing Alex was only a few yards away. Fuck, he wanted to turn on Gina, subdue her somehow, and go save the man he loved. But he couldn't take the chance Brayden was ordered to kill Alex if Gina didn't come back. He wouldn't be able to live with himself if Alex died because he got trigger happy.

"So, what's your plan?" he asked as they kept a slow march toward the cabin.

"None of your fucking business," Gina spat. She was becoming more unhinged by the second. If he didn't end this soon, he and Alex both might not make it out alive.

"Sorry, I just wanted to know why you made me come all the way out here."

"I told you. I want to tell you face to face why Alex matters. Why all of this matters. But I want him to see your face when I tell you. I want him to watch you stop caring about him, right in front of his eyes."

Matt shook his head. "Not gonna happen, Gina. Not possible." Searing pain shot through the back of his head, clouding his vision and turning his stomach.

The bitch had hit him with the gun.

"Shut the fuck up or next time I'll shoot you." Gina shoved the barrel of the gun into Matt's back and he started walking again. He placed a hand against his scalp and applied pressure. Nothing was broken, but a large knot was already popping up and tiny spots of blood stained his fingers.

He was going to fucking kill her.

"Go on," Gina said once they reached the cabin. "Get inside." She nudged him in the back and he climbed the rickety wooden planks leading up to the rotten porch. He took careful steps to the door, mindful of weak spots in the floor. "Open it."

Matt slowly twisted the knob, his nerves like live wires in his skin. As tweaked as Gina seemed, he wouldn't be surprised if she had rigged the entire place to blow, take all of them out at once. She was just fucking crazy, just unhinged enough to. But the door swung open with a long, low creak, and Matt had no choice but to step inside.

Chapter Thirty-One

OH GOD.

Oh God, oh God, oh God.

Alex knew this was the end for him. He was going to die in this place, tied up like a rabid dog in a one-room, run-down rotting shack buried deep in the woods. He would never see his mother again. He wouldn't be rebuilding the Book Nook better than before and spending his days sipping lattes and talking shop with book lovers. He would never again feel the warmth of Matt's skin against his.

Matt.

God, Alex loved Matt. He hadn't wanted to admit that fact to himself or anyone, but the truth was he was madly, desperately in love. He knew that now. He could finally come to terms with his feelings. He loved Matt. More than he ever thought possible, than he ever thought he deserved. And the love was all-consuming. Emotions controlled him now, but in the best possible way. And now, before his life with Matt had even begun, their love was over. Over before he even had the chance to experience life with someone he was so taken with. Over before he ever had the chance to show Matt how much he meant to him.

That was the worst part of all of this. Not the fact that he was going to die, or that he never understood *why* he was going to die. But because Matt would go on with his life not knowing Alex's whole heart was his.

The agony those realizations brought forth was worse than death, so he relished a tiny bit of relief knowing soon he would be free from pain unlike any he had felt before.

He didn't know what was coming after—he had been raised to believe in Heaven and Hell and all they encompassed—or where he would end up, but if there was the possibility of reincarnation, he would somehow, someway, find Matt again. They would be together. They were meant to be. He knew as much now. Deep down, in the darkest, most protected corners of his soul.

He had never believed in the whole love-at-first-sight thing, or soul mates, but now... Matthew Fields *was* his soul mate. A match designed to perfection, created in the stars eons ago, sent through space and time, soaring, existing, waiting for the moment, the one exact moment when everything aligned and the two halves could be one again.

He firmly believed the moment had been the first time he laid eyes on Matt. At least in human form. He knew their souls had been drawn to each other since the beginning of time. And he knew that even after he was dead and gone, they would be drawn to each other again. They would be whole. Forever.

Alex's mind slipped in and out of psychedelic trips through the pain and fear and sadness he was experiencing, leaving him questioning what was real and what his brain had created to help him deal with his impending death. He knew Matt was real. And the cabin he was tied up in, the cabin he was dying in, was real. The rest...he couldn't be sure.

What in the world had Gina given him?

He had never gotten into the whole drug scene. They had been huge when he was a teenager—pills, mostly; any pill would do was the motto of just about every kid in school—but he stayed as far from them as he could. Maybe because he had grown up with a mother who used drugs to cope with life, with stress, with him. Yes, she was successful. A shark when it came to business. She always had been. But when it came to life, and particularly being a mother to Alex, she simply couldn't cope. So antidepressants and sleeping pills became her best friends. Alex didn't want such a life for himself. He wanted a future, success, love. So whatever Gina had shoved in his mouth and made him swallow was wreaking havoc on his virgin senses.

Right after she snatched him from his house, Gina had forced him to take two white, round pills. Then she put a black bag over his head and shoved him into the back of a large van with no windows. Before he knew what was happening, he was seeing rainbows come to life in his head, swirling and dancing and turning his stomach on end until he was ready to puke. By the time the van had stopped and Gina was dragging him out of the back, his mind was all but gone.

He spent the next he didn't know how long trying to overcome the nausea while fighting off dragons and ogres and monsters he had never seen before, all conjured by his drug-hazed mind. He was able to settle down, though, once the effects eased up a bit. He was still high or rolling or whatever term was used now—he could tell because no matter how much he tried, he couldn't focus on any one thing for more than a few seconds—but the euphoria wasn't as severe. He could make some sense of things— his hunger, his dry, scratchy throat, the fact day had already turned to dark. How long had he been there?

He struggled to sit up, his hands bound behind his back with rope that had long since worn the skin of his wrists raw. He was almost out of breath by the time he sat upright with his back against the wall. He must have still been suffering from the carbon monoxide poisoning he now knew Gina—and Brayden—had been behind.

Where was Brayden? Thoughts of his ex-boyfriend flooded his mind like a raging river, images and memories and pain and hate filling every crack, every crevice, until Matt and his mother and his hopes and his dreams were all gone. The only thing left was Brayden. He wanted to puke again.

He fought to focus, blinking over and over to draw the warped room into view. The haze dissipated a bit, the dark ebbing enough for him to make out a table and chair.

And the door.

God, what he would give to somehow find the strength to drag himself to the door. To flee. To live. To run to Matt and throw his arms around him and tell him just how much he loved him. But his body was spent. His mind was far too warped to conjure enough common sense to lead him out of the ropes and the cabin and the woods.

He was stuck.

He was dead.

Alex closed his eyes and took a deep breath, trying to slow his erratic heartbeat and nerves. He swallowed over and over, trying to moisten his dry throat enough to speak. After a deep, calming breath, he found his voice.

"I love you, Matt," he said into the dark loneliness surrounding him. "Wherever you are, please always remember that. I love you. I will always love you. Wherever life takes you after me, just know I will always be there. Loving you."

Tears ripped jagged tracks through the dirt caked on his cheeks as they spilled from his eyes, and he let them fall, memorized each one's torturous journey, and the pain they took with them. With each tear, he grew more and more at peace with what was coming, with the fate he had been given. He would smile in the face of death, not let Gina see his fear, his sadness, his heartbreak. He wouldn't give her that victory too.

He opened his eyes when he heard the crunch of leaves, the scraping of shoes on the porch, the hand on the doorknob. Gina was back. Now was time.

Time for him to die.

He opened his eyes when the door creaked open. He wanted to see Death come for him. Wanted to look the monster—Gina—in the eyes as he left this world. He wouldn't cry anymore. Not for her. He would be strong. Resilient. He would show no fear.

Everything imploded when he realized Matt standing in front of him, and then his world went dark.

Chapter Thirty-Two

MATT CAUGHT SIGHT of Alex just as his eyes rolled back and he slumped forward. He forgot about Gina and the gun in his back and sprinted across the room, catching Alex before his head hit the floor.

"Jesus," he whispered, emotion gripping his words. He cradled Alex's head in his hands and brushed sweat-soaked hair from his face.

Alex's skin was on fire, burning up. What the hell had they done to him?

He cried as he gave Alex a quick once-over. Nothing seemed broken, no visible cuts. He was physically okay, other than severe rope burns on his wrists, but Matt had no fucking clue the emotional damage he had endured. Given Gina Stanton's own fractured psyche, he imagined the horrific things Alex had suffered.

"I'm so sorry," he whispered into Alex's ear, praying he could hear his words. "Forgive me, Alex. I love you." Alex didn't respond, and Matt's heart broke for the thousandth time. God, he had failed the man he loved. Again.

He didn't save Cameron. And now he couldn't save Alex.

"Get up." Gina was at his side, her gun inches from his face. But he didn't give a fuck. He didn't care about anything anymore. Not after seeing Alex so broken, so lost. He only wanted to protect him. Save him.

Get. Up.

Get up. Get up. Get up.

The voice in his head was pleading with him to do what Gina demanded, to keep playing the game; playing was the only way to save Alex. Though it went against everything inside him, he had no choice but to listen, laying Alex down with ease on the dirty cabin floor and standing up. He stared hard at Gina, rage boiling beneath his skin.

"What?" he snarled through his tears.

She just looked at him, her gun aimed at his chest. Her eyes were glassy, dead inside. "You love him," she said, "but you don't even know him. Not the *real* him. You love a fraud. A fake."

"What the hell are you talking about? And why do you give a shit what I do? Or who he is?" He glanced around the cabin. "And where is Brayden Cooper? He put you up to this?"

Gina laughed. "Brayden was an idiot. A big baby. He couldn't stomach any of this. That's why I'm here. He didn't put me up to anything."

A few seconds passed before her words registered in his overwhelmed mind.

Was.

She said Brayden *was* an idiot.

"Where is he?" Matt asked again. "What the fuck did you do?"

"My brother never did stand up for himself." Gina raised an eyebrow at Matt's confusion. "Oh... You didn't know I'm his sister, did you?" He just stared at her, shock seizing his voice. Gina Stanton and Brayden Cooper— brother and sister? Damn. The truth came out of nowhere. "Yeah, I'm his big sis. His protector. I'm the one who's been bailing his ass out since he was old enough to walk.

Did you know he used to piss his pants? Of course you didn't. But it's true. Little shit would just let 'er rip whenever he got scared. At school, at home, he didn't care." Gina got lost in her memories and the gun lowered a bit. Matt followed her movements intently as she went on.

"I used to scare the hell out of him on purpose," she said with a devious smile. "I'd yell for him to come to his room and then hide in his closet or behind the door. As soon as he walked in I'd jump out and grab him. He'd scream and scream, and sure enough, the whole room would reek of piss." She laughed at the memories of her and her brother's life as she circled the room, pulling her aim from Matt.

"He was a bed wetter, surprise surprise. Did you know they say bed wetters become serial killers? Who knows if that's true. But Brayden was too much of a fucking pussy to ever kill anybody. Hell, if I hadn't been around, he never would have made it this long. So weak. So fucking pathetic."

Matt took advantage of the lull in the story—and of Gina's seemingly subdued state. "You protected your brother," he said, moving forward a step. "Taking care of him is a good thing."

Gina was nodding as she slid her gun back and forth across the top of the wooden table sitting in the kitchen area of the single-room cabin. "He never appreciated me though. He never even said thank you. Even when I kept our shit-pile of a father from touching him...he never once said thank you."

Matt was beginning to piece together Gina's fracture with reality, how she could go so far as to kidnap somebody. And maybe even kill her own brother.

He had dealt with people like her before back in Seattle. One case, in particular, stuck with him, and his mind recalled the memory as Gina slid a chair from beneath the table and slumped down into it.

He had been just a candidate at the time, only with the Seattle Fire Department for just under six months, when they were dispatched to a domestic violence call along with the police. The door to the apartment had been barricaded and the cops thought they might need the truck's ladder. Turns out they didn't, but Matt stayed at the top of the ladder extended up to the apartment's living room window just in case the officers needed help.

The wife was bloodied and almost unconscious, curled up on the dingy brown carpet, and the husband was pressing the barrel of a pistol into his temple as he paced back and forth across the room, mumbling over and over. Matt had to strain to make out what he was saying.

They made me. They made me. They made me.

The guy, they later learned, was schizophrenic, and he had stopped taking his meds. He later told detectives his parents—who had been dead close to a decade—told him he had to get rid of his family.

They found the couple's three children in their beds, single gunshot wounds to their heads. The case fucked Matt up for a while—and haunted him ever since.

He shook off the memory and the feeling of dread that tagged along and refocused on the current gun-wielding psycho in front of him. The case that started his career and what was going on now weren't exactly the same, but he knew well enough to not keep pushing someone so unstable. He would only make a fucked-up situation a hell of a lot worse.

"I'm sorry you had to go through all that," he said, trying to keep his voice calm and steady.

Gina cut her eyes at him as she stood up and began pacing the room. "Fuck your pity. I don't need shit from you." She stopped her pacing and faced him, tapping the gun against her head as she said, "Except maybe to wake the fuck up. This guy"— she aimed the gun at Alex and Matt bit his lip to keep from jumping her—"isn't who he seems. He's...he's the real monster. Not me."

Matt swallowed back the urge to lunge for her. To tear her apart. He wanted to end this before things went too damn far to come back from.

"Why do you—I mean, why is he a monster?" As much as it pained him, Matt knew he had to move the blame to Alex. Blaming the one person Gina saw as evil was the only way to keep her calm, keep her talking. Her talking gave him more time to figure out how to stop her.

Gina turned away from him and shook her head. "What he did... He's the real reason my brother died."

So, Brayden *was* dead. And Matt had been wrong about him. Sure, he was a piece of shit, but he hadn't been behind the attacks on Alex. Gina had done everything all by herself. But...why?

"What did he do?" He dared to take another step toward Gina. He wanted as much distance between them and Alex as the tiny cabin would give him. When things turned and he had to make his move, he didn't want Alex to get hurt.

More head shaking from Gina, then, "He should be the one telling you this. Not me. He's getting off easy." He could sense she wanted to make a move toward Alex. No fucking way he could allow her the chance.

"No," he said sharply. "You tell me. He would just try to lie his way out of it anyway."

Matt showing support for her appeared to take Gina by surprise. He caught her lower her guard. She resumed her pacing, only this time at a much slower, much more emotional speed. Her rage had shifted into something else, something more powerful. He watched as her shoulders slumped and her face sagged, the muscles there going limp. Something was happening to her, taking over her control.

If he was going to do something to stop her, the time was now.

"The little bastard," she said, emotion gripping her words. "He asked my brother to marry him." She wiped tears from her face but never once looked at Matt. He took advantage and moved even closer to her, only feet separating them now.

"Brayden was so excited. He loved Alex. More than anybody. Every fucking day he planned their wedding. Flowers, cake, tuxes...he even paid for some cheesy ass gazebo by the water for the ceremony." She took a long pause, her emotions over the memories bombarding her, then added, "They were happy."

Matt was a conflicting ball of emotion himself. Alex was going to marry Brayden? If he had, Matt never would have known him. Not in the way he does now. He wouldn't have fallen in love with him, ready to start their lives together.

If what Gina was saying was true, of course. She was fucking certifiably crazy, so the leap wasn't a huge one to imagine her dreaming up an entirely fictional life for her brother. But Matt could see how raw and vulnerable she was, recalling Brayden's once-happy life. Her words seemed all too real to him.

"What happened?" he asked, curiosity outweighing his fury—at least for the moment. A part of him wanted to know what Alex had done. What, in Gina's warped mind, was so horrible, so incredibly bad she believed it killed her brother.

She was laughing and smiling now as she wiped away more tears. Her eyes were darting all over the place, her mind no doubt going in a million different directions.

"The son of a bitch left my brother at the altar, that's what. Didn't even have the fucking balls to call off the wedding before Brayden and our friends and every damn body we knew showed up at that stupid ass gazebo." More crazy laughing, more tears, and then, "Brayden was completely humiliated."

"But you weren't...were you?"

"Fuck no, I wasn't. I was *pissed*. So mad I wanted to rip his head off his fucking shoulders!" Her rage rose again, stronger and more dominant this time.

Fuck.

Matt needed to reel her back in, get her calm, keep her on the low, straight line of the emotional roller coaster she was riding.

"Then what?" he asked. "How...how did Alex kill your brother?"

The weird, creepy smiling and laughing stopped as abruptly as they had started, and Gina was crying again. A bit more vocal this time, tiny sobs escaping her tough but thin exterior.

"He..." She stopped and started a few times before finding the courage to say the one thing he knew had fueled her breakdown. "He tried to kill himself two weeks later. Slit his own wrists. *Slit his fucking wrists.*"

Chapter Thirty-Three

MATT COULDN'T WRAP his mind around what Gina had said.

Brayden Cooper tried to kill himself. Because...

Because Alex had dumped him.

Son of a bitch.

Almost in an instant Matt was imagining himself as Brayden. He imagined the pain, the embarrassment, the suffering he would have to go through over losing somebody like Alex. Unbearable didn't come close to describing that pain. But he couldn't imagine taking his own life regardless.

But the emotion Gina displayed, the pain...her story *had* to be true. Alex had broken off the wedding—in the wrong way, yeah—and Brayden became unglued. Then Gina followed his mental breakdown, to the point of trying to ruin Alex's life like she believed Alex had ruined her brother's.

Matt ignored his own feelings and turned his attention back to Gina. She furiously wiped away the pain from her face, catching glimpses of the anger still there, simmering just below the surface. She was like a fucking grenade with the pin pulled, just waiting for the hand squeezing tight to let go.

"Did..." Jesus, he had to be careful, so very careful. If he said the wrong thing, she was gone. She was so close to the damn edge already. "Did Brayden say he was upset because of Alex?"

"He didn't have to. I found his note. He didn't know I did, and I never asked him, but... You have any fucking idea what it feels like to read your own brother's suicide note?" She looked at Matt, her eyes so full of tears he imagined she struggled to see him.

He shook his head slow, trying to show sympathy he didn't have. "I'm an only child."

Gina smirked. "Sometimes I wish I was." A darkness fell over her face then. "Guess I am now."

Son of a bitch...he *did* feel sorry for her. Which pissed him off even more.

"Well, just so you know, it sucks. Bad. Finding his note fucking killed me. Seeing how that bastard over there destroyed him. I just...I couldn't let that go."

"I...I understand. Really." And he did. He understood how seeing someone you love hurt so much could change a person. Hell, he was living proof. Cameron's death destroyed him in every fucking way possible. And now, with Alex lying unconscious on the floor only a few feet away from him, bound and held captive by this psycho, he was being torn into jagged pieces all over again. "Wh— why did Alex dump your brother? At the altar?"

Gina laughed. "Oh, the little prick tried to say Brayden cheated on him. Bunch of lies from a bullshitter."

Of course. Brayden cheating explained why Alex hated him so much. Alex had loved Brayden—he was going to marry him, for God's sake—and Brayden ruined everything by cheating. Alex must've been destroyed. Like Matt was when he lost Cameron. Damn, they were more alike than Matt thought.

"I had to do something about," Gina went on, pulling him back to the present. "I had to... I wanted him to pay." The crazy, frantic, desperate Gina was back, her rage fueling her again. She crossed the room toward Alex, the gun in her hand lifting as she made her move.

Now or never.

Without a second thought, Matt lunged after her, body-slamming her with every ounce of strength he had in him. They flew through the air and crashed into the wall at the back of the cabin. The jolt disoriented him only for half a second, but unfortunately that was long enough for Gina to get the upper hand.

She kneed him in the gut and hit the side of his head with her gun and stars burst behind his eyes. His stomach spun, and nausea crashed into him like a fucking freight train. He fought like hell to ignore the pain and dizziness as he gripped Gina's arm and twisted with every ounce of his strength. He felt the bone beneath the skin crack and scrub together, her excruciating screams like screech owls in the dead of night.

He found his second wind and shoved her off him. As she crumpled to the floor, he frantically began searching for the gun. He had broken her arm, so he knew it had to have fallen somewhere at his feet.

But it hadn't.

Gina was still holding the fucking gun.

Son of a bitch.

Matt charged in her direction, everything around him seeming to move in slow motion. He could see her, writhing and roiling on the floor. He saw her grip the gun with her good hand. He could see her aim at him as he rushed toward her.

He sensed the vibration when she pulled the trigger. Watched the muzzle ignite in a blaze of flame and smoke. Felt the bullet crash through the skin of his shoulder and bury itself in the muscle there.

He flew backward almost as fast as he had been sprinting forward. He slammed into the floor like a rock, his head smacking the hardwood with all the speed he had mustered, blinding him with a shockwave of pain and light. He gripped at his shoulder and yelled out, squirming around on the floor.

God, the pain was fucking overwhelming. He had never, in all his years in this field, taken a bullet. A few days in the quiet, seemingly idyllic town of Cliffside, and he was lying on the floor of a secluded cabin, fucking bleeding out.

A loud commotion forced his eyes open. The room was a spinning whirl of blurry color, his mind giving in to the sleep threatening to consume him. He wanted to just close his eyes again and never reopen them.

But he knew he couldn't.

He had to find Gina.

He blinked over and over until he was able to make out shapes. There was Alex, still on the floor, still unconscious, unaffected by the fighting and the gunshot.

More blinking, more scanning the tiny room that all of a sudden seemed massive, until he found her.

She was standing right in front of him, the gun on him again.

He could practically see the rage pouring out of her like boiling lava, pulsing and ebbing like a ripple on water, permeating the room. He could feel her anger, her hatred, her drive.

He stood there, helpless, as she squeezed the trigger. He heard the gunshot.

But he didn't feel anything.

Maybe he was already dead. Maybe the first bullet had been closer to his heart than he'd thought, and he was gone.

But he wasn't gone. He was still there, still breathing. How?

He had to force his eyes open, the pain in his shoulder traveling across his body, making everything go numb. He knew he was on the verge of blacking out. If he did, this would all be over. Gina wouldn't miss again, and he would be dead. Then she would do the same thing to Alex. Kill him like a horse with a broken leg, a bullet to the head. Quick. Painless. Wrong.

Though he couldn't explain how, he was overcome with a strange, calming peace. He had always wondered how he would feel when he faced death. Would he be scared, weak, unready? Nope, he was none of those things. He wasn't afraid. He wasn't feeling sorry for himself. He wasn't wishing he had more time.

He was...content. He let go of everything he had been holding on to—his career, his old life, even Alex—and gave in to the darkness reaching out to him. He let the black hole consume him, devour him, eat him from the inside out until there was nothing but emptiness left.

He was gone.

Chapter Thirty-Four

ALEX WOKE UP two days later at Cliffside Memorial Hospital in a room eerily similar to the one he had woken up in before. The bed was the same. The gaudy brown chairs against the wall were the same. The equipment and wall colors and flat-screen television bolted to the wall—all the same. But next to him, just to his left, was something different.

Another bed.

And sleeping in the other bed was Matt, the man he loved.

Matt was alive. He survived.

They both had.

Just as he had wanted since the second he laid eyes on him, he and Matt were together. He could, for once, rest.

MATT WOKE UP a full day after Alex, groggy and in fucking excruciating pain. His entire body pulsated with anger like someone had dropped him into the world's largest meat grinder, his bones and muscles on fire every time he even thought about moving them. He had wires coming off of him in every damn direction, feeding into the unknown below and behind his hospital bed. A multitude of beeps sounded around the room, and he followed them until he found the one thing he thought he would never see again.

Alex.

God, he looked perfect. Absolutely fucking perfect, asleep in the bed next to him. He was hooked up to machines just like Matt was, an identical strip of clear tubing tucked beneath his nose and hooked over his ears. Matt adjusted his own oxygen line, wincing when he moved his hand. The damn thing was in his line of sight, and he wanted nothing to block his view of the man lying only a few feet from him. He never again wanted to take his eyes off of Alex. In a fraction of a second, he made the decision to quit his job, give up the dangerous, unpredictable life of investigating arson cases, and just *be* with Alex. Wherever life took them, he didn't care as long as *he* became *them*.

"It's about time you woke up." He recognized the voice before his eyes found the source. He smiled as wide as he could through the pain when they landed on Gregson.

"Hey, Captain." Matt's voice was more reminiscent of the sound sandpaper makes against rusty metal than an actual human. He wished like hell someone would take the razor blades out of his throat too.

"You sure as hell know how to do things up right, Fields, I'll give ya that." Gregson was smiling, Matt could see, as he stood up from a chair against the wall and made his way to Matt's bedside. He looked tired, from what Matt could tell, given his vision was blurry at best. Good, but tired.

"Don't like to half-ass my job," Matt joked, pulling a laugh from the captain. He had never heard such a sound from him before. His laugh was kind of nice. A bit odd, but nice.

"Yeah, well, don't think this is gonna get you any time off, you hear? Teagues has already called. Expects you back at work first thing tomorrow." Gregson nudged him in the side, and Matt had to bite his lip to keep from flinching.

"Aye, aye, cap'n," he said, with as much humor as he could muster. He would wait until he was better to tell his boss and peers he was done with being a fire investigator. Done with the line of work in general. But there was a conversation meant for beers down at Olly's Bar back in Bangor.

"Okay, I'm gonna get out of here so you two can get some rest." Gregson looked over to Alex and then said, "You both look like hammered shit."

Matt laughed then immediately regretted it. Pain shot through him. He tried to play things off like he was fine, but if he'd had a gun right then, he definitely would've shot himself.

Then he remembered why the hell he was in the hospital in the first place. He had been shot. Crazy firefighter-turned-vigilante Gina Stanton had shot him. But...Matt thought she killed him?

"Captain?" he called out, stopping Gregson before he left the room. Gregson moved back toward the bed and raised an eyebrow. "What...what the hell happened?"

"What do you remember?" Gregson asked.

"Not much. I know I was hit. And Alex was..." He couldn't even say the words. Just rehashing what he had seen, Alex unconscious on the floor, bloody and beaten down...the memory was too fucking much for his exhausted mind to handle.

"He's fine," Gregson said with reassurance, picking up on Matt's spider-webbed emotional state. "And you are, too, Fields. You're both fine, and you're both gonna *be* fine. I'd call this a good ending to a bad situation. Nothing else really matters."

"What happened?" Matt asked again.

Gregson's frown slid back onto his face, but he gave in. "Gina Stanton was killed in a remote cabin in the woods a few miles south of the Canadian border. A clean kill, as far as the law is concerned. And because of said shooting, a fire sergeant and a civilian were saved in the process."

"I don't want the press version," Matt stated. "Tell me what happened in there, please. I need to know." And he did. He wouldn't be able to move on if he didn't. If he didn't get the details of just how the hell he and Alex made it out alive, the unknown would haunt him forever, drive him fucking mad.

Gregson ran a hand over his wrinkled face and up through his graying hair. He had decades of experience at perfecting his poker face, but for some odd reason Matt could see right through him to what he was feeling. "You know something, Fields, I was gonna invite you to join my weekly poker game I have at my house on Saturday nights. But after this, I think I'm gonna have to reconsider. Because you are one lousy ass bluff."

Matt's face twisted with confusion until his mind conjured the memory of what happened *before* the cabin. Of the events that unfolded at Brayden Cooper's house. The phone call from Gina. His lie to the captain.

Son of a bitch. Gregson knew.

"You must've thought I was born yesterday, huh?" Gregson asked with a smile. "Only explanation for the shit show you tried to give to me in Emory. Hell, son, I knew what you were doing. Just took me a little longer than I thought it would to find you."

"Wait... *You...*"

"Like I said, the kill was a good one. A necessary one. Any cop worth his shit would've done the exact same thing."

"Gregson, I—"

"Nope, none of that." Gregson shook his head and moved toward the door. "I was doing my job, nothing else. And I was happy to. Would do it again if need be."

Matt didn't press him further. He knew Gregson enough to know he wasn't the emotional, heart-on-his-sleeve type, and what Matt had gotten so far was about as good as he should expect.

"Thank you," Matt said with a slight smile.

Gregson nodded and headed back to the door. "Now get some sleep."

"Wait. Captain?"

Gregson huffed but let go of the door. "I ain't telling you nothing else, Fields. These lips are sealed."

Matt held back his laugh because the pain hurt too much. "Just one thing," he said. "What happened to Cooper?" He knew Brayden was dead—he remembered Gina confessing to killing her brother, in her psychotic, demented way—but...had they found him?

"CSU found his body stuffed in a freezer in the basement of his house," Gregson explained, gripping the door again. "Crazy bitch slit his throat and shoved him in there like wild game."

"Jesus."

"Tell me about it. Now, don't ask me anything else, you hear? I gotta get home before my wife sends out a damn search party." He opened the door again and stepped out, but ducked back in to add, "Hey...good work out there, Fields. You'll make a hell of a detective someday."

Matt smiled as the man he had grown to respect disappeared, the door falling into place behind him.

"Hey there." Alex's voice pulled his focus from Gregson. He ignored the pain and turned to his left.

"Hey, you," he said with a smile. "Man, am I glad to see your beautiful face."

Alex smiled back. "I feel the same way." He looked weak, Matt thought, but good regardless. He wanted to jump out of his bed and go to Alex, hold him and kiss him and never fucking let him go. He had to settle for slowly, painfully extending an arm out and splaying his fingers. Alex took his cue and slid Matt's outstretched hand into his.

"I love you," Matt said. "Jesus, do I love you."

"I love you, too, *Sergeant*."

He laughed. "We gotta come up with a better nickname."

"Hey now, I kind of like Sergeant." Alex shook his head. "I think I'll keep it."

"Even if I'm not a sergeant anymore?"

Alex's eyes grew wide, and then a perfect smile spread over his face.

"Very funny," Alex said. "I see the one-of-a-kind sense of humor of yours emerged unscathed."

"If so, it's the only thing that did." Like with his boss, he would broach the subject of quitting his job another time.

Alex's smile turned into a grimace. "I... I am so sorry about this." Tears pooled in his eyes. "My God... Because of me, you almost died."

"What? No, Alex, don't say shit like that."

"It's the truth." Those tears spilled out, and Alex wiped them away. "Brayden was my ex. And she was his sister. If I hadn't..."

"What?" he asked when Alex stopped talking. Alex

looked at him, and Matt caught the truth there, deep in his eyes. "Hey, none of this is your fault. If Brayden did...what he did, that's on him, not because you didn't marry him. People don't kill themselves because of what other people do. The pain they go through, the self-deprecation... Those things live inside them. Deep down, where others can't see to step in and help."

"I was so naive," Alex said. "I know the day I left Brayden was just a few months ago, but...God, so much has changed since then. I was immature, scared. When he and I talked about marriage I just...jumped on the idea, you know? I was stupid."

"You were not stupid. You wanted the good life, as they say. Marriage, a family. There's nothing stupid about wanting to be happy, Alex. The timing was just wrong. That's all."

Alex rolled onto his back and exhaled. "I keep trying to tell myself the same thing."

Matt hadn't expected the conversation to go the direction it was headed, but since they were going there, he was ready to ask the question he knew he would long before now.

"Do you, uh, still want it?" he asked timidly.

"What?" Alex asked back, rolling onto his side again and propping his head up with his hand.

"That life. Marriage. A family. Do you still think about being married and spending the rest of your life with someone?"

Alex let his head fall to his pillow. "Yes," he said, his eyes locked on Matt. "I do."

Matt's heart swelled so much he thought his damn chest would explode. Every nerve in his body was alive, pulsing, pushing away the pain. He forced himself to move, roll over so he could see the man he loved.

With hope in his heart, he said three words he hoped would change their lives forever.

"Then marry me."

Epilogue

MATT SCOOPED ALEX into his arms the second they got out of the car.

"Hey!" Alex yelled as his feet were pulled out from under him. "What do you think you're doing, *Sergeant*?"

"I thought you were gonna come up with a new nickname," Matt said, planting a kiss on his new husband.

"Hmm..." Alex brought a finger to his lip and let it linger, playfully pretending to think hard before saying, "I could always call you...Marshal Fields. Has a nice ring, don't you think?"

Matt dug a finger into Alex's side, making him yelp.

"Don't even. I'd rather have Sergeant."

"You know, I *could* switch things up every time you get promoted. You're Sergeant now, then Marshal, then you could be... What comes next?"

"Chief," Matt said begrudgingly. "But if you think for a second I'm—"

Alex cut him off with another, more passionate kiss, sending shivers all over his damn body, and Matt forgot all about the fact he had kept the job he was so ready to give up six months ago laying in his hospital room. But when Alex had said yes, he would marry him, Matt knew he had to stay put. Well, stay with the marshal's office. But his work would now be done in Cliffside. And no chance in hell he was planning on leaving town. Not unless Alex wanted to. No, he knew he had to keep the job that had brought the two of them together. And if he were being honest with himself, he never could have walked away from the one thing in his life he was good at, anyway.

Well, the *second* thing.

He kissed Alex with passion and fire as Matt carried him up the walkway and onto the porch of their house. The place had been Alex's up until the day they both said "I do" in front of their friends and family, but now the home was theirs.

Theirs.

Damn, Matt loved that word.

The ceremony had been perfect, intimate, and the day was the happiest he had ever been in his life. All the pain of losing Cameron, of coming close to losing Alex, just went away when he and Alex had walked hand in hand down the aisle while everyone applauded.

Matt never in a million years thought he would ever reach this place in life. Not after Cameron died. Before, yeah, he could see being married. Being happy. But after the accident that took the man he loved all because he was too mad to forgive him... The night had changed Matt. For the worse. He gave up on happiness. On marriage. On love. He settled. Settled for being alone. Being...content with what he had. Frankly, spending the rest of his life in a self-built isolation chamber was all he thought he deserved, given how things went down with Cameron.

Then, he met Alex, and like a blow to the gut his life was upended, renewed, like someone had pressed the restart button and gave him a second chance. Alex coming into his life blindsided him. Falling for him so fast. Loving someone again. But the surprise was the best thing that could've happened because it brought him to life again. He knew now he could be happy. Truly happy. With Alex.

Now, he was living that life instead of just dreaming of the possibility.

And it was perfect.

AND ALEX HAD been over the moon too. He had been through so much in his life, lost so much. But now he had the man of his dreams. And he had just broken ground on his new store, the Book Nook, Too. The life he had been looking for was in his grasp. Finally. Finding happiness was all he had ever wanted.

When he was younger, before the machinations of his parents and their tumultuous relationship swayed his judgment, Alex wanted nothing more than to meet someone and fall in love and live happily ever after like the princes and princesses in the fairy tales his nannies used to read to him at night. He had always been a romantic at heart, always holding out hope his very own Prince Charming would swoop in and save him, and they would fall madly in love and spend the rest of their lives in their very own happily ever after. He never thought his dream would come true until he met Matt.

His very own Prince Charming.

"Wait," Alex said just as they were about to go through the door into the house. *Their* house. Matt looked down at him and his heart beat wildly in his chest. The love he had for Alex was overwhelming him.

"What?" Matt asked. "Are you okay?"

"Yeah, I just..."

"What? Tell me." He held a marked persistence.

"If you carry me across the threshold," Alex said, "does this mean I'm the wife?"

Matt couldn't help but laugh. "Who cares," he said with a smile. "As long as you promise to love me forever, you can be whatever you want." Alex smiled, and Matt couldn't resist adding, "And you do all the cooking and cleaning."

Alex playfully smacked his cheek, and Matt pretended the tiny slap hurt and Alex smiled. "Watch out, *Sergeant*, or you'll be single before you know it."

"Not a chance." Matt kissed him again and opened the door. Before they crossed the threshold to begin the life both of them couldn't wait to live, Matt said, "I love you, Alex Porter Fields."

Alex smiled and slid a hand from behind Matt's neck and up to his cheek, giving the rough skin there a soft caress.

"Ditto."

Acknowledgements

A huge thank you to NineStar Press for giving me the opportunity to share Alex and Matt with anyone who might want to visit with them for a while. A special thank you to Stacey Jo for her awesome editing skills—you made this story so much better. And to the uber-talented @NSnowDesigns for such a gorgeous, perfect cover!

For Missy @glorydaysgirl, who was there for the first read-through and gave valuable feedback. You're the best!

And to the readers who take a chance on an unknown and give this book a read—you guys ROCK.

About the Author

My love of writing began when I bought my very first book when I was barely a tween. It was adult and long and much too mature for my young mind, but it forever changed me and made me fall in love with reading. I love getting lost in the pages of a novel over almost everything else (except maybe TV; that's my jam!), and writing is yet another wonderful escape that hooked me from the start.

I live in a very small, very hot and humid city in the south, where I long for colder days and am envious of those who see snow every year.

OUT OF THE ASHES is my first foray into the world of m/m romantic suspense, and I am loving it!

Email: authormjjames@gmail.com

Twitter: @AuthorMJ_James

Website: www.mjjamesauthor.blogspot.com

Also Available from NineStar Press

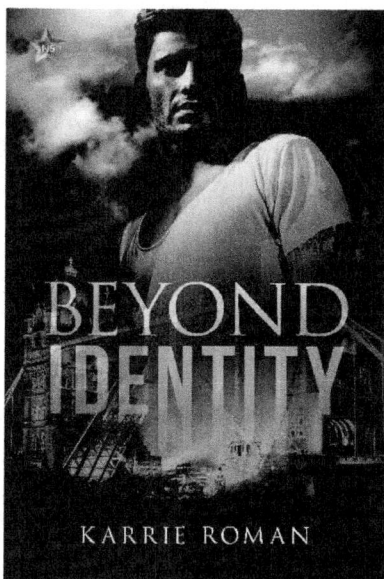

Connect with NineStar Press

www.ninestarpress.com

www.facebook.com/ninestarpress

www.facebook.com/groups/NineStarNiche

www.twitter.com/ninestarpress

www.tumblr.com/blog/ninestarpress

Printed in Dunstable, United Kingdom